oⴄⴄⴄⴄⴄⴄⴄⴄⴄⴄo

Acclaim for Laura Restrepo and
LEOPARD IN THE SUN

"*Leopard in the Sun* is like a tremendously suc-
cessful work of journalism, making contemporary
events seem intelligible and poignant."
—*The Portland Oregonian*

"Restrepo combines prose swollen with sensory
description and magical exaggeration with a jour-
nalistic precision."   —*Booklist*

"Finely crafted fiction."   —*Library Journal*

"Restrepo is a writer to treasure."   —Alastair Reid

ALSO BY
LAURA RESTREPO

The Angel of Galilea

LAURA RESTREPO

LEOPARD IN THE SUN

Laura Restrepo has been a professor of literature at the National University of Colombia, as well as publisher of the weekly magazine *Semana*. In 1984, she was a member of the Peace Commission that brought the Colombian government and the guerrillas to the negotiating table. She is the author of several novels, among them *The Angel of Galilea*.

LEOPARD
IN THE SUN

LAURA RESTREPO

TRANSLATED BY STEPHEN A. LYTLE

VINTAGE INTERNATIONAL

VINTAGE BOOKS   A DIVISION OF RANDOM HOUSE, INC.

NEW YORK

FIRST VINTAGE INTERNATIONAL EDITION, SEPTEMBER 2000

Copyright © 1999 by Laura Restrepo

Al rights reserved under the International and Pan-American Copyright Conventions. Published in the United States by Vintage Books, a division of Random House, Inc., New York, and simultaneously in Canada by Random House of Canada Limited, Toronto. Originally published in Spanish by Grupo Editorial Norma, South America, in 1993. Copyright © 1993 by Laura Restrepo. Originally published in hardcover in the United States by Crown Publishers, New York, in 1999.

Vintage is a registered trademark and Vintage International and colophon are trademarks of Random House, Inc.

The Library of Congress has cataloged the Crown edition as follows:
Restrepo, Laura.
[Leopardo al sol. English]
Leopard in the sun / Laura Restrepo; translated by
Stephen A. Lytle. — 1st ed.
I. Lytle, Stephen A.
II. Title
PQ8180.28.E7255L4613
1999
863—dc21
99-13509

Vintage ISBN: 0-375-70508-2

Author photograph © Jorge Mario Múnera
Book design by Barbara Sturman

www.vintagebooks.com

Printed in the United States of America
10 9 8 7 6 5 4 3 2 1

TO IVAN

for such happiness in these fierce times

ACKNOWLEDGMENTS

The following people lived each step of the writing of this book and are part of it because of everything they contributed in spirit, company, support, assistance, suggestions, corrections, or all of the above: Helena Casabianca de Restrepo, Carmen Restrepo, Andrea Marulanda, Pedro Saboulard, Ramón Marulanda, Mónica Marulanda, Mireya Fonseca, Fabiola Castaño, Javier Marulanda.

This is a fictional novel based on research of real-life events. The following individuals contributed key information: Ricardo Villa (may he rest in peace), Jorge Alí Triana, Hernando Corral, José Araújo, Armando ("el Pato") Fuentes, Alfredo Daza, Hermel Daza, Alvaro Restrepo, Misael Guerra, Campo Cabello Barquero, Manzur Agustín Serra, Rolland Pinedo Caza, Alcira Weber, Moisés Perea, Hernando Marín, Wilder Guerra Currelo, Francisco Pérez Van Leden, Franklin Gómez, Jorge Bruges Mejía, Alvaro Gómez, Alvaro Castillo Granada y Los Gambos, Enrique Delugen Brito ("el Pachá"), Serapio Faruteso, Cristóbal Redondo, José Amaya, and Manuel Redondo.

I also have old debts of gratitude to Eduardo Camacho Guizado, for teaching me to read when I was studying at the Universidad de los Andes in Bogotá and to Plinio Apuleyo Mendoza, for teaching me to write when I worked at the magazine *Semana*. And to Gabo, of course, because his genius half stuns and half illumines us.

Beyond them lies a yellow desert,

speckled by the shadow of

the stones, and death awaits

there like a leopard lying

in the sun.

LORD DUNSANY

LEOPARD
IN THE SUN

"THAT GUY OVER THERE, *sitting with the blonde, that's Nando Barragán.*"

Word runs quickly through the dimly lit bar. It's him, Nando Barragán. A hundred eyes steal furtive glances at him. Fifty mouths speak his name.

"There he is. He's one of them."

Wherever the Barragáns go, they are followed by murmuring, cursed through clenched teeth, secretly admired, deeply hated. They live on constant display. No longer allowed to be themselves, they have become what people say and think about them, living legends, constructed from the lies told about them. Their lives are no longer their own, but have become public domain. They are idolized, repudiated, imitated, and, most of all, feared.

"Sitting there at the bar, that's the boss, Nando Barragán."

The words glide across the dance floor, passing from table to table, and are multiplied in the mirrors on the ceiling. The palpable fear is diminished somewhat by the black lights, but a sharp tension cuts through the clouds of smoke, disrupting the tempo of the boleros coming from the jukebox. Couples stop dancing. The beams of light from the mirrored balls glow blue and violet, warning of danger. Palms become sweaty and hair on the backs of necks stands up. Ignoring the whispers and detached from the commotion that his presence produces, Nando Barragán, huge and yellow-skinned, smokes a Pielroja cigarette as he sits on a tall stool at the bar.

"What color is his skin?"

"Burned yellow, just like his brothers'."

His face is pocked with holes as if he had been attacked by birds, and his nearsighted eyes are hidden behind black Ray-Bans with reflective lenses. A greasy T-shirt shows beneath his guayabera shirt. From a heavy chain over the ample chest, hairless and glistening with sweat, a solid gold cross of Caravaca, heavy and powerful, hangs ostentatiously.

"The Barragáns all wear the cross of Caravaca. It's their good luck charm. They use it to ask for money, health, love, and happiness."

"They may ask for all four things, but the cross brings them only money. The others, they've never had and they never will."

Next to Nando, on another stool, a corpulent, formidable blonde crosses her legs provocatively. She is squeezed tightly into a black elastic bodysuit, a disco mesh, through which a large amount of mature skin and a satin bra, size 40C, can be seen. Her colorless, plain eyes are heavy with mascara, eyeliner, and shadow. She throws her head back and her long blond hair whips her back like stiff straw, revealing black roots. Moving with the sensuality of an alley cat, she has the mysterious dignity of an ancient goddess.

Nando Barragán looks at her adoringly and his crude warrior's heart melts drop by drop, like a holy taper burning on an altar.

"The years have been kind to you. You're beautiful, Milena. Just like you always were," he says, then punishes his throat with the raw smoke of his Pielroja.

"And you, all covered with gold," says the blonde, her voice hoarse and sensual. "When we met you were poor."

"I'm still the same man."

"They say you have cellars full of dollars, all piled up. They say your dollars are rotting, that you have so many you don't know what to do with them."

"They say a lot of things. Come back to me."

"No."

"You went with that foreigner to get away from here. You went so far you forgot all about me."

"It was a bad memory. They say you leave only widows and orphans behind. What evil things have you done to make so much money?"

The man doesn't respond. He downs a shot of whiskey and chases it with Leona Pura. The sparkling bubbles of the clear soda bring back a vague memory of children playing baseball in the dirt, with broomsticks for bats and bottle caps for balls.

THE MONSALVE gang enters and all hell breaks out. Nando Barragán and the blond woman are still at the bar, their backs to the entrance, and the burst of shrapnel throws them into the air.

"Nando and the blonde were talking and kissing, with their legs intertwined, when they were shot. I was there, in the bar, and I saw it with my own eyes."

No. That night Nando never touched Milena. He treats her with the respect that men have for the women who have left them. He talks to her, but he does not touch her. All he can do is look at her longingly.

"How do you know how he looked at her if he was wearing sunglasses? It's just talk. Everybody says what he thinks, but nobody really knows anything."

People are not so naive, they know what's going on. Nando's suffering was plain to see, like a faded aura around his body. When he's with Milena he loses his reflexes. He can't sense the danger lurking around him, because it's overshadowed by a deep anxiety that makes him forget everything but her. And he trembles. She's the only person who's ever made him tremble. She's the only one who ever said no to him.

"Despite everything he was a hopeless dreamer, a lost cause."

When he's got his feet on the ground he's unbeatable, relentless. He's shrewd and lightning quick, like a whip. But when she appears, even if only in his memory, he falls into a soft, innocent drowsiness, like a recently fed puppy, or an old woman on Valium. The night they meet, after many years apart, Nando is not capable of thinking about anyone or anything else. He's not worried about running into his cousins and enemies, the Monsalves. Maybe he's even forgotten about them for an instant.

In honor of Milena, who can't stand weapons, he's not carrying his Colt .45, the one bearing a prancing horse on its ivory handle and filled with bullets marked with his initials. His guard is down and he's vulnerable, thinking only about his love for Milena, begging her forgiveness.

That's why he doesn't notice when the Monsalves enter the bar. Everyone else hears the black curtain at the door as it is pushed aside and sees the silver silhouette of a thin man and his three companions. The couples hug to protect themselves from what may happen. The cocktail waitresses slip under the tables. But not Nando. He doesn't notice anything; he's lost in his memories and his longing.

From the back of the bar, along the hallway by the rest rooms, comes a gust of cold air that smells of plumbing and old cigarettes. On the ceiling a strobe light flashes a hundred rays of light, each fading quickly like camera flashes—on, off, now I see you, now I don't—illuminating the newly arrived figure, phosphorescent and ghostly.

It's Mani Monsalve. Physically, he looks like Nando Barragán. They could be brothers. Even though they hate each other, their blood is the same. They are cousins. Mani is younger, not as tall and fat, or as ugly, and he has greener skin. His expression is harder and his features are more defined, with one in particular that makes him instantly recognizable: a half moon stamped on his face, a waning crescent that starts at his temple, brushes the corner of his left eye and continues its curve across his cheekbone, stopping just short of his nose. It looks like a half mask, a deep, indelible monocle, his evil scar earned in some scuffle or gunfight.

"Nando Barragán, I've come to kill you," shouts Mani Monsalve. "Twenty years ago today you killed my brother, Adriano Monsalve. It's blood for blood. Take out your weapon so we can fight like men."

"I'm unarmed," responds Nando.

"It sounds like a comic book, a Western. What did Nando say? Gasp!? Oh no!? Those people never said anything. They never warned anybody. They didn't exchange courtesies. They just shot."

"No, they had their laws and traditions. Anyway, after the first shots the lights went out, and whatever happened next took place in the dark. Maybe the owner of the bar had the foresight to switch them off, who knows? But what I do know is that they were shooting in the dark."

People are going crazy, shouting, blindly trying to flee the invisible bullets. They hear mirrors and bottles smashing, then the police sirens. The Monsalves probably take off when they hear the sirens, because later, when the lights come back on, they're already gone. Nando Barragán crawls out from behind the bar, wounded and covered with blood, but still alive. The only other injury is the damage to the bar. It's destroyed, but only Mani and Nando had shot, no one else, as if it were a private duel between the two of them.

"That's how it was with those people."

"How do you know? Didn't you say the lights went out? And how did Nando shoot? Maybe he wasn't unarmed after all?"

"*Some say he was unarmed, others say they saw the Colt in his hand. One thing for sure is that he was badly injured and Mani Monsalve escaped without a scratch.*"

"*Milena wasn't hit either. Maybe she was protected by all that fine flesh. Nando had as many holes in him as a colander, but none was life-threatening. The worst one destroyed his left knee and left him lame for the rest of his life.*"

"*It wasn't the left; it was the right.*"

"*Everybody has his own version, but from then on he walked pretty wobbly. He learned his lesson that day and was never seen in a bar again. After that he was careful and stayed hidden. We never saw him with Milena again either. She took him to the hospital that night, saved him from bleeding to death, and then went back to her foreigner. She vanished completely and no one has seen her since. Nando Barragán never saw her again either, except in his deliriums of lost love. They say his bodily wounds healed, but the ones in his heart never did. He was tortured for the rest of his life, mostly from not being able to forget that woman.*"

"*She never loved him?*"

"*They say she did, but she ran away from him and his wars, from the bad things that surrounded him.*"

ON THE WAY to the hospital, Nando Barragán tells the blond woman his sad story, as the blood seeps from his wounds and the ambulance rattles over potholes in the broken asphalt. He thinks he's telling her, but he's actually muttering a delirious string of incoherent thoughts she can't understand, but somehow already knows.

The siren wails frenetically in Nando Barragán's ears while a clumsy nurse pesters him with cotton balls, transfusions, and tourniquets. Bouncing around in the stretcher, sliding back and forth between this world and the next, Nando struggles to keep Milena's face in focus. She crouches at his side, bathed in red by the spinning light on the hood. His life is draining from him without pain or compassion and he is talking incessantly, like a hemorrhage. He feels an urgent need to tell intimate details about his life and gushes hurriedly like a drunk, or a gossipy neighbor. He wants to unburden himself of his bad memories as you get rid of a bad tooth. He wants to cleanse himself of guilt and regrets, so he confesses to Milena, Santa Milena the Impossible, the Unattainable, the holy priestess with her red robe and miter.

"Don't leave me alone in agony, Milena. Protect me when death comes. Absolve me, Milena, forgive my sins. Anoint me with holy oils. Don't let me die."

THE STORY Nando Barragán tells Milena during the agonizing ambulance ride begins on a dirt road swept by clouds of dust in a desert town.

He is twenty years younger, and walks the street nearly naked. Large, ungainly, yellow, and naked except for a loincloth like those worn by the desert Indians, a pair of black Ray-Bans, and an old Colt .45 at his waist.

"The same pistol he used the rest of his life?"

"Yes, but he hadn't added the ivory handle yet, and he hadn't begun using the silver bullets with his initials."

He was a heavy adolescent, oversized, walking like King Kong through the dusty street. The craters in his face haven't yet dried. A voracious acne, boiling in full eruption, is devouring his neck and cheeks.

Behind him, trying hard to keep up, trots another adolescent of the same age, smaller, rougher, greener, with deep, narrow eyes above a pointed nose. There is a family resemblance between them. They have the same profile, the same way of tilting their heads, of balancing their bodies, of pronouncing their r's and s's. Everything and nothing, different, but the same.

It's his first cousin, Adriano Monsalve. His best friend and partner. The same blood. He's suffocating in his clothes, swimming in a dark double-breasted suit with wide lapels, bell-bottom slacks, cuff links in the stiff shirt cuffs, a narrow tie, and platform shoes. A handkerchief pokes out of his breast pocket. Everything is too big and scratches and chokes him, because none of it is his. Nando has lent it to him for his trip to the capital, his first, to close the sale on a load of contraband Marlboros.

"Nando, these clothes don't fit."

"You'll have to put up with them. Later you can buy all the clothes you want."

"Nando, they're choking me."

"I told you, you'll just have to put up with them. It's cold there."

"I look ridiculous."

"You'll look fine there."

"Grandmother says it's bad to wear someone else's clothes, because the owner's luck wears off on you."

"That's just a stupid old superstition."

The boys walk together toward the offices of the Golden Condor, the bus company that will take Adriano to the capital, and buy a ticket for the six o'clock bus. It's barely three and they stand on the corner to wait. Nando, the huge naked Cro-Magnon, stands immovable in the full sun, and Adriano, sweating profusely in his dark suit, stands in the shade under the eaves of the bus station.

A team of mules, adorned with tassels and silver fittings, faded and tarnished like a Christmas tree still on display well after the holidays are over, passes by, raising clouds of dust. The cousins choke on the earth-laden air and cough up coffee-colored saliva while they go over the specifics of the deal they are about to close. Adriano writes the number of his contact in the capital on a piece of paper, writes it on his hand too, in case he loses the paper.

They got started in the contraband business forgetting an old tradition. Until now their families, the Barragáns and the Monsalves, have survived in the desert by bartering sheep. From the beginning, they sat together in the middle of the barren landscape, among the sedimentary rocks and prehistoric winds, mountains of salt and limestone and gaseous emanations, where life was meager and was measured with an eyedropper. They stole water from the rocks, milk from the goats, and rescued the goats from the claws of the tigers. The ranches were next to one another, surrounded only by desolation and sand.

Except for the fact that the Monsalve children were green and the Barragáns were yellow, there was no difference between them. They called their fathers and uncles Papá, their mothers and aunts Mamá; any older man was called Abuelo, and the adults, without distinguishing between grandchildren, children, nieces, or nephews, raised them all together, by the dozen, in heaps, on sheer will, dry figs, and leaves.

Nando Barragán and Adriano Monsalve are the same age. When they turned fourteen they struck out together looking for work. Adriano bought some orange-colored stones from the coast called *tumas* and sold them to the Indians in the Sierra, who strung them into necklaces. He became a businessman. Nando learned how to smuggle foreign cigarettes across the border. He became a *contrabandista*, a smuggler.

In only a few short months they both knew clearly which business was better. Adriano left the *tumas* for the Marlboros and in time several other brothers joined them. Following this twisted path, the new generation of Barragáns and Monsalves joined a world in which men are organized in gangs, drive jeeps, travel hundreds of miles at night, learn to shoot, bribe public officials, and get drunk on Scotch. They carry rolls of bills in their pockets, loudly challenge their enemies, laugh uproariously, make love to prostitutes, and hit their wives.

The sons brought color televisions and stereos to their fathers' packed-mud huts. They shooed pigs and chickens from the kitchen to install double-door refrigerators, and buried rifles in the goat barns.

That afternoon, standing on the corner, Nando and Adriano were getting bored waiting for the bus.

"Marco Bracho died a year ago today," says Nando, as if to himself.

"His widow must be celebrating the anniversary," says Adriano, looking the other way, speaking to the wall.

"Should we go for a little while?"

"What if the bus leaves me?"

"Just a little while."

"Let's go."

They walk through deserted streets to the outskirts of town until they are enveloped in the delicious smoke of a roasting goat. It comes from a fire in a large hut with no walls. Inside, outlined against the smoke, they can barely see drowsy women with heavy shawls stirring huge pots on the fire and tending roasting animals sacrificed on sticks. Some are nursing babies while the men pass around bottles of rum or sleep in hammocks.

Outside, in a patch of hardened clay crossed with old tire tracks and stained with puddles of motor oil, several trucks are baking in the sun, filled with illegal cargo, prohibited goods, well-camouflaged but predictable: weapons, canned foods, cigarettes, liquor, electronic devices. There are huge Pegasuses, imposing Macks, powerful Superbrigadiers, towering Mercedeses, napping like dinosaurs, slowly digesting diesel fuel in their belching intestines. Only these gigantic, shiny bodies show the true size of the desert, where the huts are nothing and humans are mere insects.

Nando and Adriano stop at the entrance, their eyes teary from the smoke and their appetites whetted by the smell of roasted meat. They are handed a bottle of rum.

A dark, attractive woman approaches and tells them to sit. She doesn't hide her body beneath her shawl as the others do, nor does she cover her hair with a kerchief. She is stuffed into a satiny dress that outlines her breasts, stomach, and rear. The open sleeves reveal her arms and her meaty, cushioned armpits. It's Soledad Bracho, the widow. Dead Marco Bracho's wife. She offers them cigarettes.

"Poor dead man, what he's missing," says Nando so the woman can hear him, and he gives her a slow, sensual look from behind his black glasses. Adriano laughs.

"The two little cousins," she says. "Wherever one goes, the other follows."

They laugh again, but not as loud, a little uncomfortable. She moves among the men, serving the other guests. She returns to their table, bringing cigarettes, roasted goat, and white rum. They eat and drink in silence, watching her come and go, watching her from the front and from behind, studying her strut and her swaying hips.

At five o'clock Nando says, "Brother, you have to go."

"There's still time."

Soledad Bracho approaches, displays her cleavage under their noses, smiles, touches their faces as she sets down their plates, cleans crumbs, removes empty bottles. They see the birthmark on her chin, smell her perfume, feel the fine, silky hairs on her arms. They manage a glimpse of her nipples, which peek out, then hide again.

"The old lady still looks good," says Adriano.

"That's a dish I've already had," replies Nando.

"That's not news to me, cousin, I've had some too."

They laugh and give each other conspiratorial pats on the back.

"That's why she said that wherever I go, you follow."

"What she said was wherever I go, you follow."

Adriano hangs his jacket on the back of his chair and takes off his shirt and tie, which falls to the ground like a colorful snake.

"Pick up my tie, you're stepping on it," orders Nando.

Adriano picks it up and ties it around his neck, over his bare skin.

"That's better," says Nando. "Now put on the jacket too, and the shirt, because the bus is about to leave."

"The bus already left, cousin."

"I'm telling you for the last time. Get yourself to the capital. You're bothering me here."

"Why don't you go to hell."

The rum dances in Adriano's pupils as he stands up shakily, seeing crooked and walking in a zigzag. He approaches Soledad Bracho and puts the tie around her waist — wasp-thin among the mountains of satin — and pulls her against his body. He breathes in her ear, blows on her neck, presses his hardened, feverish sex against hers, which is soft, pleasant, inviting.

Nando watches them and his cheeks flush with fury. For the first time that day he takes off his black glasses to be sure of what he is seeing. The couple rocks side to side, carried away by the rubbing and grinding, and Nando's eyes bulge and become inflamed. Adriano and the widow brazenly caress and fondle each other, as a bitter, heavy displeasure rises in Nando's esophagus. Adriano lifts the satin, inserting his hand, and Nando is overcome with black waves of jealousy.

Adriano opens the zipper of his trousers and in that instant activates the mechanism that leads to his ruin. He pushes the red button. His cousin's alcohol-deadened brain receives the signal clearly. A vertiginous ecstasy explodes in Nando Barragán's head, without past or future, without conscience or consequence, glowing with anger and blinded by pain. A superhuman force takes over his body and suddenly his distorted face, drained of color, reflects the bril-

liant flash of insanity that has overcome him. He stands up and separates the lovers with a sharp, brutal punch. The woman is pro-
pelled against the wall and his cousin is thrown to the ground on his
back at Nando's feet.

The other patrons gather around, shouting, calling for help, but
in the midst of the chaos Nando hears only the secret, persuasive
call of the Colt, tickling him in the ribs, heavy, bulky, available, saying, Here I am.

Adriano raises his arms to protect himself. He tries to laugh,
struggling to make a joke, to give soothing explanations to Nando
Barragán, enter into negotiations with him. But the big hulk pins
him to the ground, choking him. And there he remains, mute and
pathetic, begging for forgiveness with a pair of sunken eyes, flooded
in panic and hope, reluctant to say good-bye forever to the light
of day.

Nando, the Terrible, pays no attention to his pleas. The short
circuit blocking his mind at that moment only allows him to understand how much he detests the abject being he's pinning to the
ground. And he shoots him in the chest.

The echo of the shot causes the widow, dazed and astounded,
to lift her hand to her head and arrange her hair in an automatic,
inane way.

Mortally wounded, Adriano looks at his cousin as if to ask what
happened. He tries to speak, to pull himself together, to return to
normalcy. Until finally he gives up, surrendering to eternity, desolate and still, a cadaver.

The smell of powder, sharp and sweet like marijuana, seeps
into Nando Barragán's being through his nasal passages. It whips his
brain and clears away, in a single lash, the satanic rage and the
drunkenness. Suddenly, he understands that he has killed his
cousin, and the overwhelming realization of having committed that
irrevocable act falls upon him.

Time is suspended for Nando. He knows he has entered the fathomless domain of fate with no possible return. Yellow, disoriented, suddenly vulnerable and hollow, he struggles to control the shivers that shake his soul and he looks around with a lost expression that will dominate his factions from now on.

He puts away the weapon, suddenly cold and silent, kneels next to Adriano's body, and, with awkward tenderness and unhurried, almost feminine movements, Nando begins to dress the still-warm body, as if dressing a newborn baby. He puts the shirt on and buttons it, fighting with the cuff links that refuse to go through the holes. Then he picks up the tie from the ground, wipes it off, ties it around Adriano's neck with a Windsor knot, and adjusts it, making sure it's straight. He puts the arms through the sleeves of the jacket, closes the double row of buttons, and fixes the lapels. Nando wets his index finger with saliva and rubs away the telephone number written in ink on his cousin's hand. When he finishes, he announces softly:

"I am leaving this wretched place and I am taking my cousin Adriano with me."

He puts on his Ray-Bans, hoists the body over his shoulder, and walks away, like a gorilla carrying its offspring.

THE BODY OF Adriano Monsalve slung over his shoulder, Nando Barragán walks for a dozen days and nights in the desert without stopping to eat or sleep. On the horizon, to his right, twelve blood-red dawns appear; to his left, twelve sunsets of the same color fall. He is on a miserable plain in the sovereign reign of nothing, burdened with a sick conscience and a dead body, weighing him down like a cross. Endless expanses of burning sand scorch his feet and the broiling sun blinds his eyes and cracks his skin. There is no water to slake his thirst or shade to calm his hallucinations. No peace for his repentant soul.

"Is all that real, or is it a legend?"

"It's real, but in being told so often, it has become a legend. Or the other way around, it was a legend and then became real. But this is just the beginning."

The body remained intact during the desert crossing. Fresh and proud, as if nothing had happened, no odor, no stiffness, very comfortable on Nando's shoulder. The dead man appears alive and the living one appears dead. They keep each other company during the interminable days in that desolate sand that start where the world ends. Together they fend off the overwhelming loneliness. They even talk with each other. It's nothing important, the same dialogue repeated until it becomes singsong.

"Forgive me, cousin, for killing you."

"You're going to pay for it. You can keep the widow, and the guilt too."

"I don't want either of them."

In the deepest part of the desert, where the sound of the sea cannot penetrate, they find what they have come looking for. A hovel in a nest of desolate winds, square with two open doors, one to the north, the other to the south. Gale-force winds tear through the structure, howling like tormented souls, whistling, crying, tumbling against themselves, like cats fighting or lovers playing, and then they become indifferent and leave for the open desert, each wind in its own direction.

Nando enters the rancho, carefully stretches out Adriano's body on the dirt floor, and sits by his side, to wait. It's the first time that he has rested in many days and he sinks into sleep, undulating like the surrounding sand dunes, and has a vision.

"Something terrifying appeared before him? A supernatural being?"

To tell the truth, he only dreamed of Tío, his uncle, a simple, rustic old man whose singular peculiarity was his extremely advanced age. His old pre-Columbian body was badly punished by arthritis and arteriosclerosis.

"Tío, I killed my cousin Adriano Monsalve," confesses the sleeping Nando Barragán.

"Yes, I see," says the old man.

"You are the only one who knows the laws of our people. I have come for you to tell me what I must do."

"First, you must take the boy away from here. Don't leave him for the sand and wind to devour; bury him deep, in dry, black soil. Then come back here to me."

Nando blindly obeys. He journeys with his cousin until he finds noble, inviting soil. He says good-bye forever to Adriano, and upon his return, which has taken a long time, he sees the old man waiting for him in the same spot, like Gandhi or a child from Bangladesh, whipped by the hurricane trying to carry his flimsy, naked body off to heaven. With that miserable appearance, Tío delivers the most relentless of sentences. From his toothless, foul-smelling mouth come the terrible words that will sink the Barragáns and Monsalves into hell on earth.

"You have spilled blood of your own people. This is the most serious of mortal sins. You have declared war among brothers, which will be passed down to your sons, and the sons of your sons."

"That is too cruel," protests Nando. "I want to cleanse my guilt in good faith."

"Among our people, blood pays for blood. The Monsalves will avenge this death, you will pay with your life, and your brothers, the Barragáns, will do the same and the chain will not be broken until the end of time," the old man shouts angrily, deaf to Nando's pleas.

"If I go to a priest," Nando tries to argue, "he will bless me and give me a penitence of prayers, rosaries, fasts, and whipping. I will endure it and be in peace with God."

"There is no priest or blessing that can help you. The church hasn't been through here since the days of Pablo VI, and he only waved as he flew over in an airplane on his way to Japan. This is a land without God: the only thing that matters here is what our ancestors said."

"I could look for a judge to try me and imprison me. I would serve my sentence and return to freedom, in peace."

"No judge, lawyer, or tribunal comes here. Those are luxuries for foreigners. Our only law is written in the sand by the wind and our only justice is meted out by our own hands."

Things have always been, and will always be, as Tío, the old prophet, holder of truth and expert in the inevitable, says and Nando capitulates. He lowers his head, swallowing bitter saliva, locking his gaze on the ground, and accepts his cruel fortune.

The old man begins to recite the code of honor, laws passed on from generation to generation, the rules of war, which must be respected.

"The Barragáns and Monsalves can no longer live together," declares the voice of the ancestors. "They must leave the land where they were born and raised, where their forefathers are buried. They are banned from the desert. One family must live in the city and the other in the port. One cannot trespass upon the territory of the other. If you kill your enemy, you must do so with your own hand; no one may do it for you. Fighting is done man to man, not by third parties. You must not harm anyone unarmed or unaware, nor surprise anyone from behind."

"When can I avenge the deaths of my family?" asked Nando, his back to the wind, having already accepted his role in the nightmare as if it were the only reality.

"Only on *zetas*, which fall nine nights after a death or when a month has passed, or a year. On *zetas* your enemies will be waiting for you, so you will not catch them unaware. When one of them is killed, you will do the same. On *zetas* you will defend yourself and your family, because the Monsalves will come for you."

"Is that all?"

"You will not harm old people, women, or children. This punishment is for men only."

"Tell me how I must bury my people."

"In their best clothing, dressed by the one who loved them most. You must place them facedown in the coffin, and when you remove the body from your house, the feet must go first."

"Who will win the war?"

"The family that eliminates all the males of the other."

"Is there something that can be done to avoid all this misfortune?"

"Nothing. Now go and make sure all deaths occur according to this law."

Tío dissolves into his sighs, lost in the hurricane like a fart in the storm. Nando Barragán exits through the southern door and follows a straight line through the boundless yellow desert, heading for his family to guide them on the path of their new fate.

"He managed to leave behind the desert and gradually forgot about Tío and even crying over Adriano's death, but he never awakened from the hallucination. Over time he confused it with vigilance and resigned himself to living with it."

"It was more than resignation. There was pride. The art of vengeance became a question of honor."

THE RUDDY sun disappears, its licking flames extinguished, and Nando Barragán finds himself in a green-tiled cube, cold and inhospitable. The burning colors of the desert, the incandescent reds, oranges, and yellows, have dissipated, and the world is now sterile and green, mint green, optical green, doctor's-scrub-suit green.

Painfully symmetrical tiles cover the walls of the recovery room in the hospital, ranged in identical parallel rows on the too high ceiling, on the too close walls, on the floor that rises and falls unstably. Nando Barragán feels as if his aching body were floating among the cold, water-colored surfaces. His consciousness, still asleep, swims in green skies of anesthesia while lashes of an inexplicable and deep pain shake his mistreated body, waking him. He detects a strong odor of disinfectant.

"It smells like cleaning fluid," he thinks in his first flash of lucidity. "I must be at the circus."

He dreams for a moment about the elephants at the Egred Brothers Circus. They seem very old and battered, and he remembers himself years earlier, already an adult, eating pink clouds of cotton candy, dazzled by the wildcats, the trapeze artists, the magicians, all seen for the first time.

The circus vanishes and Nando returns to his oppressive green world. He dreams that Milena is approaching him, her made-up face expressive and her lips moving. She speaks words that fall like drops of light in the dark pool of his lethargic brain.

"Do you love me, Milena? Are you telling me that you love me?"

She is no longer a bishop. The phantasmal red shadows have receded, and once again the black leotard covers her worldly form.

"I'm so thirsty, Milena. Put your hands in the green water and give me a drink. I want to drink from your hands."

"They operated on you, Nando." Her voice emerges from the depths of the sea. "They took out the bullets. You're fine. The doctors say you're not going to die."

"Is that you, Milena? You didn't leave me?"

"No, but now I'm going."

A SLIVER OF a moon breathes sweetly over the night in the port. The black waves are heavy, like docile mammals approaching in a herd to lick the foundations of the big house. The illuminated terrace levitates over the water, like a UFO, and in one of its corners, protected from the breeze, is an intimate table with two places set, a white linen tablecloth, crystal wineglasses, a vase of red roses. Nelson Ned is crooning a romantic song on the stereo.

"It sounds like the set of a soap opera."

Even worse. It is. Their life is pure *telenovela.* At least inside the house, because outside it's a horror movie, with bright lights shining all night, closed-circuit television to detect intruders, bodyguards who pass making their rounds, and dogs trained to kill.

A woman is leaning on the balustrade of the terrace: tall, young, perfect, with the ideal curves of a fashion model and wearing a vaporous dress of pearl gray muslin.

"She wouldn't be that perfect."

Yes, she is. Before she got married, Alina Jericó de Monsalve was a national beauty queen. Now she's looking out at the infinite darkness, letting the warm breeze tangle her long chestnut blond hair and humming irritably with Nelson Ned. She forgets everything, standing there, and just lets time pass.

Until she looks at her watch. She sees how late it is and a dark shadow covers her beautiful face. She looks at the watch again, first with annoyance, then with anxiety, and finally with despair. She bites her carefully manicured nails, her brilliant, white teeth mercilessly attacking them, peeling off the Revlon polish, ripping off hangnails. Drops of blood appear, but she ignores them and continues gnawing like a mouse.

Alina goes into the house, where everything is new and expensive—luxury in Miami pastels. Her high heels dig into the soft white carpet. She enters the kitchen, which is fully equipped with microwave ovens and multiuse electric appliances, and approaches the cook, an old woman wearing a polyester sweater to protect herself from the air-conditioning.

"What did you make, Yela?"

"Sea bass, rice with coconut, and roasted plantain."

"Did you chill the wine?"

"Why should I, when he only drinks Kola Román?"

"It's getting late and he's still not here."

"Don't wait any longer, child. Don Mani won't arrive until dawn."

"How do you know?" asks Alina, as if begging her not to answer.

"He's out there somewhere, probably killing somebody."

"But he promised me he wouldn't," she says without a shred of conviction or hope.

Alina Jericó de Monsalve, the ex–beauty queen, walks slowly to her bedroom, her shoulders drooping and her spine pricked with the needles of stress. Her gait is no longer studied and coquettish, her smile no longer practiced or radiant, as it was when she strutted the runway at the national beauty pageant amid camera flashes and thunderous applause. She enters her large marble bathroom, takes two Bayer aspirin from a bottle, and swallows them with a drink of water, to see if they can help this sadness.

She considers going to sleep, but decides against it and goes to the TV room, where she falls into an overstuffed chair. The former beauty queen takes off her shoes, folds her long, perfect legs beneath her, and presses the on button on the remote control. On one station a politician is being interviewed. On another a TV star is kissing a Mexican actress. Alina watches for a while without really seeing them. She rocks a little in her chair, hugging her legs, murmuring to herself, given over to self-indulgence. The TV star and his lover have stopped kissing and are arguing jealously as Alina begins to feel drowsy. She stretches her aching back, relaxes, and falls asleep.

The midnight *telenovela* ends and the final newscast reports an attempt on the life of Nando Barragán a few hours earlier in a bar in the city, but the slumbering Alina doesn't hear the news.

"Should I bring you your dinner, Miss Alina?" says Yela, awakening her.

"I don't want to eat."

"Then go to bed, child. I'll turn off the lights."

Alina goes to her room, removes the muslin dress and pearl necklace, and puts on a transparent negligee. She lies down on the king-size bed with its satin sheets and fixes her gray eyes on a spot on the wall.

Now she's overtired and frightened, at the mercy of a sharp feeling of abandonment. A single thought drills at her brain. Her husband has forgotten about her, but not to be with another woman; that she could deal with. She knows she is young and beautiful; she could put up a good fight and come out the winner. No, despite her commitment to her husband, she cannot deny her husband's true passion: killing other men.

Hours later, a pinkish dawn emerges in the sky, and the sea, speckled with foam and seagulls, awakens. Alina's eyes, still open and burning from insomnia, remain glued to the same spot on the wall, her heart ruminating on the same ominous feeling of despair, as the silhouette of a man appears at her bedroom door.

He's thin and wiry, not yet thirty, but the greenish tint of his skin caused by too many sleepless nights makes him appear older. His dark temper is immediately discernible, but he's tall and strong and well built. His tennis shoes and the unbuttoned, untucked shirt give him the air of a young gang member, but the heavy bags under his eyes hint at many years of nightmares. His gaze is magnetic and his face is attractive despite the wide half-moon scar covering the left side, lowering his eye and wrinkling his cheek.

Mani Monsalve leans silently on the door frame, looking at his wife's messy blond hair and her model's body tense with exhaustion from waiting. She doesn't see him, but she feels his presence.

"Did you kill Nando Barragán?" she asks without turning to look at him.

"I don't know," he says. He approaches the bed and, carefully, as if he were about to touch an electrified wire, tries to caress her.

"Wash your hands first," she says.

Mani enters the bathroom, carelessly removing his clothes and dropping them on the floor. In the steaming shower, he relaxes under the powerful stream of water. He returns to the bedroom naked and damp, his hair dripping, the minty taste of Colgate on his breath. He gets into bed, reveling in the smoothness of the satin sheets. He turns on the wide-screen TV that he had installed on the ceiling. In slow motion and without sound, he watches a succession of images from an old Western movie. He allows his mind to empty, as he becomes enraptured with the galloping horses, and moves closer to his wife, putting his arm beneath her head and hugging her.

Upon contact with her husband's still-damp body, she softens and the mountain of anger accumulated during the night melts away.

"It's over," he says convincingly. "Forget it."

She wants to forget, to believe that it is over, that it won't happen again, to be happy. She just wants to forgive him, hold him close. She just wants to be able to stop worrying. She is about to open her body and soul to him without reproach or condition, as she does every night, but she calls upon her last thread of willpower, her last drop of character.

She says, "Do you remember when you promised to stop the fighting? You haven't kept your word. I am going to make you a promise and I will keep my word." She pulls away from her husband, sits up on the bed, and looks at him with resolve, not daring to blink.

"You look so sexy when you get angry," he says.

She doesn't give in to his teasing and continues: "When I get pregnant I am going to leave you, because I don't want my child to be killed for having your name."

"That morning Alina Jericó threatened her husband, but he didn't hear her because he was already asleep."

He's not asleep. Mani Monsalve closes his eyes and doesn't answer, but he does hear her, and he will never forget her words.

2

"THE MONSALVES *lived in the port and the Barragáns in the city?*"

"*Yes. After Tío's curse expelling them from the desert, they separated. Nando Barragán became the head of his family and Mani Monsalve the head of his. The two families grew and became wealthy, but each one on its own, because they only dealt with each other to kill each other.*"

"*You mean after the first death, there were others?*"

"*After the first death, war broke out for many years. Just today, there was crying and the church bells rang. The first death was followed by the second, third, tenth, and on above thirty or forty. For each Barragán that perished out of vengeance, a Monsalve died, and vice versa. That's how the chain of blood was fed and the cemetery filled with gravestones.*"

"*Did they always make their living from the black market?*"

"*No. That was just at the beginning.*"

"*Then how did they make so much money?*"

"*Everyone knows, but no one will say.*"

"THE PEOPLE *in the Silverado that just went by were the Barragáns. Their bodyguards were in the Toyotas following it. Look, you can still see them.*"

At daybreak the caravan of five vehicles speeds through the city streets, a Silverado and four four-door Toyota jeeps with Venezuelan license plates. They breeze by like a gust of wind, tires squealing and burning, making a show of their power, climbing the sidewalk on corners, claiming the right of way, ignoring traffic lights, forcing students to jump out of the way, splashing water from puddles onto women buying milk, striking fear into the hearts of the lottery-ticket vendors and the dogs in the plaza.

"In this city the people aren't awakened by roosters, but by murderers."

"Which one is Nando Barragán? The man driving the Silverado?"

"Yes, the one with the dark glasses and the cigarette in his mouth. The one who looks like a big criminal. The other guy is his kid brother Narciso Barragán."

It's a gray metallic Chevrolet Silverado pickup truck with flaming orange stripes on the sides. The windows are closed and inside the air-conditioning hums coolly.

Nando Barragán barely fits behind the steering wheel and has to tilt his head forward to keep it from hitting the roof. His body is less bulky than before. The attempt on his life at the bar didn't kill him, but it reduced his weight.

The younger man traveling at his side, his brother Narciso, is the financier. At twenty-seven, he manages the family's hugely profitable dirty businesses, keeping track of all the money that comes in under the table. He is reclining low in his seat with his head laid back and his eyes closed, half asleep, off somewhere in his mind, unaware of his surroundings. His usual state.

"How could anyone have seen them with the windows closed? The Silverado has tinted windows precisely so no one can see inside."

Everybody in the city knows what Narciso looks like. They know his eyes from memory, even people who have never seen them. Large and black, they're the fierce eyes of the people from the desert. The moist, fevered gaze of a Bedouin. Or an epileptic. His eyelashes are heavy and seductively long. His closely cropped beard and his dark, silky mustache don't scratch the skin of the women who throw themselves upon him, because he uses brilliantine.

Everything else about him is ordinary. Medium height, maybe a little too skinny. Hidden beneath his mustache, his lips are too thin. Teeth, who knows? It doesn't matter. Anyone who looks at his eyes would swear he's the most handsome man in the city.

Narciso always dresses in white from head to toe. Shirt, pants, Panama hat, Italian leather loafers, soft as slippers, no socks. That's how he is. Immaculate, impeccable, like a nurse, or a girl at her first communion.

"They say no one has ever seen a stain on his clothing, not even blood. But that's because he never gets his hands dirty. He handles cash, not weapons. He's the money man and he leaves the dirty work to his brothers. Everybody thinks he's a coward, but his friends say he's not. They say it's not out of cowardice, but because killing just isn't his style."

A dedicated playboy, Narciso Barragán falls in love with all the beautiful women he meets, deeply and from the bottom of his heart. When he tells them that he loves them, he becomes as emotional as a poet, and desires ardently to make them his, to worship them, all of them. He cries when a woman leaves him and he would give his own life for each of his innumerable lovers.

Part of his success as a seducer lies in his singing ability. He writes songs and plays the guitar. They call him El Lírico. Some people say he has the most beautiful voice they've ever heard. Others say it's nothing special; it's his way of gazing off into infinity as he sings that makes it unique. His brothers chastise him. Wandering around preoccupied with his verses, he becomes careless, giving himself up to a bohemian lifestyle, falling in love, forgetting about business for days at a time.

He goes by in the Silverado like a silver flash, traveling the streets of the city, and people see him sitting next to Nando, though the closed, tinted windows make it impossible to see him. Not only do they see him, they can even detect a hint of his cologne in the air.

"There are women who swear it's not his eyes that are so attractive, but his cologne."

It's a sweet, persistent fragrance that envelops him and is absorbed by clients who shake his hand, women who kiss him, even friends who stand near him. It clings to everything he touches: pool cues, female buttocks, telephone receivers, automobile steering wheels.

"If a woman is unfaithful to her husband with Narciso Barragán, his indelible odor denounces him. There is talk of money that passes through his hands and months later still carries his scent. Some say it is Drakkar Noir by Guy Laroche. Others insist it's an expensive women's perfume, or patchouli, or incense, even essence of marijuana. No one agrees, but when the authorities want to locate Narciso they find him easily, no matter where he hides, by his smell."

Today he goes by in the gray Silverado headed somewhere on the outskirts of town. But it's not common to see him in the big war machine belonging to his brother. Narciso's car is totally different. It's sumptuous, unlike any other, made to order directly from the factory, the only one like it in the country, the world even. It's a violet Lincoln Continental limousine, twenty feet long.

"Violet?"

Furiously violet, Holy Week purple.

"Inside and out?"

Only outside. The interior is upholstered in tan leather.

ALTHOUGH THE asphalt has turned into taffy beneath the fiery morning sun, the gray Silverado glides swiftly like a yacht on a still lake. The two brothers travel in silence.

Nando is lost in thought, giving free rein to nostalgia, and Narciso is comfortable in his drowsiness, not thinking about anything in particular. There are two Toyota jeeps with bodyguards in front of them and another two behind. The caravan leaves the city far behind and arrives at a miserable village surrounded by dirty sand and swampland.

The lead jeep is farther ahead, zigzagging around several amphibious huts and sliding through puddles of petroleum onto a beach covered in sour-smelling garbage and industrial waste. It stops at the last hovel, which is set apart from the others. The jeeps' doors open and the gang of bodyguards spills out—Pajarito Pum Pum, El Tijeras, El Cachumbo, Simón Balas. They surround the place snorting prepotently and waving their black automatic weapons. They search and sniff, and when they're satisfied the place is empty, they signal their bosses.

Nando and Narciso Barragán descend from the Silverado and enter a kitchen with no walls and a roof made of greasy tin blackened by smoke. Piles of rusty tools, broken lamps, stems of dry banana stalks, cowhides, wooden buckets with staved-in bottoms, faded Christmas ornaments, replacement parts from cars, tractors, and airplanes, and multitudes of other, unidentified materials lie scattered about.

Everything is rusted, worm-eaten, and worn out. Narciso, accustomed to contemplating beauty, looks around and his soul shrinks.

There's a table that was once blue, and a few stools. Off in a corner a coal stove is lit; in another dozens of candles burn on an altar covered with multicolored statues of saints, chipped crèche figurines, replicas of the childless virgin, and sheepless shepherds. Mixed in with this holy populace are a few pagans: porcelain ballerinas, plaster dolls. In the center of the crowd stands a figure larger than the rest, with a black cloth draped over its shoulders. Its glass eyes overflow with sorrow, and sparse, but human, hair covers its delicate head. A broom is held firmly in the figure's hands. It is Fray Martín de Porres, the mulatto patron saint of lepers.

Nando Barragán cups his hands around his mouth and shouts, looking out at the trash-strewn beach, "Roberta Caracola! Mamá Roberta!"

There is a movement off in the distance. Nando calls out again and something resembling a human emerges from behind a pile of empty bottles and stumbles over the remains of an old boat. The figure approaches, trotting like a dog, swerving around empty cans, rags, broken bottles, tampons.

It's a tiny old caramel-colored woman, completely wrinkled, with indefinite, incomplete features, like a poorly formed plaster statue. She's missing her nose and maybe her lips, or eyebrows. No one knows for sure because no one can bear to look her in the face. Her fingers are missing the last joints, or maybe she has no fingers at all.

She scurries over to the kitchen and stops, dwarflike, in front of Nando Barragán, who asks her, "How are you?"

"Oh, sort of falling apart a bit," she answers in a mushy voice. "What brings you here, and who's that with you?"

"I've come for your blessing. This is my brother Narciso."

Narciso looks at the old woman with his astounded playboy eyes, horrified. He's never seen anything like this in his life and he's trying to figure out the foul-smelling monster in front of him. Finally he understands and a sudden dizziness makes him lean against the wall: it's leprosy. The old woman has leprosy. Or, maybe, a biblical leper has incarnated in the form of this ragged old woman.

"Narciso's nerves were on edge and his stomach was churning. That visit to the leprous witch was one of the most difficult tests of his life. He simply could not bear sickness, old age, physical decay. Wounds, sores, and deformities appalled him. He couldn't look at blood without getting upset."

Ignoring Narciso, the old woman mumbles litanies, babbles sacred tongue twisters and prayers, thanks the Virgen del Carmen, the patron saint of difficult tasks. She goes on to invoke other virgins and martyrs. She exorcises demons, obstacles, enemies, and dangers, and finishes by showering blessings on the piously lowered head of Nando Barragán. Then she says, "Make an offering to Fray Martín de Porres."

"He's a worthless saint who only makes miracles for women and sick people," laughs Nando.

"Swallow your words, Nando Barragán, because he's the most vengeful saint of them all. If you don't please him, he'll take revenge. You better fear and respect him."

"I'm not afraid of any saint, but I am afraid of you," answers Nando, as he gives the old woman a wad of bills and asks her to read his fortune in a cup of cacao.

She puts the pot on the fire, brings the liquid inside to a boil three times, and pours two cups. She brings them to the table, one in each hand, placing her mutilated fingers ostentatiously in the boiling liquid. She scrutinizes the two men. She wants to know how far they are willing to go. "Drink it," she says.

Nando takes the cup, not thinking twice, and drinks its contents in one gulp, burning his tongue. He puts the cup on the once blue table. Narciso doesn't touch his cup.

Roberta Caracola locks her dry, dull eyes onto the boy's soft, damp eyes. He tries to explain: "Don't be offended, Señora. If I don't drink the cacao, it's not out of dislike. It's because I want my fate to remain a secret."

"I don't need to read any cup to know your fate, because it's written plainly on your face. You're a poet and poets fare badly in war."

Narciso loses control and becomes pale. He stands up, barely refraining from smacking the rotting, meddlesome old woman. He angrily tells Nando that he'll wait for him outside. He goes back to the Silverado, turns on the air-conditioning and the cassette player. The beautiful young man struggles to calm the rapid blinking of his eyelids and closes his precious eyes, trying not to think of anything. But he can't.

THE PLACE smells of urine, soap, and dirty rags. It smells like prison.

The breathing and swearing of a hundred and thirty prisoners crowded into twenty cells hangs thickly in the dark air of the passageway. A hundred and thirty pairs of lungs breathing the same rectangle of stagnant air passing from man to man, cell to cell, transmitting tuberculosis, syphilis, rabies, dementia.

"What is it with that Fernely?!" comes the distant howl of the guard.

Immediately the news is murmured along the passageway, cell to cell. The gossip occupies the inmates' attention the entire morning. Fernely, alias the Communist, is free. The same man who talked like a leaky faucet when he arrived at the prison two years ago. They put the pressure on him and he squealed. He ratted on his buddies. That's the price he paid to save his life.

In prison they nicknamed him the Communist, but nobody knows if he is one. And nobody believes the story that he's an arms dealer; more likely he's an assassin for hire. A killer, pure and simple, operating on his own, or a paramilitary soldier, or a guerrilla or counterguerrilla, God knows which. Maybe all of them at the same time, or in turns.

There's an endless list of accusations against him, but they're going to let him go, because someone on the outside bought his freedom. Someone, someone powerful, bought his freedom. They say it cost a hundred thousand dollars. In exchange for the money, they say, the file disappeared and the authorities declared him innocent.

He never lacked money; everybody knows that because they've seen him buy privileges. Some *patrón* is backing him. Maybe that's who's rescuing him now.

Holman Fernely's money certainly wasn't used to buy affection or company. The two years he was locked up he spent holed up in his cell, lonely as a mouse. He didn't make any friends, because he didn't trust anyone. He never talked. He didn't waste his time with the human race.

No woman ever visited him, not even his mother, and mothers never fail a prisoner, no matter how ruined his life is or how low he has fallen. Fernely didn't have any family, lovers, or friends. Even the prostitutes who paid visits didn't want to be with him. They thought he would contaminate them, and that any girl who went to bed with him would remain infected with his sadness for the rest of her life.

Fernely never spoke to anyone. He was only heard to repeat sayings every now and then, and only when absolutely necessary. But he used only common phrases. He had no imagination for speaking and could only repeat words that others had spoken before. Maybe he didn't speak his own words so that no one could figure him out psychologically.

"What's with that Fernely?!" howls the guard again.

The sound of footsteps is heard at the end of the passageway, unhurried, in a straight line, toward the front door. The man taking those steps can't be seen because there are no lightbulbs and the covered windows don't let in any light. He moves in the darkness like a black hulk. Tall and thin. From the sound of his steps it's obvious that he's wearing rubber flip-flops. A halting shuffle to who knows where.

The thin man passes the rows of cells on either side of him. Invisible arms, like branches in the night, stretch out from between the bars, touching him, pulling on his clothing. Voices from the darkness echoing the same hopeless whispers that resonate each time someone goes free.

"Don't forget about me when you get outside."

"Remember your neighbor, brother."

"Leave me a memento. I was your buddy. A little money, your radio, your chain . . . "

"Leave me your blanket. I was your only friend."

He doesn't hear them, nor is he moved by their lies. He crosses the sea of pleading arms without answering or even bothering to look at them. He doesn't say good-bye to Crazy Rat, Dry Blood, Good Boy, Witch Face. He doesn't distinguish between them, Crazy Blood, Dry Boy, Rat Face, Good Witch. They're all the same to him. The transvestites fawn over him, Lola, Katerín, Margarita, with their falsetto voices, plucked eyebrows, nylon stockings, and all their other legitimately feminine attributes. They're wasting their time with him. A pair of authentic breasts can't move him, much less fake ones.

He walks along indifferently, with an empty expression, until someone confronts him.

"How did you get them to let you go? Did you rat on your mother?"

He doesn't respond.

"So what are you, guerrilla, paramilitary soldier, *sicario*?"

Still no response. He leaves them all dying to know.

Finally he arrives at the end of the corridor. He approaches the guards and reaches out his hand so they can stamp him with the exit stamp. There is a tattoo on his forearm that says "God and Mother."

The prisoner in flip-flops goes out to the patio and is illuminated by the faded winter sun. He is tall and ugly, with ash-blond hair, thinning and strawlike, and a sparse beard.

He looks at the white sky and takes out a handkerchief to rub his eyes. They're red and puffy from chronic conjunctivitis, which keeps them filled with thick tears. He pulls a bottle of medicine from his pocket, puts a drop in each eye, and rubs them again with his handkerchief.

He crosses the patio without looking at the line of prisoners waiting with their plates for their food rations. He comes to a gate. Another guard stamps his tattooed arm and lets him pass.

Fernely approaches an improvised altar with burning prayer candles. He kneels in front of the Virgin of Mercy, closes his infected eyes, and prays that he dies before he has to return. He repeats the same prayers as the other released inmates, without adding or omitting words. Even his dialogue with heaven is prefabricated.

He goes through some empty lots that serve as playing fields and arrives at the last gate, the one leading to the street and freedom. No one prevents the prisoner from passing through because all the charges against him have been dropped, by miracle or by bribery: assassination, desertion, breaking and entering, illegal use of explosives, illegal possession of weapons, extortion, kidnapping. If there's no record, then there's no guilt. The man is innocent and can no longer be incarcerated.

His identification card is returned and he is handed a paper bag containing a pair of shoes, but he gestures that he prefers to wear the flip-flops.

"Out of curiosity, Fernely," asks the last guard lazily, "what occupation are you going to pursue on the outside?"

"That's for me to know and you to find out."

A late-model Mercedes is waiting for him at the prison gate. Holman Fernely looks for the last time at the high cement walls without enthusiasm.

"After a while, crocodile," he says. Then he shuffles across the street in his flip-flops, gets into the Mercedes, and rides away.

DAWN BREAKS over the city as a boy sleeps in the suffocating darkness of his room. It's Arcángel Barragán, Nando Barragán's youngest brother. He's dreaming that a blue iguana is watching him from the lighted interior of a crystal ball. Though it's enclosed, the reptile is not upset and doesn't try to escape. It remains there inside, comfortable and tranquil, looking out at the world with resignation.

Arcángel Barragán is lying facedown in his bed, covered by a sheet. His pulse is slow and his breathing is barely perceptible. Rather than being asleep, he appears to be unconscious, to have escaped from life. Like the iguana in his dream, he is trapped inside a bubble. Docile, even-tempered, isolated from the dangers of the outside world, he doesn't notice the heat of the locked room.

The glint of sunlight filtering through the crack in the wooden shutters falls upon a cowlick in his hair, illuminating it. His skin has the color and sparkle of honey. A small gold hoop perforates his left earlobe. His profile is silhouetted against the pillow, so fine and soft that it could be a child's, or a woman's.

The boy moves, rolls onto his side, and the sheet slides to the floor. Naked, he lies there radiantly, like a being fallen from heaven, barely stirring as he breathes. There is a bandage on his right arm. From his neck hangs the cross of Caravaca, like the one his brother Nando wears.

The room is too spacious to be a bedroom. It is full of weights and exercise equipment; there's even a basketball hoop in one corner, and four brightly colored pinball machines lined up, one next to the other, against the wall.

A woman dressed in black enters. She has removed her shoes to avoid making noise. She is already past thirty but not yet forty; her eyes are hard and her eyebrows thick.

"In the barrio they say she looked just like Irene Pappas, the Greek actress."

She never speaks. She's mute. She is La Muda Barragán, Nando and Arcángel's maternal aunt.

"They say that La Muda didn't speak because she didn't want to, not because she couldn't."

They say a lot of things about La Muda, because they can't stand her silence. They find her aggressive and pedantic. People don't like those who don't share their secrets, or confess their weaknesses, and she is a woman of granite, capable of withstanding torment without complaining or running off to hide or to tell someone.

"They say that once she couldn't bear it any longer and cried on the shoulder of her boyfriend."

"Not true. She never had a boyfriend because she wore a chastity belt her whole life and it was always locked with a key."

"Who made her wear it?"

"No one. She simply decided to protect her virginity with the contraption."

"Who had the key?"

"No one. She locked it herself, threw the key in the toilet, and flushed it down."

"And she never wore colors. Not even gray or white."

She never wears colors. In this she is as strict as the rest of the Barragán women. Since they began burying their men they wear only black, although their clothes have a greenish sheen from so much use. Custom dictates a year of mourning for each death, and the women can't finish one before the next one is added on. It's like what happens to prisoners with long sentences—their lives are shorter than their punishment.

When La Muda enters her nephew's bedroom she doesn't feel the dense and humid heat that has accumulated during the night. Like her chastity belt, her black dress acts as armor against sensations and feelings.

She kneels beside the sleeping boy and gazes at him for a long while. She watches him so long that she sees his dream; he's looking at the blue iguana inside the crystal ball. She learned to read other people's dreams a long time ago and she can actually see them, like movies.

La Muda's eyes are fixed upon her nephew. Her thickly lashed eyes are indecipherable, like the Holy Mysteries and the Holy Father, who judges but doesn't forgive. Her eyes see everything but don't tell anything.

"What La Muda must have seen with that penetrating stare."

"They say she could see through walls, that's how she knew everyone else's secrets."

The woman observes the celestial beauty of the young man and lets time pass. For five, ten, fifteen minutes, she contemplates his young body, so smooth and fresh, so still and empty, abandoned by its inhabitant, who has left to fly high in a dream without consciousness or memory, far from that bed, that room, this world. La Muda moves her hand and caresses the honey-colored skin on his back, barely brushing it.

She gets up, leaves the room, and then returns with a tray bearing a cup of coffee, a flask of hydrogen peroxide, cotton balls, tweezers, gauze, adhesive tape, and a bottle of syrup. She opens the room's two windows that look out onto an interior patio and wakes Arcángel by shaking his shoulder. She hands him the coffee.

"Last night I dreamed that you were touching me," he says, with his voice still buried in the back of his throat.

"No," she indicates with her head. "You dreamed about an iguana," she thinks.

Arcángel, still asleep, drinks the coffee with his eyes closed. When he finishes it he takes the bandage off his arm. A bullet has left a wound that won't heal. La Muda kneels at the side of the bed again and devotes her energies to healing. She cleans the infection with tweezers and cotton balls, pours some hydrogen peroxide on it, and scrubs the unhealthy flesh as if she were scouring floor tiles.

The pain wakes the boy up and he laughs and yells, tries to prevent his aunt from continuing by grabbing her wrist, then laughs again and lets himself be dominated by her, since she's stronger. She holds him down firmly, like a cowboy branding cattle.

Arcángel's forehead is damp from the pain in his arm and his aunt gives him a spoonful of syrup and wipes the sweat with a handkerchief moistened with alcohol.

"Clean it more, Muda," he begs. "Even though it hurts. So it will heal."

But he doesn't want it to heal. He would remain there all morning offering his arm, bearing the pain, just to be near her. He wants to prolong this daily torture that he would gladly bear as long as she doesn't go away, as long as she doesn't let go of him. He doesn't want to wait for the next day, the new ritual of cotton balls and disinfectant, for her hands to touch him again. He notices unhappily that the wound is getting better and fears that when it closes up she won't come in the morning anymore to cool his forehead with a handkerchief dampened with alcohol.

"What monstrousness—that child Arcángel was in love with his aunt. That's why he didn't like other women."

"Yes, he liked others. He has several girlfriends and he makes love to them. They're trusted girls from the neighborhood, from families that they know. La Muda brings them to his room and locks them in with him, because Arcángel is prohibited from leaving it, for his own safety. Nando gave the orders. He takes better care of Arcángel than he does himself. Especially since the attempt on Arcángel's life."

Arcángel was wounded in the arm three months earlier, in an attempt on his life in the capital. It happened in an engineering classroom in a private university, where Nando had sent him to keep him away from the war and the business.

"You must study and prepare yourself," Nando suddenly told him one day as he ate a plate of beans. "And live far from here. I want your life to be different. The rest of us are stupid. I want you to be intelligent."

Without further explanation or asking his opinion, Nando sent him off to the capital with two of his men to watch him night and day. The trip was made in secret to avoid risk, and he arrived at the university with a false identity, a faked high school diploma, since he hadn't finished yet, and under definitive orders to stay away from anyone who might recognize him and from women who might fall in love with him.

To hide the perfection of his features they cropped his hair, which only made them stand out more, and they fitted him with fake glasses. Thanks to the monthly stipend that Nando sent, Arcángel, who now went by the name Armando Lopera, lived surrounded by luxuries, but overwhelmed by the cold mountain air and the relentless loneliness that he didn't dare break by exposing himself.

Despite the elaborate precautions, the Monsalves found him and launched an attempt upon his life. They failed only because at the moment they shot him another student accidentally intervened, taking the brunt of the gunfire and giving his life for someone he didn't even know by name. Nothing remained of the incident except a mention on the crime page of the paper the next day, the wound in Arcángel's arm, and an astonishment stamped forever on his soul, which is why he is now thought of as an ethereal creature.

The boy had to leave the capital and return to the city, forgetting forever his university studies and any prospect of a normal life. His older brother's zeal to keep Arcángel alive and free from harm was so great that he kept him locked in the largest and most inaccessible room in the house, under the constant care of La Muda. Nando bought him the pinball machines so he wouldn't get bored and the gym equipment so he could keep in shape, but most of all to correct a strange defect that Arcángel had acquired, along with the astonishment, as a consequence of the attempt on his life. He had the habit of walking on the tips of his toes, as if he wanted to avoid contact with the ground.

Like the rest of the members of the clan, Arcángel follows every detail of Nando's orders. It never occurs to him to question them, much less disobey them. Nando's word is law. He told Arcángel to stay locked up, and Arcángel obeys. It's discipline. But also natural inclination. The animal in the forest is distrustful of the outside world, and breathes tranquilly only in the dim light of its lair.

When he works out, lifting weights or shooting basketball, he always does it with the same movements, precise and studied, again and again and again until he reaches a hundred; then he starts over. For him it's become a habitual, repetitive routine, like a caged animal pacing to kill time and ward off anxiety.

La Muda prepares his food with her own hands and serves him on an irregular schedule, whenever she thinks he might be hungry. He eats very little, only two or three bites off each plate, then pushes it away and dives into a painless sleep that stretches on and sticks to him like gum, from which he can't escape until his aunt comes and rescues him by waking him.

The pinball machines have become an addiction. He stands in front of them and grabs them as if he were going to penetrate them. He fondles and caresses them, pushing them forward and pulling them back, shooting the mercury-colored balls with precision, handling the flippers with mastery. He transmits the rhythm and energy of his hips to the machine and holds it like a woman on a dance floor. Connected to the machine body and soul, he becomes one with it, swept up in the same impulses and reflexes. The wound on his arm doesn't bother him because it's anesthetized, like his brain, caught up in the hypnotic trance the machine induces in him.

One of the machines features images of a counterguerrilla mercenary, with an eye patch and a wild man's face, crawling through a tropical jungle and submerging into malaria-infested swamps. Another shows a band of Amazon women with enormous breasts, hair falling to their ankles and fluorescent eyes demanding blood. They carry clubs for breaking skulls.

"But they say his favorite was the intergalactic one."

His favorite is the intergalactic one. Guided by his expert hand the silver balls fly into space, crash against the planets, bounce off stars, light up the Milky Way, then fall into black holes. Arcángel spends entire nights with that machine, lost in its artificial firmament, accumulating bonuses, multiplying his points, and creating a ruckus of ultrasonic chimes and electronic bells.

If Arcángel receives visits from girls, it's because La Muda sneaks them in. She puts one in his room every two or three days, being careful not to bring the same one too often, in case they develop an affection for each other. He is courteous with all of them, but withdrawn, and doesn't say anything or ask anything, not even their names. He doesn't seduce them, or force them. If they voluntarily offer themselves to him, if they undress on their own and get into his bed, then he makes love to them; if not, then he doesn't.

When he takes them he doesn't do it with the same passion with which he plays pinball, but in the same routine way he exercises. When a timid girl comes, one who doesn't take the initiative, he treats her with the same courtesy afforded the rest. He offers her a drink, some coconut cookies, and lets her go.

No one else has access to his enclosure. Not even the doctor, because Nando has ordered La Muda alone to take care of him.

"Couldn't it all have been arranged by La Muda? She could have made Nando fear for Arcángel's life in order for her to control the boy's life."

"Who knows? What is certain is that while Arcángel was locked up, La Muda was his only contact with the world, his umbilical cord. He clung desperately to her and she was happy to take care of him. Maybe that was their way of expressing their strange, warped love for each other."

But the danger was real; the enemies were watching. The incident in the capital demonstrated to the Barragáns that there was no hiding place where the Monsalves couldn't find them. The simple truth is that Arcángel is safe only isolated in that room, in the center of that house, which is guarded around the clock. Because it's the Barragáns' house, even though it looks like all the other houses in the barrio, it's a fortress that the Monsalves have never been able to penetrate in their many attempts.

The other male Barragáns, including Nando, can show their faces, expose themselves, risk getting killed, because their deaths are already taken for granted. They have accepted this as part of the wages for their job, the risks of their war. But when it comes to Arcángel, the baby, the cherished heir, the one destined to survive, no precaution is too great and no one can be trusted, because as intense as is Nando Barragán's desire for his youngest brother to survive, even more so is the Monsalves' for him to die.

Curious people like to scrutinize the privacy of others and invent intrigues where none exist. La Muda Barragán probably loves Arcángel only as a nephew and is concerned only with his well-being and safety. If not, if she is motivated by hidden intentions, then why would she choose the girls and bring them to him herself? She acts as his procuress.

"Few people believed the story of Arcángel's girlfriends, because no one saw them go in or out of the house."

They aren't seen because she brings them in clandestinely by one of the secret entrances in the cellar. She does it so he won't be alone, so that he'll experience women and not grow up warped.

"Maybe that's all there was between aunt and nephew, healthy familial love. But who knows?"

"With those people you never know."

MANI MONSALVE and his wife, Alina Jericó, are in the country buying Paso Finos. Horses with pedigrees and genealogical trees, which are pampered like children and cost more than a new car.

"Even more than jewels, or expensive clothing, Alina liked her husband to buy her fine horses."

"They say that five years ago, when she turned twenty-four, he gave her a black stallion with regal bearing, the finest creature on four legs that had ever been seen in that part of the country. They say that no one could ever ride it because the Barragáns had put a spell on it that gave it the whirlwind sickness: instead of walking forward it twisted its neck and twirled in circles, digging a hole in the ground like a drill."

The sky is blue and cloudless. No airplanes or pollution spoil its beauty, no urban noises break the silence. The sweet smell of the tall, silky grass greets their nostrils, and the breeze, blowing warm and tender, awakens happy shivers on their skin.

Nothing in the landscape has been placed there by man except the sterile wooden fence with its white tips. The primordial countryside extends flat and green as far as the eye can see, bright and vivid where the sun beats, deeper green, almost blue, where there is shade.

"It sounds like paradise."

"Sounds more like a camouflage military uniform."

Mani Monsalve and Alina Jericó are seated alone on the hot, fragrant grass in the shade of an ancient ceiba tree, hugging.

"Their story seemed like a telenovela, *but it wasn't. Something always came up to spoil the happy ending."*

At this perfect, luminous moment they aren't thinking about business, or war, or their earlier unhappiness. They are happy and in love and they want to believe it will last forever. Alina is radiant in her riding clothes, with her hair in a youthful braid. Mani is a gentle, solicitous husband, and he whispers into her ear that he'll spend the whole day with her, something they haven't done since they first started dating. There is no hurry, no danger; there are no bodyguards, no machine guns. They have their whole lives before them, and behind them is a past they have given up and want to forget. They wait patiently for the trainer to show them the horses one by one so they can choose the one they like best.

"Horses were Alina's weakness, and when Mani wanted her forgiveness, he bought her one."

"No. Her weakness wasn't horses. It was Mani Monsalve."

First comes a spirited chestnut with trembling lips, spitting foam. Alina doesn't like him. She says he turns his hooves to the outside and she points out several other defects. Mani, on the other hand, notes his good temperament and asks his wife to ride him. The trainer dismounts and offers the reins to Alina.

"She was known for being a wild rider."

"It was gossip, nothing more. Like all the other stories, made up."

"She had grown up in the country, riding horses since she was very young, and she did it very well, with class. They say her greatest pleasure was riding, and his greatest pleasure was watching her ride."

Alina easily dominates the chestnut. She moves him into a cadent step and, using the reins and her heels, makes him lift his head and follow her lead. "I really prefer the sorrel," she shouts to Mani.

But Mani Monsalve doesn't like the sorrel because he has three white hooves, and Mani believes the old saying that one is good, two better, three bad, four worse.

The trainer appears with a beautiful white mare, but Alina won't even look at her.

"Take her away," she orders, without further explanation.

Then a splendid animal is brought out, a spirited young stallion with a star on his forehead. Mani becomes excited when Alina mounts and the animal grows bolder. Their eyes sparkle with enthusiasm. "This is our horse," says Mani, convinced, ecstatic.

"That morning they lived another chapter of an old story."

When they were married, Mani promised to withdraw from his clandestine businesses and the battle with his cousins and to take her to live on a hacienda. They would establish their own stable of horses, have children, and watch them grow up on the backs of the animals, like centaurs.

Mani's first step toward the fulfillment of his promise was to buy Alina five hundred acres of paradise.

"One night Mani Monsalve dreamed about the most beautiful hacienda in the world in the middle of a promised land, and when he woke up he searched the whole country for it, until he found it and built a house like the one in his dream."

He became the owner of a plot of virgin land at the edge of the sea, bordered by a ribbon of beach with fine white sand, to which the mountains descended, populated by mountain lions, wild goats, long-tailed monkeys, deer, iguanas, and macaws. A jungle forest where giant caracoli trees, used by the Indians to make canoes, grow in profusion. There are saman trees, which are full of flies, carretos with red bark, petreas, blooming guayacans, birds of paradise with their carnival plumage, wax palms towering hundreds of feet into the air, dwarf Malaysian palms, and fat coconut palms, heavy with fruit.

A stream of fresh water, fed by the melting snows from the sierra, full of shad and trout, empties into the transparent, submissive sea. Above, at the peak of the mountain, where deer bathe in the moonlight and tigers take their nightly walks, huge black rocks with pre-Columbian markings outline an ancient religious site.

To this Eden, where the white Norwegian whales and the huge sea turtles, marked with tags by Californian ecologists, go to die in peace, Mani Monsalve and Alina Jericó went too, like Adam and Eve. They built a palace of bleached wood with a soaring straw roof and surrounded it with curaçao and cayenne flowers and wild orchids. And they built fifty stalls for their Paso Finos.

"People who saw the place swear that the stalls were more like three-star hotel rooms."

Alina furnished the ranch with the help of professional decorators, supervising all the details herself, and called it La Virgen del Viento, the Virgin of the Wind. They bought horses one by one, only the best show horses. They traveled wherever it was necessary, to inspect and buy them.

Everything was ready and Alina was waiting for Mani to set the date for the move. She spent her time imagining the moment when their final happiness would begin: jungle, children, horses, sea, peace, Mani at her side, a healthy life in this bit of heaven on earth.

She daydreamed of beautiful, regal horses, but when she slept she was tormented by a recurring nightmare in which a black mare in heat, blind and riderless, emerged from the darkness and kicked down the walls surrounding her. Alina so dreaded the nightly visit of the phantom animal that she forbade Mani ever to buy her another mare, a radical obstinacy that halted the reproduction of horses at La Virgen del Viento and that her husband finally accepted as a respectable but incomprehensible whim.

Mani Monsalve kept postponing the date for the move and asking his wife to understand, explaining that he had to leave things in order before he could retire. It wasn't easy, but she tried to understand and be patient.

Each time he informed her that he still wasn't ready, he would send several dozen roses to appease her. She halfheartedly arranged them in vases and tried to make the best of the situation.

Meanwhile, they had settled into a luxurious residence fifteen minutes from the port. It was a temporary arrangement and Alina didn't even bother to unpack her trunks, because she knew they would be leaving any day. So she bore without complaint the constant traffic of the bodyguards and armed men that wandered through her house as if it were their own. They slept on the couches in the living room with their machine guns leaning in the corner, devoured huge quantities of food, urinated in the potted plants, and played Chinese checkers on the terrace where she sunbathed. They arrived like evil birds—to deliver messages, request orders, or report problems—always just when she thought she had found a moment of peace alone with her husband.

"They called them bodyguards, but they were really a gang of assassins. Ordinary and prepotent. Alina hated them, without ever realizing that deep inside her own husband was one of them."

Alina consoled herself by thinking that all would soon change, and she put up with Mani's erratic schedule and sudden trips, his long silences and the streaks of dark emotions that often overtook him, all the while imagining the horrendous activities in which he participated, but about which he never spoke.

Alina Jericó waited patiently because she knew it was only a matter of days. As soon as Mani could get everything organized they would flee this world of threats and death and invaded privacy, to start over alone in a new life—a real life with real love.

"It's like I said, they were living a telenovela *that could never have a happy ending."*

"Their curse was to have dreamed of paradise, created it, and then never be allowed to enjoy it."

After a couple years of postponements, Alina finally understood that the date of the move would never come.

"La Virgen del Viento has been erased by the wind," she complained.

Then he would become animated, tell her stories, make calculations and promises, and send her absurd quantities of roses. To convince her that this time it would happen, he would take her to buy a new horse that he would send to the hacienda to wait for them with the others. A professional trainer, charging astronomical fees, would keep the horses in shape, ready for the day when the owners would come to ride them.

Meanwhile, the ranch, with the jungle animals, the cool stream, the trainer, the domestic staff, the covered furniture, the Jacuzzis, the Olympic-size pool that had never been used, was growing older and falling into disrepair.

Until today, that is. Until this clear morning when everything will begin to change. Their dreams will come true and Mani Monsalve will see his wife riding the young stallion along the beach at La Virgen del Viento. The sacred promise she had made him at dawn a few days earlier, that she would leave him if she got pregnant, obsesses and torments him. It echoes painfully inside his head, clinging like a sappy tune. He is ready to take her to live in the country, to give her a different life, a child, anything to avoid losing her.

Seated on the fence made from tree trunks at the edge of the clearing, he realizes that this is the moment to grab the bull of destiny by the horns. He looks at his wife, beautiful, strong, and sure of herself, fully capable of keeping her promise. He convinces himself that nothing in his life is more important than she is.

"It's now or never," he thinks with determination. "This horse with the star is a lucky omen. That star is telling me to retire from the fight, before it's too late."

"It was already too late, but he didn't know it."

"It was always too late for him, for all of them."

At the same moment that Mani Monsalve had finally resolved to take off in a new direction, the exact instant, a jeep approaches, interrupting the quiet afternoon and frightening the animals, bursting Mani's hopes as if they were soap bubbles.

Tin Puyúa climbs out of the jeep. A short, slight man, he is hyperkinetic and alert. He's Mani's right hand, his confidant, the man who efficiently dispatches the most important orders, from choosing roses for Alina to liquidating shady business partners.

Tin Puyúa is always tense and hyper, plugged into an invisible electric current. He climbs out of the jeep without even turning off the engine and hurriedly speaks to Mani, without finishing his sentences, as if he has no time.

"Mani, your brothers sent me to tell you they're waiting for you," he says.

Mani is suddenly transformed into a man of war and business. His lips disappear, turning his mouth into a thin line. He rubs the half moon on his face and is immediately disconnected from his surroundings, the horses, the blue sky, from healthy pursuits, love, the future.

From a distance, Alina sees the jeep, guesses Tin Puyúa's words, pulls the horse up sharply, and in a single instant moves from bliss to disgust, from gratitude to resentment. She bitterly waits to hear the words she already knows.

"I have to go, Alina," shouts Mani in his other voice, the public one, the voice of the young organized crime executive.

"I know," she calls back icily. She knows too that it's not worth chastising him, or asking for explanations or crying.

"Buy the horse you like best," he says. "Buy all of them if you want. Enjoy the rest of the morning. Ride all you want. The driver will take you back when you're ready."

The two men get in the jeep and disappear down the road among the carob trees. Still astride the horse, stopped in the middle of the clearing, with her teenager's braid and her riding outfit, Alina sits, stiff and absurd, like a useless mannequin that the owner of a store has tossed out on the sidewalk to be hauled away with the trash.

3

SEVEN OF THE thirteen Monsalve brothers are still alive, and are assembled in a building they own in the port city, five stories of polished marble, with a parabolic antenna on the roof and polarized windows. It's an enormous, modern building in a style never seen before. In the center of an old neighborhood of houses with patios graced with tamarind trees and wicker rocking chairs, the headquarters of the Monsalve clan stands glaringly apart as if grafted from another world.

"It looked like an office building, but it was really an armored fortress, and it contained such a large army of armed men that everybody in the neighborhood called it La Brigada, the Stockade."

Six of the brothers sit in silence around a glass-topped table with chrome legs. They all have greenish skin with fine features and are wearing guayabera shirts, boots, pistols under their arms, diamond rings on their fingers, and gold chains around their necks and wrists. At the head of the table sits a dry, ragged man with prominent cheekbones, hollowed cheeks, and a crown of curly, graying hair. He's smoking a strong-smelling cigar, which emits heavy clouds of smoke. That's Frepe, the eldest.

Mani stands in the doorway, leaning against the frame, drinking Kola Román from the bottle. He's running the meeting but doesn't sit at the table with his brothers; rather, he keeps his distance. He's the head of the clan, but he doesn't mingle with the others. He moves differently than they do, speaks and dresses differently. He wears Levi's, and Nikes, and an open shirt revealing pewter religious medals hanging on his chest. There's not an ounce of gold showing on his body. Since childhood he has disdained his primitive brothers, and as an adult he cultivates the differences between them as an efficient way to reinforce his authority.

Today he feels uncomfortable and out of place. He arrived after the meeting had already begun, excusing his tardiness by explaining that he had to take care of personal matters.

He was delayed, he said, because he was buying a horse. The others were surprised to hear this. He even surprised himself when he said it. With these people no personal reason, much less a horse, is cause for missing an appointment.

But Mani is thinking about something else, preoccupied with private concerns. The right side of his brain is involved in the discussion, but the left side is focused on Alina and her recent threat, and on the young stallion with the star on his forehead that they didn't buy, and now certainly won't ever buy.

"Mani's weakness was his wife, but his brothers didn't know it."

He seems unsettled and scattered, not focused and energized as he usually does. For days now they've been talking behind his back about how he's been acting different. They've always accepted him as the leader even though he's the fifth son, because he knows how to multiply their money and because, until now, he's been the strongest in the war against the Barragáns. The worldly style that he's begun to develop is not understood or valued by his brothers, who are cultivators of rustic, unadorned machismo, and who interpret his style as an affectation and a weakness.

Mani wants to clean up his image and catch up with the times. His prestige as an assassin has begun to bore him, because it cuts his possibility for social ascendance and threatens to distance him from Alina Jericó. He fell in love with her in part because she wasn't like any of the women in his family, and in part because he understood that her middle-class beauty and high school education would be his key to other worlds. But he knows that's not enough; changes and adjustments must be made in his personal style. So, for a couple of years he's been toying with the idea of laundering money to start businesses with quasi-legitimate facades, more or less convincing, to open the doors of society to his family.

While Mani is trying to climb the hill, his cousins and enemies, the Barragáns, walk a flat path. They have remained the same, day in and day out, rich or poor, living in the same barrio, in the same house, eating the same black beans, with their mourning women, sullen children, and their wads of bills hidden under the mattress. No matter what happens in the rest of the world, they are an insular clan from the deepest corner of the desert, the rarest of animals, faithful only to ancient, traditional beliefs, always removed from the mainstream, hostile and strange in the eyes of everyone else.

"That's how Nando and all the others were."

Not Mani. Mani wanted to become part of the modern urban world, where illegality and violence flow beneath the surface like canoes on black water while above there are tuxedos, mutually beneficial agreements with highly placed military officials, beautiful women who spend fortunes on clothing, baptisms conducted by bishops, close friendships with prominent politicians, striking offices with white-collar employees, and investments in public and private businesses.

The piece that was hardest for Mani to fit into the puzzle of his transformation was the war with his cousins, the endless war that taxed the bulk of his energies, his nerves, and his income. Furthermore, it placed the Monsalves in a position of constant tension and strife, keeping at bay the discreetness necessary for clandestine business. The fratricidal war is viewed with repugnance by potential partners and new friends, managers and advisers, the mayor, even the parish priest, who openly chastises them from the pulpit.

"The local newspapers mentioned the dirty war and the butchery, monstrosities of all sorts. We fellow residents of the barrio scanned the papers looking for notices of them. We made bets about who would die next. Their stories sparked a lot of gossip and morbid chatter. But that didn't make the Barragáns lose any sleep. They were accustomed to it and had come to expect it. But not Mani Monsalve. He aspired to appear in the social pages, not the crime blotter."

Mani is still leaning against the doorjamb. He finishes his Kola Román in one long gulp and goes to the bar for another. The smell of tobacco coming from Frepe bothers him and puts him in a bad mood, which he can't hide. The comments the other brothers make irritate him with their grotesqueness and ignorance. He can't stomach them. He's never felt so distant from his brothers as he does today.

Until recently they were united by their ferocious hatred for the Barragáns, the thirst for vengeance that held them tighter in complicity than any blood ties ever could. All for one and one for all in a fever for death that devours more readily than the jealousy of a newlywed and more easily than the flame of an ignited passion. Their hatred is complete and perfect, like the universe. It is the mother and father of everything else. It swallows everything and converts itself into its own reality, outside which there is no other reason to live or die.

While his brothers revel in this obsession, Mani has begun to cast it off, little by little, without seeking to, or even noticing. He hasn't forgiven the Barragáns; it's just that they don't matter as much. Still hating them, he distances himself from them, as one forgets his first love over the years but never really stops loving her.

Out of place at the meeting, Mani is trying to gain ground in his brothers' eyes, trying to regain control. But Frepe has already stepped in and taken his place, leapt forward in firm possession of his role as eldest brother, demanding recognition and demonstrating leadership.

"It's wrong, wrong, wrong," says Frepe, sucking on a fat cigar. "It's just not enough to fight the war with the Barragáns, we have to win it."

The statement hits Mani like a kick in the gut. He has no response. He has certainly led a fierce battle against the Barragáns, but he has never been able to achieve a significant advantage over them.

"This phenomenon is peculiar to our country — fighting endless wars where everybody ends up losing."

It's peculiar to them too. Blood is spilled and men die on both sides. No *zeta* passes without payback; no death is left unavenged. But in the final balance, no one loses and no one wins; it's just a perpetual, uncontrollable war. War is queen by divine design, and the two family armies abide with her resignedly, like someone who suffers a hereditary abnormality.

"We have to end this business now. What are we waiting for?" asks Frepe, pounding the table as his brothers look at him in agreement.

Win once and for all? Wipe out their enemies and forget about them? It sounds wonderful to the Monsalve brothers, elementary even. They are so accustomed to war, so enraptured with it, that they never considered the advantages of getting out from under it. But how?

Mani doesn't have the answer. His capacities as a leader are neutralized by another force of equal magnitude but opposite charge: Nando Barragán. They have invested their entire lives in a duel to the death, and it's a tie.

Frepe knows; he has the answer. Mercenaries.

"Frepe was the first to propose they hire professionals to get rid of the Barragáns. Not Mani. Mani wouldn't have dared to talk about sicarios. But Frepe was different."

Sicarios. Hired killers. The word makes the brothers bristle, like a stream of cold water running down their spines. Killing the Barragáns themselves, that's what they're supposed to do, that's the tradition they've upheld. No one outside the family is allowed to participate.

After a noisy and combative initial refusal, the brothers begin to capitulate, one by one. They reconsider. The proposal has attractive advantages. It would allow the brothers to do just the dirty work and delegate the really horrible stuff to third parties.

Mani remains alone. He is the only one who disapproves and he argues angrily, defending the old rules. "The Barragáns respect them," he says, "and we have to do the same." When they don't listen, he threatens them and points a finger at Frepe. But he knows he's already lost.

Frepe smells victory and looks at Mani condescendingly. "Times change, Mani," he says. "Tradition gets left behind," he proudly explains with the superior attitude of an older brother. Frepe is full of arguments in support of his position and is growing more sure of himself. "This is not the same war as before," he says. "Either we take the lead, or we've lost."

Mani's hesitant silence causes Frepe to pull an ace from his sleeve. The older brother shows he is more than just talk. He tells his brothers that he has already hired someone to train and manage a squad of professionals who will begin the liquidation of the Barragáns.

He's an expert with many years of experience, fully recommended by associates who know him. Frepe has been in contact with him for several months and has paid a hundred thousand dollars to get him out of jail. Now he's here, in the building, anxious to go to work.

"Bring him in," Frepe orders.

A long silence is broken by the sound of a pair of rubber flip-flops dragging along the corridor.

Mani steps aside and Holman Fernely enters the office.

"DID ROBERTA *Caracola, the leprous witch, read the chocolate grounds for Nando Barragán?"*

"Yes, he asked her to, so she did."

Nando Barragán drinks the boiling liquid in three quick sips and swirls the cup to mix the chocolate grounds, all the while holding it delicately in his enormous hands so as not to break it like an egg. Then he places it upside down on the table, letting the residue from the cacao run down the sides of the porcelain cup in rivulets, eyes, lakes, windmills, and other whimsical shapes that outline a man's destiny.

"So what did she tell him?"

Roberta Caracola waits seven minutes to allow everything to appear. It wouldn't do for a drop not to fall and reveal a fundamental piece of information.

"Seven minutes, no more, no less?"

"Exactly seven, like the seven days of the week, or the seven wonders of the world."

For seven long minutes, while the old woman waits silently, Nando listens to the sound of the wind dragging trash across the beach.

Finally Roberta Caracola takes the cup in her incomplete hands, brings it to her nearly blind eyes, and studies it with the air of a scientist looking for microbes.

"There is an answer that cannot be found here," she says. "Why are you still in business if you have all the money that you could ever spend?"

Nando Barragán replies that it's because of the war. He says that maintaining the war against the Monsalves is very expensive and that to preserve his life and the lives of the rest of his family he needs a lot of money.

Roberta Caracola moves her scaly neck in a solemn tortoiselike gesture and makes a recommendation.

"Forget about the war. It's not a good thing to be killing your relatives."

Smelling the foul odor emanating from the sick woman's ravaged skin, Nando says he can't, that he is under orders to fulfill the sacred obligation of collecting debts of blood.

"Then do what you must," says the witch, unwilling to waste the few remaining words of her life. "But watch out, Nando Barragán, never paint your face white."

"You say the strangest things," he replies. "Why would I want to paint my face white?"

"You listen to me. Do you want to hear anything else?"

"Tell me how many children I'm going to have."

"Not even you will be able to count them."

"And how will I know that my end is near?"

"The day it won't get hard for you. When that happens, you won't have much time left."

Nando lets out a long, exaggerated laugh that is heard all the way to the city. What he hears sounds funny because he is infamous for his sexual appetite, for being the greatest breeder of the species. He tells the old woman that the day that it won't get hard he'll be so old that he will be able to die in peace.

"Who knows?" says Roberta Caracola, as the voice of the woman suffering a terminal illness is drowned out by the powerful laugh of the giant man. "Go now," she orders, "because I'm not going to tell you anything else."

MANI STEPS aside and Holman Fernely enters the office where the Monsalve brothers are assembled. They look over the recent arrival from head to toe, somewhat disappointed. They offer him coffee, and as they watch him drink, they notice he is so weak that he spills it. They read the tattoo on his arm: God and Mother. They watch him drop medicine into his watery eyes.

"Ever since that day we saw a lot of Fernely in the barrio, going in and out of La Brigada. Fernely wasn't an impressive-looking man. Quite the opposite. We often asked ourselves if this scrawny fellow with the swollen eyes and sparse hair really was an infamous assassin for hire. No big belly, no hair on his chest, no cold stare of a true mercenary. He looked sick, the way he dragged his flip-flops and constantly rubbed his eyes."

Fernely sits quietly in his chair. He looks at the most famous inhabitants of the port city with indifference, as if they weren't even there.

"The neighbors say that Fernely was always either silent or repeating clichés. Some thought it was a sign of prudence, others thought he was mentally defective or just too lazy to think."

He listens to the Monsalve brothers talk about an upcoming *zeta*, but he doesn't know what a *zeta* is and he doesn't give a damn. They explain that it's the anniversary of their brother Hector's death and that they must commemorate it by retaliating against the Barragáns. They begin to talk about possible victims. Of the eleven Barragán males, four are still alive. Nando, the eldest, is a tough bone to chew. The others are Narciso, the poet; Raca, a godless, lawless being; and Nando's favorite, the youngest, Arcángel, whose arm they wounded several months ago in an unsuccessful attempt to kill him.

Holman Fernely listens to them without interrupting, without showing signs of impatience. Or of life. He is fixated on his burning eyes, and he keeps blinking in a vain attempt to soothe them under the damp protection of his eyelids. After a while, when he feels he has heard enough, he speaks.

"Narciso should die."

He has spoken the obvious. It was already clear to everyone present. For that reason, his advice is accepted unanimously.

"Let Narciso die, for being lazy."

"The enemy must first be ruined, then exterminated," declares Fernely, leaving the Monsalves perplexed. For them it's obvious that Narciso should die, but for being so ostentatious and so soft, such an easy target. What Fernely's strange logic proposes is something else: wipe him out because he handles the finances, the client lists, and the contacts.

"The enemy must first be ruined, then exterminated," repeat the Monsalves, convinced, pleased with their unanimity.

"Later, alligator," says Fernely unenthusiastically as he leaves to begin studying his target and making a plan of action.

WE KNEW *the Barragáns' house only from outside. Since we had lived in the same neighborhood all our lives, they recognized us and let us pass by undisturbed or sit on the curb to talk. They took care of the barrio. Their men patrolled day and night. They left us alone, but they didn't let strangers get too close.*

Once a quiet barrio, boring really, ours had became chaotic. When one least expected it, pow, pow, pow, and everybody ran to the street to see what had happened, bang, bang, bang, and they all wanted to know who was dead. Many of the homes had been damaged by the Barragáns' war against the Monsalves. Each assassination or confrontation left a scar on the streets of our barrio and we grew up

with them as constant reminders of the most important moments of
our local history.

Not even the most respectable or private properties had escaped
becoming crime scenes. An attempt was made on Helvencio Barragán's life inside the parish church, leaving nine bullets embedded
in the altar. The tenth bullet, and the most profane, hit the chalice.
Helvencio had taken refuge in the church, thinking they wouldn't
dare attack him in such a sacred place. But they dared, and they
killed him.

They dared everything. The ice-cream parlor was the favorite
hangout for the local boys and girls because it had a large window
looking out onto the main street where one could sit and watch people
go by. That window was shattered by bullets twice in one year. After
the second time, the owner gave up and replaced it with steel bars.
Another time a bullet caused an explosion in a gas station, and now
all that stands on that corner is blackened rubble. There were bullet
holes everywhere, in walls and windows. There were even bullet holes
in the tiny park where the old men gather to play dominoes. A broken
column at the entrance of the public school always reminded us of the
day it was knocked over by a car full of Monsalves fleeing after an
attack.

A lot of damage was caused over the years by the fighting. Every
block had its own bloody story. Gunshots were so frequent that we
called our own barrio, where we were born and had grown up, La
Esquina de la Candela, Death's Corner. People who didn't live here
called it that too.

The children delighted in telling stories about the war to visitors,
and some were better narrators than others, giving more color and
detail to the stories, while others had better memories, and others still
could imitate perfectly the sound of bullets being sprayed from the
machine guns and the squealing of tires. A few could even act out in

slow motion the impact of the bullets on a body, or a scene from a kick fight or knife fight.

The visitors were always impressed by what they heard. They saw too, because we organized tours, like in museums, taking them to different locations: here they assassinated a Barragán as he was leaving his brother's burial, we would tell them, and they could put their finger in the bullet holes in the cemetery wall. Or, those windows were smashed during an attempt against so-and-so, or they found so-and-so in this laundrette after he had been killed.

Our barrio, which had been just like every other, now had its own tradition, its own folklore. It was dangerous living here—mothers forbade their children to play in the street, and even greater fear crept in with nightfall, but at least we had something to talk about. We had invented our own source of pride. The Barragáns were protagonists in something spectacular, something worth telling.

We didn't like them at all and we rarely dealt with them. Or rather, they never dealt with us. They tolerated us, but nothing more. Maybe because of mistrust. They didn't trust their own mother. It was enough that they let us pass their house without searching us. For that we were grateful, for that and for their not bullying us around.

They had established their roadblocks and logged everyone in the barrio into their memory banks. Anyone they had not seen before, or didn't know whose son he was, ˜r whose cousin, wasn't allowed to pass. The barrio was their territory, and we had grown accustomed to that. We respected their governance and vigilance, first because we couldn't confront them, and second because in spite of everything else, it had its advantages. In La Esquina de la Candela no one was robbed, no one was assaulted, and there was no delinquency or vagrancy. But it also had its disadvantages. We were sitting on a powder keg, waiting for the Monsalves to attack. Or for the Barragáns' defense, which sometimes was worse for us.

The Barragán women were less sociable than the men. They always wore black, and when they left the house to go to the market, or to the doctor, or to mass, they walked quickly without stopping, without speaking to anyone. The men were less evasive, but they weren't friendly either.

So when they announced Nando Barragán's wedding and the rumor circulated that everyone in the barrio was invited, none of us wanted to miss the opportunity. Not out of affection, because they disgusted us, but in order to see their fortress from inside. To study them up close—the morbid curiosity of wanting to see the monster's entrails. Everyone in the barrio wanted to experience it in person; no one was about to wait for the others to come back and tell about it. At first there were only rumors of uncertain origin. We didn't know whether it was true or just malicious gossip. But the invitation changed that, because now we knew we were really going to see everything up close, like at a movie premiere.

None of us had thought Nando Barragán would ever get married, so the wedding announcement took us all by surprise. He had made many women pregnant, but none had ever complained or pursued it, because they were afraid of him.

It would never have occurred to even the boldest father to make a claim for damages for his daughter, much less demand marriage, or even ask for money to help raise the child. On the contrary, the girls gave birth and then gave the babies their own last names to prevent the Monsalves from taking them, since they were offspring of the jefe of the Barragáns. It was a cursed name, much better not to carry it.

But, at the same time, the men in the barrio envied Nando a little, because there was no virgin he had not deflowered, no lonely widow he had not consoled. No woman was out of his reach. When he couldn't get it by being nice, then he got it by being mean, or any way he could. With a style like that, who thinks about marriage?

His brother Narciso, the one they call *El Lírico* because he's so beautiful and writes poetry, was also a womanizer, but in a different way. Nando went with any woman, as long as she wore a skirt. Well, even that's not true, because he'd go with women in jeans, shorts, or hot pants, or whatever.

Narciso, on the other hand, was highly selective and chose only the best. He liked models and TV actresses and had no problem conquering them. Never by force, like Nando, but with style, using his reputation as a handsome playboy, his bullfighter's striking looks, and his good manners. He was also proud of his success with mature, worldly women. They had to be at least high school graduates, but preferably college graduates. He liked lawyers, doctors, engineers, any profession, as long as they were pretty. Teenagers and uncultured women were not for him, the former because they were immature, and the latter because they were coarse. He was proud of being able to select only the finest, and disdained the rest.

Not Nando, who had such an appetite that he devoured whatever was placed before him. His sexual prowess was infamous in the barrio. He had even had sex with a sixty-year-old woman. People said a lot of things, most of which were only half-believed. But this is for sure: once he had been with a woman, he never wanted to see her again.

His wedding was a surprise for several reasons, but most of all because everyone thought, or at least everyone said, that his only love was Milena, the blond rehabilitated prostitute who refused to marry him. There was much talk of his desperate love for Milena and many people thought that he acted as he did with other women out of spite, to avenge her disinterest in him.

The women said that the only one who could marry him was Milena. We didn't know her, had never even seen her, but she had become a character in the drama. So there was great confusion when we learned that she was not to be the bride. And even more when we found out who it was: Ana Santana, the most ordinary girl in the bar-

rio. The least interesting, the least mysterious. She was a seamstress and everyone in the barrio would go by her house to ask her to size their clothes up or down, or fix the hem of a dress, or spruce up a pair of pants or an overcoat, to keep us in style.

Ana Santana wasn't the most beautiful, but she wasn't the ugliest either. She wasn't very intelligent, but not completely stupid. She was nice, but not too nice. Not fat or skinny, but normal, like any other. In short, she was an ordinary girl, the most ordinary of all. The most surprising thing was that she wasn't pregnant when she got married, that it wasn't an obligatory wedding but a willful one. All the more reason for us to be there when Nando Barragán said "I do." Hearing is believing. Until he said it in public, in front of everyone, no one was going to believe that he had let himself get caught.

On the day that the invitations arrived, Ana Santana's house, which was a block and a half from the Barragáns', was inundated with women from the neighborhood. They were upset because they thought they knew everything that happened before it happened and this time they were caught unawares. None of them even suspected that Ana and Nando were dating. And that's because they weren't, but rather they met one day and within a week had already set the date. So the hens flocked to Ana's house with an astonishing array of pretexts: one woman came for the piece of wool she left a month ago, another came to borrow some cloves and cinnamon — any reason they could think of to get in and gather a little information. And she told them all the same thing.

Ana's story was that a few days earlier she had been awakened at dawn by a song called "Caballo Viejo." On Ash Wednesday, when she passed by the Barragáns' house, she heard the same song again, at full volume. It stuck out in her mind because it was a religious holiday.

The next day, Maundy Thursday, the same thing happened again, and she decided to voice her protest against this disrespect. She rang self-righteously, emboldened because she felt her religion was being made fun of, but she would never have dared if she had known who would appear at the door. None other than Nando Barragán himself. The living legend, in flesh and blood, opened the door in his undershorts and his black sunglasses, with a cigarette in his mouth and the medal on his chest, and asked what he could do for Ana. She swallowed her words, immediately dropping the idea of complaining, and remained silent, staring dumbly at the half-naked giant awaiting a response in the open doorway.

He asked again what she wanted, still with a pleasant tone. Then a light went on in her head. She had an inspiration from the Holy Ghost. It occurred to her to ask, in a whisper of a voice, whether he might lend her the record so she could tape it. He asked her if she thought it was a pretty song, and she answered that it woke her up each morning. He apologized sincerely and said he would lend it to her. Ana took the record and, though that was the extent of their conversation, in that instant she fell in love. And she nearly fainted later that evening when Nando Barragán himself knocked on her door with the pretext of collecting his record.

That's how the romance started, like teenagers. At least according to Ana, whose dreams were soft and pink and had nothing to do with Nando Barragán's dark legend, his history of conquering women without bothering to court or even flirt. And since he never told his account to anyone, Ana's story about the record became official.

Ana received other visitors too. The fact that the marriage would convert her from simple seamstress to multimillionaire didn't escape many people. And some simply came to warn her about the dangerous situation in which she was about to put herself.

They told her a thousand stories about Nando's thousand lovers. "Don't think he'll leave them for you," they said to her. "You'll become number one thousand and one, and the one at home always gets the worst end of the deal." They warned her about her future husband's illicit businesses and the war against the other part of the family. "From the moment they are born, your children are going to be threatened," they reminded her. "Neither you nor your family will have a moment of peace. Money, yes, all you want, but never peace or love."

Some distant relatives came from a town on the other coast to tell her about an unknown occurrence. "Open your eyes, Ana," they told her. "This is not the first time Nando Barragán has proposed matrimony." They told her that during a visit to their village he had gotten involved with a young mulatto virgin, whose father protected her like a pearl. Nando Barragán thought he would do what he always did, drag her behind some trees and have his way with her.

The girl's father turned out to be a huge black fisherman whose formidable body had been shaped by many years of pulling lobsters from the bottom of the ocean. When he saw that some newcomer was about to ruin his treasure, he stood firmly in front of Nando Barragán and threatened to kill him. Maybe Nando had a little respect for the black man's monumental size, or he saw in his eyes that this man really was going to try to kill him, because instead of picking a fight he pulled a wad of bills from his pocket and offered it to the father in exchange for fifteen minutes with his daughter.

The father became more indignant than before, but just before he could pounce, like a wild animal on its prey, he took a good look at the stack of money, which must have been more than the whole town earned in a year of harvesting lobsters.

"I accept your offer," he said to Nando, "but only if you marry my daughter."

Nando laughed—it was the most absurd thing that had ever been proposed to him—but he stopped laughing when he realized that the father wouldn't settle for less. Nando offered to double the money for just the fifteen minutes.

"I don't want any more or less than what you've got there," declared the man firmly, "but you've got to marry her."

Meanwhile the young girl appeared from behind some banana trees, and when Nando saw her he couldn't control himself. He was desperate to have her, but he was in a hurry. He had to travel on to close a million-dollar deal and he was chained here, wasting his time on this.

"Twenty thousand dollars for ten minutes and it's a deal," he said.

"Ten and marriage," countered the father.

Nando understood that there was nothing else he could do and he was adamant that he was going to have that girl at any price. He shouted, "All right then, damn it, go get the priest."

The fisherman smiled triumphantly, showing all his teeth.

"There's only one problem," he said. "We don't have a priest in this town."

On the verge of losing control of his criminal anger, Nando Barragán looked around at the townspeople gathered there, old people, women and children, all in a circle watching and enjoying the spectacle. In the crowd there were two nuns, teachers at the school, dressed in white, with wide starched hats, like the wings of a seagull.

Nando took the elder nun by the arm.

"Since there is no priest, this holy sister is going to marry us," he announced.

The old woman was horrified and tried to put up a fight, but that was more than Nando was able to bear. He pulled his Colt revolver from his waist and put it against the starched seagull on the woman's head.

"Either you marry us right now, or everyone here dies," he shouted.

The nun married them as best she could and the father took the money. Then Nando grabbed the girl, took off his Ray-Bans, opened his zipper, deflowered his wife in seven and a half minutes, and took off, disappearing forever down the highway in his metallic gray Silverado.

Ana Santana listened to the story in silence, and when her relatives had finished, she thanked them for the information and bid them farewell. "A marriage performed by a nun isn't valid here, or in Timbuktu for that matter," she said dryly, and never allowed anyone to speak about the incident again.

Ana was told many more stories, and her friends told her they were worried about her happiness. But she turned a deaf ear to their pleas. Either she already knew her fiancé's past or she didn't care about it, because she never changed her mind.

It was just as well for us, because if Ana Santana had hesitated, there wouldn't have been a wedding, and everyone was ready for the wedding.

LA MUDA Barragán, barefoot and dressed in black, cloistered in her impenetrable, silent world, dusts the pinball machines and gym equipment in her nephew Arcángel's room with a red rag.

"Why did they call her La Muda Barragán if that wasn't her last name? Wasn't she a maternal aunt?"

That's how they refer to all the women in the family. Severina, Nando and Arcángel's mother; La Mona, their sister, a wild, mannish woman who carries weapons and frightens men, the only girl in a family with eleven boys; the wives of the married brothers; their daughters; La Muda herself; and the other maternal aunts.

"All closed up in that big house, dressed in black and not interested in knowing anything about the rest of the world. We made jokes about them in the barrio. We said they were a harem, or a coven of witches, or a flock of evil birds. It would never have occurred to any of us to fall in love with a Barragán. And of course, they never even looked at any of us. The old women were all dried up from so much suffering and giving birth, and the younger ones had been turned to stone by their family war. They had no time to be females, or mothers. They were frigid and sterile. Or at least we thought so."

The men are in charge outside the front door; inside, the women rule. The women put up with one another but struggle under a tense living situation characterized by jealous battles for domestic power.

"In La Esquina de la Candela there was no fight, no matter how private, that didn't become public. A lovers' quarrel, the smacks of a jealous husband, even an argument over a soccer game, these things became major scandals and were widely commented upon. But we never heard a word about the conflicts between the Barragán women."

The conflicts are intimate, secret rages that never explode into open dialogue. They are breathed in the air, but never expressed, and then disappear as if by magic in emergency situations. When it comes to defending their men and their children, the Barragán women act as one body. They forget their petty fighting. But they still exist, and they're strong. Each one is a general competing for power.

They say that Severina, the matriarch, is the top authority, the backbone of the family. But the truth is that each one, in her own way, controls her own bit of territory. And, by extension, exercises control over some of the men.

Severina is the master over Nando, her eldest son. She loves him so intensely that she subdues and suffocates him. He doesn't move a finger without consulting her. At the age of forty he still gets mad and argues with her every now and then, like a rebellious teenager.

"Some of the neighbors thought that Nando's surprise marriage to Ana Santana was an attempt to jab once more at his mother."

La Mona, the wild animal who follows Nando in age, looks just like him. She is a living portrait of him, except she's shorter and wears skirts. Despite her name, which usually means blondie, her hair is completely black. They call her La Mona because she's like a monkey, another meaning of the word. She is responsible for Raca, the penultimate brother, who is living proof of the old adage that the apple doesn't fall far from the tree. They are not physically similar, but are temperamentally and ideologically identical. He's just like his sister, but worse. Inconceivably worse.

And then there's La Muda, of course—withdrawn like her Indian forebears, cloistered in her virginity and her silence—and her curious relationship with her nephew Arcángel.

"La Muda never allowed anyone direct contact with Arcángel. Except the girlfriends she herself selected."

That's not true. Arcángel also has a best friend, a corporal in the army named Guillermo Willy Quiñones. Their friendship began a year ago and is cultivated with weekly visits by Quiñones, which La Muda tolerates.

"Then someone else had access to Arcángel's secluded quarters?"

Yes. That corporal, Guillermo Willy Quiñones, the only man with foreign blood who is allowed to enter the Barragáns' house. On his visits he brings Arcángel gifts of old issues of the magazine *Soldier of Fortune* to entertain him, and since Quiñones understands English and Arcángel doesn't, he translates the articles. They spend hours talking about weapons, operations, special commands, mercenaries. They are swept up in the passion of a violence in which neither participates actively. Other times they work out on the gym equipment, or they sit and listen to Pink Floyd albums. Quiñones is proud of having memorized the words to the songs, and he translates them for his friend.

"And La Muda permitted this friendship?"

If she didn't permit it, it wouldn't have existed; not even a fly moves in Arcángel's room without her authorization.

"In the barrio they said that La Muda, who didn't speak, was the one who spoke loudest in that house."

La Muda controls the little, indispensable things, without which none of them could live. She oversees the half dozen servant girls who live in the back patio and do the domestic work.

They call them girls, but they're really slaves. They sleep on straw mats and work in exchange for food. They are between nine and fourteen years old, the daughters of poor families who can't afford to support them. The Barragáns received them as gifts and now they're family property, like the mules and chickens and the rocking chairs on the patio.

At the head of her platoon of girls, La Muda takes care of the domestic activities, which are monumental in that huge family. The slave girls obey her minutest signal. They have learned to interpret the meaning of her facial expressions and the orders she gives with her hands. The practical functioning of the Barragán house, which is more a citadel than a house, depends on La Muda. If she doesn't buy the food, no one eats. If she doesn't do the cleaning, the dirt overtakes them. If she doesn't pay the telephone, water, and electric bills, the services are cut off. If she doesn't make the children fill notebooks with vowels and consonants, they grow up illiterate without any of the other adults losing any sleep over it.

La Muda finds someone's lost shirt, somebody else's cartridge case, a cough remedy for still another. She gives purgatives to the children, sets out poison for the cockroaches and traps for the rats, mends socks, polishes shoes, waters the garden, trims the fruit trees, checks to make sure there is toothpaste in the hall bath, that this one drinks his milk and that one doesn't put his feet on the table, and it is in her managing the everyday things that she establishes her invisible power. Without her the house would fall apart, and the family knows it but would never admit it.

Severina's authority is absolute. Her matriarchal presence is all that is needed to put everyone in his place. Mona, however, commands with punches. She hits anyone who doesn't obey, or she throws a dish, or screams obscenities. She's in charge of inventory, the cleaning and maintenance of the weapons, and the munitions supply. Since she's a woman she doesn't play a direct role in the war, but she has the strength of a bull, which reveals an abundance of testosterone in her body. She shoots better than her brothers and can arm and disarm a rifle faster than any of them.

La Muda is alone with Arcángel, in his locked room. She's cleaning the dust with a red cloth and he's watching her work, lying on his bed, unable to keep his eyes off her.

"To us, who only saw them from the street, La Muda was nothing more than thick eyebrows, a steely glare, and a shapeless form wrapped in black."

Arcángel looks more closely and sees a great deal more. The excessive clothing she wears ignites his imagination. He fixates on the only part of her that is not hidden, her bare feet. In the rapid, silent steps of those young feet, the boy deciphers the code that allows him to guess about the rest of her body. With his best friend, Guillermo Willy, he sometimes talks about women. They make lists of the ones they know, they laugh like grown-up men, using crude, uncaring language to describe them. Arcángel dreams about La Muda, but he doesn't dare mention her, and he bites his tongue in indignation and jealousy when Guillermo Willy does.

"In the barrio they say she's an overweight spinster," Guillermo Willy tells him.

"It's not true; she's beautiful."

"They also say she wears a chastity belt."

"It's not true."

"Yes it is. Rojas, the blacksmith, swears he made it for her with his own hands years ago. One day she even drew it on paper, to show how it was to be made—a sheet of steel with two orifices, one in front, protected by thirty-six teeth, and another in back, with fifteen teeth."

"They're lies. Shut up."

La Muda flies around the room dusting and picking up dirty clothing. From the bed, her nephew follows her movements. He looks at her feet, admires her hidden body, desires her ripe flesh, thinks he can smell the warmth of her sex, imagines the metal pressing against it. In her brusque, energetic movements, in the way she holds the broom and shakes the red rag, the boy is captivated by a secret, hypnotic worship. He sees life itself when he looks at her and wears himself out trying to understand her. He wishes he could find the key to open the locks to such forbidden and armor-plated wonder.

"Muda," he begins, and she stops cleaning to look at him. "Is it true that you can speak? Talk to me. Say anything."

HOLMAN FERNELY spends a week following every move Narciso Barragán makes. During that period he collects the necessary information to plan the details of his assassination.

"*The Monsalves needn't have hired a professional to do that. To follow Narciso's trail all one has to do is follow the scent of his cologne.*"

All that stuff about his cologne is folklore, and Fernely is a professional who doesn't rely on hearsay. He is guided by facts, by what is certain. He is a criminal scientist.

"*There was no need for so much science and technology, because the victim was so wide open.*"

Yes and no. Just by remaining inside the city limits, Narciso and the other Barragáns are granted a sort of immunity, which comes from the territorial pact between them and the Monsalves dating back to that day when Nando Barragán presented Adriano Monsalve's cadaver to Tío in the desert. According to that pact, the families would leave the desert and one family would go live in the port and the other in the city, and neither could trespass on the territory of the other. If Narciso gives himself the luxury of not watching his back, it is because deep inside he trusts that the Monsalves will not enter the city.

"*Unless it were a zeta . . .*"

Unless it were a *zeta*. During the twelve hours that a *zeta* lasts, the territorial pact is lifted and there is only one rule: one side attacks and the other defends itself. One side tries to kill and the other tries to avoid being killed. Each death is avenged on the ninth day, at the end of a month, or the end of a year. Each death is avenged, and the avenging causes a new death. The *zetas* multiply like cancerous cells. All the attempted assassinations by the Monsalves in the city, and by the Barragáns in the port, have taken place on some anniversary. Always.

"Nando was always on the defensive, zeta or not."

Since the attempt in the bar that ruined his knee, Nando takes precautions, and so do the other surviving brothers Raca and Arcángel. Not Narciso. Narciso believes only what he wants to believe, and slinking around clandestinely doesn't fit with his playboy image, his matador ways, or his seductive siren song. He's like the bull-fighters and superstars; his spectacular display of beauty requires a public with lights, music, sets, and applause.

If a Monsalve surreptitiously tries to enter the city, the Barragáns immediately find out and liquidate him, because they have eyes and ears in alleys, on street corners, behind lampposts. So when the Monsalves enter, they do it carefully, on the *zetas*, armed to the teeth and in caravans of bulletproof vehicles. They invade the village, destroying like the Huns, like pirates attacking, like the bad guys in a Western movie.

"And the Barragáns wait for them with all the weapons in their fortress."

Fernely's plan is different, defined by a completely different style. They pay him to kill, and he does it quickly and without scruples. He doesn't respect laws or ethics. Nothing can cause him to feel remorse, and that's why he is infallible as an assassin. As an unknown outsider, it is easy for him to enter the city without being noticed and circulate at will, passing himself off as a street vendor selling contraband Milky Way bars. He clings to Narciso like an evil shadow and only needs a few days to penetrate his subconscious and learn the intimate secrets of his behavior.

The first thing he learns is that his victim is always thinking about women. If he is dancing with one, he takes advantage of the moment between songs to call another on the telephone. If he becomes involved in some business deal, he gets tangled up with the wife or daughter of his associate. If he sees a movie, he gets excited about the actress. When he takes part in a legal proceeding, he seduces the women lawyers and judges. He executes his seduction like a priest, and he is so fascinated with his moves that he has become a slave to his own charm. His energies are diluted by wanting so many women, and he can never find the perfect amount of love—he can't tolerate women not loving him, but he becomes exasperated when they love him too much. He wants them all and they all want him. So his life is spent in a devout, absolute, pluralistic offering of himself, and to such a degree that he has no chance for repose or real intimacy, much less time to be concerned with his personal security.

Holman Fernely doesn't need to know anything else. He knows that there is no target more vulnerable than someone in love, and Narciso depends on the love of women as a fish needs water and humans need air. The only reason he doesn't kill Narciso immediately is not because of complications but because he has received explicit orders from his benefactors to wait for zero hour.

4

THIS IS THE DAY everyone's been waiting for, Nando's wedding day. The Barragáns are finally opening their doors. Well, sort of. Outside the front door they have assembled a private army to check everyone who enters, physically searching gentlemen, ladies, children, the bride's godfather, the maid of honor, whomever, to make sure no one's carrying a weapon.

Although the invitation is for the evening, many guests arrive early in the afternoon to make sure they are first, only to find others already there sitting on the curb waiting for the party to begin. And there are fake guests—bodyguards camouflaged amid the multitude, Pajarito Pum Pum, Simón Balas, and El Cachumbo, dressed up like farmers, acting silly, but keeping an eye open to prevent security problems.

"How were we supposed to know who was who in that crowd when everyone seemed disguised?"

When the doors open, the guests stampede in, screaming and shouting, like crazed fans in a sports stadium, and run around the house inspecting everything, taking pictures, sticking their noses in every corner, like tourists at the zoo.

"We had imagined treasures, or tunnels, or torture chambers, or who knows what strange things inside that house, but it was an ordinary house, just like ours, only larger, much, much larger."

Inside, the descending hordes don't discover the riches or mysteries that they are expecting. They see only out-of-fashion furniture scattered around the rooms and corridors, as if the passing of years, more than human will, had been responsible for their arrangement. There are locked rooms that no one is allowed to enter. They peek between the cracks in the old wooden doors and see only empty space. In a bedroom they are surprised to see a brass cot lost among mountains of corn kernels. In another, a goat is tied to the leg of an armoire.

In a small prayer chapel that smells of incense and dead rats they discover oil portraits of each of the dead members of the family, with multitudes of lit candles beneath them. There is a large plaster saint, complete with robe and sword but no nose. There are also a crucifix, candelabra, and tapers. An unused coffin, standard size, waits hidden behind a curtain, ready for the next funeral.

"Death never caught those people unprepared. . . ."

When the place has been thoroughly scouted, Ana Santana makes her appearance on the arm of a maternal uncle, since her father is deceased.

"The arrival of the bride deflated us again. We were expecting a stunning dress with veils and lace like the one Grace Kelly wore when she married Rainier."

Ana doesn't seem dressed for a wedding so much as for a first communion. She made the dress herself, a simple, insipid thing of cheap sateen and, although the beauty salon has curled her hair and dolled her up with eyeshadow, powder, and rouge, she's the same plain girl as always, not ugly, not pretty. The assembled guests look at her more with pity than admiration, and think of her as a dove entering a lion's den.

The Barragán brothers are not in sight, nor are their women. The guests are received and attended to by the slave girls and a few inexperienced waiters, who appeared to have been trained the day before.

"*Because they had been trained the day before. They were actually trusted peasants who had been brought in from the Barragáns' farms. For security reasons, the family never hired strangers, because they didn't want to run the risk of being infiltrated by the enemy. We hadn't seen Nando, the groom, but a rumor was circulating that he was closed up in a small office transacting business. Like Marlon Brando during his daughter's wedding in* The Godfather."

First Nando takes care of private matters, then he appears in the middle of the party. He is dressed as always, wearing the same Cuban guayabera shirt that he has worn for years.

"*Maybe it's not the same one. He might have several that look alike.*"

As a gesture of deference to his guests, he is seen today for the first time in public without his black Ray-Bans. He has the slow, beady eyes of someone who has removed corrective lenses, and the guests struggle not to look at him directly for fear of being drawn into the intimacy of his gaze, previously hidden in shadows and now suddenly exposed to the light of day. With his round, unknown eyes, he lumbers through the crowd, greeting everyone with ostentatious, asphyxiating bear hugs. The only person he doesn't hug is the bride herself, who merely receives a dispassionate, fraternal kiss on the forehead.

Nando Barragán refuses the glasses of liquor the waiters offer him. He moves to the buffet and studies it carefully, examining and suspiciously smelling each dish, like a dog, but tastes nothing. Then he disappears through the clothing hanging in the back patio and enters the kitchen.

He finds Severina, his mother, alone. She, too, is wearing everyday clothes, as if it were just a regular day. Barefoot, wearing a long black cotton shawl stamped with white flowers, a towel around her shoulders, and a plastic apron tied around her waist, she has just washed her hair with Blue Cross soap to prevent lice. Nando notices that her hair is loose, something he has rarely seen.

Although Severina has spent her entire life closed up in that house, with the exception of periodic visits to the cemetery, her sons have never seen her disheveled or newly awakened. They have no idea what time she goes to bed, or what she needs. They have never heard her complain, or laugh, or cry. Her privacy is impenetrable. She has managed to control the weaknesses of those around her, but has remained immovable in regard to her own. When the others get drunk she stays sober; when they are sick she nurses them; when they fall apart she holds herself together; when they wander off course she remains firmly in place. While they throw away money, she saves every cent. When the family's world falls to the ground and shatters, she picks up the pieces and glues them back together again.

Severina knows each of the members of her family inside and out, but no one knows her. She is a fragile, but powerful, enigma. She is always there and she has always been there, imperturbable like a prehistoric rock, yet she is as intangible as time and space. Her authority, which is absolute, stems from her quiet patience and sphinxlike mystery.

Her husband died of natural causes and seven of her twelve children have died violent deaths. From seeing so much death, it's as if she has become a being of different substance, an inhabitant of spheres beyond pain and other human conditions. She assumes her harsh destiny with an incomprehensible heroic fatalism. And although she is the principal victim in the war with the Monsalves, she has never asked her sons to end it.

The years have shrunken her and grayed her hair but it still reaches down to her waist. Nando watches her disentangle it with a fine-toothed comb, noticing that she handles the thinning strands in the same energetic manner that she needed years ago to wrangle her once magnificent cascade. "She's old now," he thinks, and is surprised at this proof that his mother is susceptible to the passing of time.

"I'm hungry, Mamá."

She goes to the lit coal stove—she never wanted to try out the electric one her sons had installed for her—and prepares her son a plate of black beans and a glass of Old Parr whiskey.

"Nando Barragán lived with the fear that he was going to be poisoned and so he never tasted a mouthful of food that was not prepared by his mother."

"The real reason was that he was an uncultured man, incapable of trying a dish that seemed new or strange."

Hidden away in the kitchen, mother and son forget about the party pounding away in the distance, like a festival in another town. Nando sits at the heavy carved table where the family has eaten, ground corn meal, and ironed clothing for twenty years. Severina approaches him from behind and, with the firm touch of a lion tamer, massages his hairy neck with her fingertips, as she has done since he was a small child whenever she wanted to calm him.

"Okay, tell me why you're marrying her. Give me one good reason," she says.

"Because a man should have a wife," he answers, concentrating on his plate of beans, chasing them with gulps of whiskey.

"You're going to destroy her, Nando."

"Ana Santana is stronger than she looks."

"Then she's going to hurt you. Look at the circus you arranged today, just to please her. We have never had strangers in this house before."

"Everything is under control."

"You always say that and things always turn out badly."

The kitchen door opens and a fortyish gentleman enters. He is fair-skinned, taller than average, and has peaceful blue eyes that go well with the healthy pinkness of his cheeks. He is wearing a white shirt and a discreet dark suit that conveys professional confidence and personal security. It's Méndez, the family's lawyer and friend.

"*Méndez had a reputation in the city for being a gentleman. He was a friend of the Barragáns', but he wasn't like them. He was single, led a tranquil existence, and never got involved in matters concerning weapons. He acted as attorney to both families, the Monsalves as well as the Barragáns, and he was the only person who, for any length of time, had been able to deal with both without becoming the enemy of either.*"

Méndez defends members of both families against third parties. He performs his work with the strictest impartiality, without drama or involvement in disputes between the two families, and, most important of all, he never takes a penny over the modest cost of his services.

He knows that he is dealing with people who are accustomed to greasing palms and buying consciences, and that the moment someone takes money from them under the table, that person becomes their slave with the obligation of unconditional faithfulness under penalty of death.

Both families respect the attorney and consider him an honest, educated man. They value his friendship and understand that it's good for both sides to have someone like him, because despite the mortal feud — or perhaps because of it — it's helpful to have an indirect connection, a means of communication via someone close but neutral.

"*At any rate, the lawyer's life was hanging by a thread; one false move on his part, or one word too many, would have broken the delicate balance between the Monsalves and the Barragáns, and his rosy-cheeked personage would rot at the bottom of a ditch.*"

Cleanly shaven and fresh, as if he were wearing new skin, Méndez enters the kitchen and greets Severina with a hug and a kiss, and Nando with a handshake.

"He was the only person outside the family that greeted the Barragáns with a kiss. Not only that, he was the only one permitted to enter their kitchen."

"Counselor!" says Severina in greeting, with an effusiveness she never uses with anyone else.

"Sit, please," Méndez says to them, as if he were the owner of the house. "I'm glad to have found you together. I need to talk to both of you."

It's about Narciso. Méndez assures them he's not spreading gossip or inside information, which he never does. He only wants them to know what is obvious to everyone: that Narciso overly exposes himself. He is frequently seen with showy women in bars and restaurants.

"If he continues like that he won't last long," Méndez warns.

"There are always women behind the deaths of my sons," declares Severina dully.

Meanwhile, outside the kitchen, the party boils at full steam and the bands blare. At times the tumult and activity blast higher, reaching a peak, and the whole barrio vibrates, shaken by the energy emanating from the Barragáns' house; then the mood cools a little, dulled by noise, fatigue, and whiskey, until the wave catches it again, raising it to the crest and exploding in a frenzy once again.

"Everything happened at that party."

Near the end of the second day, when the musicians, waiters, and bodyguards are collapsing from drinking so much rum and the improvised bathrooms are giving off a robust odor of ammonia, Nando Barragán has cut away at social distances and is reborn, shoulder to shoulder, hiccuping, along with the rest of the drunks at the party.

As always, on his right wrist is his gold Rolex watch with forty-two diamonds, bulky and shiny, not easily missed. One of the guests, an insignificant little man called Elías Manso, buzzes and spins enviously around the watch. He has the pathetic look of a poor but pretentious scoundrel — rumpled hat, straight-legged pants, little white shoes — and Nando swats him away like a mosquito with unconscious waves of his huge hands. Manso, completely inebriated, returns to the bait, locking his lustful eyes on the Rolex with its brilliant constellation of diamonds.

"Let me have your watch," he says to Nando, who doesn't hear him. "Let me have that watch," he insists annoyingly.

Nando stands up unsteadily, his anger mounting, and throws the little man to the floor with a loud shout that chills the room and scares Manso so badly that he soils himself. Nando Barragán notices this and says, "You're a filthy insect. You shit in your pants. Let's see how low you'll go to get what you want."

"No, I don't want it now. Really, I don't even like your watch," mumbles the trembling Manso.

"Don't lie to me," roars Nando. "You'd trade your own mother to have it and I'm going to give you a chance to prove it. Have them bring you a plate, fork, knife, and napkin. If you eat your own shit, slowly and with proper manners, without gagging, I'll give you the watch."

The crowd encircles Elías Manso and might have witnessed a truly repugnant act if at that moment their eardrums hadn't been blasted by a loud crash outside that dissolved into the cascading notes of the song "La Negra," played enthusiastically on fifteen guitars, twenty violins, and twenty-three trumpets by five mariachi bands hired to perform together. The deafening serenade shakes the guests like an electric shock. Everyone becomes excited and runs to throw themselves at the door to witness the new spectacle. Down the street comes a cloud of mariachis squeezed into tight gray suits adorned with silver, playing their instruments beneath huge black sombreros.

Behind them, in silent, sumptuous procession, glides Narciso Barragán's violet Lincoln Continental.

"At Nando's wedding, it was Narciso who stole the show. Imagine appearing with so many mariachis."

"He always stole the show."

"He made a triumphant entrance, like a conquering general riding into the town plaza."

At the tail of the parade, following the Lincoln, a strange enormous hulk creaks and wobbles, barely fitting in the street. At first no one knows what it is. Mounted on an open wagon and pulled by a tractor, it is round and flat, measuring twelve feet across.

It's Narciso's wedding gift to his brother Nando, a huge round waterbed with a tortoiseshell frame, complete with mirrors, full bar, fox-fur bedspread, and a profusion of fur-covered cushions of various sizes.

Narciso looks like Gardel, the Argentine tango singer and composer, with his dark hair pulled back and plastered to his head with brilliantine. He's meticulously dressed in a white bullfighter's suit with white Italian loafers as soft and pliable as gloves.

"All that white in Narciso's costume was deliberate, purposely designed to highlight his eyes, which were as deep and black as night in the desert."

"Everything about him was deliberate. He loved to create a scene."

He's accompanied by a woman right out of a fashion magazine, an expensive girl, several inches taller than he, with extra-long legs, super-straight hair, a sensuous mouth, and a V-necked dress open to her waist that reveals a great deal of her flat chest.

"I don't know what Narciso saw in her. She was as skinny as a cat."

"*He liked them like that, skeletal, modern. He used to say that you only ask for meat by the pound at the butcher shop. He liked fine women, not ordinary ones.*"

Narciso orders the mariachis to play the triumphal march from *Aida* and, with a magnificent theatrical gesture, invites Ana Santana to take his arm and walk with him. He wants to officially present his gift. They enter the living room and he lifts her with both arms, respectfully, as befits the new wife of his brother, placing her gently in the center of the fur-covered bed. Narciso calls for silence and, before the expectant crowd, flips the switch built into the headboard of that indescribable piece of furniture.

Then the most bizarre thing happens. Lovely music flows from the recessed stereo, the black and red lights surrounding the tortoiseshell frame come on, the mattress begins to vibrate, massage, and move up and down, turning first to the right, then to the left, revolving slowly on its base.

The guests are terrified and begin screaming.

"The bed is bewitched!" yells someone.

"It looks like a Ferris wheel," another guest calls out.

"Someone save the bride!" shouts still another.

Ana, somewhere between startled and amused, struggles to maintain her equilibrium, rolling among the furry cushions, tearing her white dress, losing her orange-blossom crown. She collapses in nervous laughter, begging for help, calling out for someone to stop the awful machine, then changes her mind and decides to ride the bed a while longer.

As if on cue, the musicians begin to play again and couples begin to dance. The drunks perk up and start drinking again. Coming back to life, the crowd roars and people begin climbing over one another to be first to ride the magic bed, then finally form a line to ride one at a time.

"Enough!" shouts Narciso, who isn't about to be upstaged by a bed. He turns off the machine, putting an end to the circus and resuming his position in the spotlight. He places a sombrero on his head and a red carnation between his lips and begins to sing *rancheras*, strolling the patios with the mariachis accompanying him.

His voice vibrates above the violins and the trumpets, thrilling the guests. The men howl and yell "Ayayay!!!" and the girls cry hysterically, like fans at a rock concert.

"My sweet little brother!" yells Nando Barragán tenderly, his steely arms squeezing Narciso, lifting him until only the tips of his Italian loafers touch the ground. Nando caresses Narciso's face with the rough pawing of an adoring gorilla and whispers into his ear, his voice breaking from emotion and alcohol. "Be careful. Don't let them kill you like a dog."

Once again Narciso takes full advantage of the moment. With the grace of a gypsy and the agility of a tightrope walker, he jumps onto Nando's shoulders. His white-clad body is bathed in light, as if onstage under spotlights. The room becomes as silent as a church, and from his human pedestal Narciso prolongs the moment, entrancing the crowd with ardent rays from his beautiful eyes.

Then, serenely, he responds to his brother's warning, improvising a monologue that will long be remembered in La Esquina de la Candela.

"Brother, we are shit and shit is what we will become. You and I already know this, because we are cursed. We drink until we fall. We eat until we vomit. We spend all our money. We love all the women. We look straight at death and spit in her face."

"How did the party end?"

After three days the house looked like a deserted battlefield, covered with trash, nearly destroyed by the hordes of guests, and invaded by packs of stray dogs looking for scraps of food.

Ana Santana is alone in the immense round nuptial bed, still wearing her freshly ironed nightgown, stoically bearing the abandonment by her husband with proud resignation. Nando Barragán, drunk and lying in a corner of his mother's kitchen, surrounded by a pile of sour-smelling cigarette butts, is crying over the painful memories of his blond Milena, the woman who wouldn't love him.

THE INHABITANTS of the port awaken from their siesta. Slowly they open their shuttered windows, allowing the brilliant sun to inundate their houses and dispel the rancid humidity of another hot afternoon. Mani Monsalve, who never takes a siesta, is at his desk, looking out the window. Through the polarized glass the sea takes on artificial silver tones that are more pleasing to him than the natural ones. The violet sky is splendidly unreal, like a Cibachrome photograph.

Mani is in a private meeting with his right-hand man, Tin Puyúa. He has removed his shoes and is gently rubbing his feet on the carpet, which he just had installed because the old one lost its new smell.

Still surprised by the textures and smells of the expensive things he has come to know as an adult, Mani enjoys touching the chrome desk legs, the marble top, the imitation leather on his reclining chair, the cut crystal of the vase in his hand. He breathes deeply the clean, impersonal perfume of the air freshener. He has had the walls covered in cork to isolate himself from the noise of the crashing waves because it gives him a headache. The air-conditioning is on full blast and the freezing air makes him shiver. That's how he likes it. For so many years he suffered the desert heat, and now it makes him feel powerful to be able to be cold.

Each week he is visited by a *contrabandista* who brings him the newest technological inventions and who always leaves happy, because Mani Monsalve is a sucker for anything that you can plug in. His closets are filled with electronic gadgets he doesn't need. He buys them for the sheer pleasure of it and doesn't even know what some of them are for. Mani carefully saves the packaging and the operating instructions. He has learned the little English he knows by trying to decipher them. He has an unbridled passion for intercoms, giant-screen TVs, quadraphonic stereos, digital watches, electronic games and calendars, electric blankets, microwave ovens, self-cleaning ovens, auto-rewinding cassette recorders, auto-focus cameras, and, most of all, telephones.

No two of his twenty-six telephones are alike. He has cordless, magnetophonic, psychedelic, and memory phones, anti-interference, shoe-shaped, Coca-Cola can, and Snoopy phones. His favorite, which he keeps on his desk, is transparent, and allows him to see the inner workings. It receives and transmits messages, lulls people on hold with soft music, and glows colorfully in the dark like a flying saucer.

As captivated as he is by electric appliances, he is equally disconcerted by the paintings that hang on his walls. "Modern art," explained the gallery owner who sold them to him at exorbitant prices. He reluctantly paid, let them be hung where it seemed best, and even learned the names of the artists, but truthfully, and he would never confess this to anyone, he can't stand them. He doesn't understand how they can charge so much money for a couple of incomprehensible blotches, or for paintings that look as if they were done by children. But he doesn't dare remove them. If the decorators chose them, they must be good.

He has acquired more money than he could ever have dreamed, but he lacks the judgment to spend it properly. He doesn't know what is pretty and what is ugly, what is stylish and what isn't, and that worries him immensely.

"As soon as I say I like something," he tells Alina, "it turns out to be bad taste."

That's why he needs advisers, to always be certain that he doesn't make mistakes or do anything low-class to reveal his status of nouveau riche.

As with the paintings by Obregón and Botero, there are other things Mani hasn't figured out, among them brand-name clothing. He buys it by the ton, but he doesn't wear it because it itches, or it's too loose or too tight. His fingernails are always unkempt — he hates manicurists. And masseurs, barbers, and doctors, because he has a phobia about anyone touching his body. He avoids physical contact and doesn't get near anyone, or let anyone get near him. He sleeps very little, can go days without eating, doesn't smoke or take drugs, doesn't like alcohol, and drinks only Kola Román.

"Kola Román was his addiction. He drank it by the gallon and always said it was the red aniline in the soft drink that made him so hyperactive."

"Is everything ready for tonight?" Mani Monsalve asks Tin Puyúa, looking the other way, as if he weren't interested in a response, as if he weren't even asking a question. Mani takes a piece of mint gum from his pocket and chews it nervously with his mouth open. He wants to know if the attempt on Narciso Barragán's life is all set up. "What about the plan for tonight?" he asks again without giving Tin Puyúa time to answer. He has decided to stay on the sidelines, keep his hands clean, and leave it all up to his brother Frepe. Mani wants a clean conscience so Alina can't blame him for anything. But he's too accustomed to pulling the strings and at this late hour can't resist getting involved. "How's the Narciso thing going, huh?"

Sitting on the edge of his chair and tapping the ground with the heel of his boot, as if only waiting for a chance to leave, Tin Puyúa answers his boss's question. He speaks hurriedly, tearing up pieces of paper, tossing back a strand of hair that falls across his forehead with a spastic shake of his head.

"Tonight's a *zeta*, so the Barragáns will lock themselves up in that house. Except Narciso. He doesn't care about the *zetas* and he's gonna spend the night with a model, celebrating her birthday. Fernely knows 'cause he tapped the phones. They're gonna hit him when he gets to her house. They got a public-works truck to block his car, then some guys in soccer uniforms with guns in their gear bags will jump him."

Mani listens, then turns in his chair, displeased. His gum has lost its flavor, so he spits it out. Tin Puyúa continues. "Fernely already got the truck with a little bribe and found the girl's house. Everything's ready. We're just waiting for Frepe to give the go-ahead."

"Why the hell are they making it so complicated?" asks Mani, annoyed.

For Mani killing is simple. It's done with guts, not intelligence, more like hunting animals than devising military tactics. He becomes increasingly angry at all the strange, elaborate preparations. He decides to call Frepe to tell him to drop the plan and get rid of that Fernely. The two of them should just go alone in a jeep and shoot Narciso in the head. Then he contains himself and doesn't call. He had decided not to participate in this drama, and he won't.

For the third time that day he asks Tin Puyúa what he thinks of Holman Fernely, and Tin is about to repeat for the third time that he doesn't know when suddenly the door to his office opens.

"They say that Mani jumped up and pulled out his revolver. The intrusion was totally unexpected, because no one, not even his wife, would dare enter his office without knocking."

It's Alina Jericó. Surprised, Mani puts the revolver down and invites her to sit down. "What's up?" he asks.

"Nothing," she says, and Mani immediately senses that something serious has happened.

She's wearing slacks and a blouse of loose-fitting, light-colored silk, with sandals revealing her perfect white feet. She's not wearing any makeup and the dark circles under her eyes suggest that she spent the night battling the nightmare about the black mare. Her ears peek out from behind her gathered hair, and on each delicate lobe a small but clear blue diamond glitters like Venus in the afternoon sky.

"Tell me what has happened."

"Nothing."

Alina sits in a chair in front of her husband's desk, silent. She throws a look at Tin Puyúa, her hatred for him glowing brighter than the diamonds. She abhors the assassin's nervous tics and his constant intrusion on her private life. She crosses her legs and presses her lips together. She won't say a word in front of him and Mani quickly realizes this.

"Leave us alone, Tin," Mani orders.

The boy throws back his hair with two successive shakes of his greasy head and stands haughtily. He would give his life for Mani, but he hates Alina as much as she hates him and doesn't bother to hide it. He leaves, closing the door behind him.

"Okay, now tell me what it is," Mani says to his wife, hoping with all his might that it's nothing big. His brain is saturated with the Narciso situation and he feels incapable of enduring marital reproaches right now. He looks at her with hardened eyes, already tired of the impending conversation. He adores her, just as long as she's not causing problems.

Without opening her mouth, Alina reaches into her purse and pulls out an envelope. She stands and places it on his desk, then sits again. There is a defiance in her demeanor, a touch of James Dean, that puts Mani on alert. He hesitates before reaching for the envelope, looking at his wife, questioning her with his eyes, begging for a clue, anything, but she stares back resolutely.

Mani feels lost. He doesn't know why, but he knows this is something big, fat, and heavy and there's nothing he can do about it now. It's already on top of him. He opens the envelope, unfolds the certificate inside, and reads: "Clinical Analysis Laboratory, Dr. Jesús Onofre. Señora Alina Jericó de Monsalve. Immunological test for pregnancy: Positive."

"SO EVERYONE *in La Esquina de la Candela went to Nando Barragán's wedding?"*

"Almost everyone, but not quite. El Bacán and his crowd refused."

"Who were they?"

"A bunch of domino players. El Bacán was a blind black man who was over six feet tall. His wife read him the newspapers and he talked about politics and history and knew everything, because he had learned it on his own. He was an authority in the barrio, the only one who had any power without using a weapon. He hated violence, cheating, and ostentation. His combo was a group of domino players, a group of friends that gathered on the sidewalk in front of his house every evening at six o'clock to continue the championship game they had started three years earlier and would probably never finish. One afternoon, before Nando's wedding, Bacán's wife, a huge mulatto much younger than him, interrupted the domino playing to ask for money to buy a dress for the wedding. He flat out said no. She was used to her old husband letting her have her way and asked why not. In front of his friends and the onlookers, Bacán lifted his useless, cataract-filled eyes from the dominoes and said what no one else in the barrio had dared to say. "Because we aren't going. I don't associate with murderers."

AT FOUR O'CLOCK in the morning in the city's red-light district a cream-colored Mercedes-Benz 500 SE with tinted bulletproof windows and white calfskin upholstery stops suddenly in front of a black windowless wall, broken only by a neon sign reading "The Blue Siren Topless Bar and Strip Club—Authentic Sirens to Make Your Wildest Dreams Come True." Two Toyotas with armed bodyguards pull up behind the Mercedes.

A huge man limps out of the Mercedes and enters the establishment, peering into the smoke-filled room through black Ray-Ban sunglasses. Nando Barragán pauses a few moments in order to make out the figures dancing in the darkness to the merengue hit "Devórame Otra Vez." He scans the room with a practiced eye, making a mental picture of it. In all there are twelve available women, scantily dressed: two butterflies, a peacock, two mermaids, a lollipop, two transvestites, a rabbit, a tiger, and two plain whores.

"The black Mermaid, the Peacock, and the Tiger," he says to his men, abruptly leaving and going to his car to wait.

"In the old days, before the attempt on his life that damaged his knee, Nando would arrive at The Blue Siren, order the doors locked, and buy drinks all around. Then he'd climb up on the stage to fondle the strippers, stuffing dollar bills in their G-strings, and invariably wind up taking off his own clothes."

"They say his member was ridiculously small, like a tortilla chip in the middle of that colossal body, but that in spite of his lack of attributes, he made women feel good and there was always enough left over for a second round, but they say lots of things, not all of which are true. For example, some say he was completely covered with fine hair, like a monkey, but the truth is that his skin was waxy and hairless, like all yellow-skinned people of the desert."

The bodyguards approach an immense black woman dressed like a mermaid, a blonde with a tail of peacock feathers, and a skinny girl with striped ears and a tail wearing an imitation tiger-skin bodysuit. They say something to the three women, who hurriedly cover themselves, grab their bags, and run out to the street, balancing on six-inch spike heels, pushing each other like high school girls.

The women climb into the Mercedes in a jumble of squeals and scrambling, the Peacock in front and the Mermaid and the Tiger in back. But Nando doesn't approve and rearranges things so that the Mermaid ends up in front with him and the Tiger and the Peacock are in back. The Mercedes and the Toyotas take off through the streets, tires burning and screeching. Once they are under way, the Peacock decides to open the door and in a sharp curve almost falls out of the car, but she's saved when someone grabs a plume and pulls her back in. Farther down the road they stop in front of a mariachi plaza, and at Nando's signal the bodyguards gather a trusted trio and put them in one of the Toyotas.

The caravan heads down the coast, taking a mountain road along the shoreline. The sea pounds against the rocky cliffs. The tremendous, roaring waves are black, green, and violet. Nando is steering the car at sixty miles per hour with one hand and holding a whiskey bottle in the other. He alternates gulps of whiskey with drags from the Pielroja cigarettes the women stick in his mouth. Flying low, drunk, ignoring the force of gravity beckoning him at each curve in the road, Nando fires his Colt at the signs warning of danger ahead.

The girls are exhilarated. Swept up by the car's speed and the party atmosphere, they have given themselves over to the booze and smoke and busy themselves with pleasing their host. While one kisses him another gives him a blow job and the third whispers love sonnets in his ear. They pour Old Parr down his throat and throw the empty bottles out the windows to see the brown glass shatter against the asphalt in a thousand golden stars and laugh as the Toyotas swerve to avoid the shards.

At Nando's request, the Mermaid starts a fierce striptease while she murmurs a merengue with the hoarse voice of a ruined Indian.

She unfastens a bra festooned with metal scales like medieval armor, and two monumental tits, worthy of *The Guinness Book of World Records*, burst free, nipples firmly planted in the center of each like a cyclops's eye. Each of the Mermaid's breasts is huge and black, real heavyweight champions. On the left is Frazier and on the right, Muhammad Ali, duking it out with the bouncing and rolling of the car on the road. A turn to the left and Frazier falls on Ali, pushing him onto the ropes. A turn to the right and Ali comes back with an uppercut to Frazier's jaw. In the excitement of the scuffle, the nipples harden and open like satellite disks sending pornographic messages of war.

The passengers in the front seat are packed in like sardines in a tin, as if instead of two oversized people there were four, Nando the Gorilla, the Mermaid, better known as the Whale, the huge breast Frazier, and his twin brother, Ali.

The Mermaid takes off her tailfin of wire and silver lamé, freeing the wild nest between her legs. Her sex is overwhelming and prodigious like a vortex, emitting animal fluids that further excite Nando..He pushes a bottle into the meaty Amazon cave until it disappears from sight, completely devoured, the old man with the beard on the label lost from sight.

"You tricked me, Mermaid," cries Nando, disenchanted. "Mermaids aren't supposed to have a hole even the size of the eye of a needle, but you have a canyon that if I entered, I could see your tonsils."

In the backseat, the Peacock, a blonde with long hair, has fallen asleep with her mouth and eyes open. Nando orders the Tiger to wake her up and pluck her feathers. The Tiger, who is skinny but vicious, slaps the Peacock, then shakes and bites her, but the Peacock remains mute and absent, lost in who knows what alcohol-induced purgatory. Next, the Tiger, angry and unwilling to accept failure, scratches the Peacock with her sharp nails, yanks feathers from her tail, and pulls her hair, which falls to the floor revealing a shaved head, smooth as a billiard ball.

"She doesn't want to play; she won't cooperate," whines the Tiger accusingly.

The Peacock is oblivious. Unimpressed with the whole scene, she lies there passed out on the backseat, a poor, scrawny, plebeian bird with wrecked plumage and sad breasts flattened by their own weight, her round, wigless skull exposed.

"These whores have deceived me," complains Nando Barragán childishly. "The Mermaid is a fraud and so is the blonde. This cruel world has left me only you, Tiger."

The Tiger revels in her victory and rises to the occasion by emitting low guttural sounds. She puts the Peacock's wig on Nando Barragán and she clings to his neck, licking him with her pink tongue like a kitten drinking warm milk from a saucer. She's still in the backseat and it's difficult for her to maintain a comfortable position; she leans forward over Nando, pressing her head against him, pinching his neck, breathing her foul breath on him; she knocks his glasses off his nose and tickles his ears with her long feline whiskers, impairing his driving ability.

The Tiger is not daunted by obstacles. She dedicates herself with renewed vigor to properly performing her function and manipulates his masculine features with obvious experience and guaranteed results. She plays arpeggios with her long fingers, flourishes with her soft fingertips, and massages him with her palms. Through the rearview mirror he watches her remove her tiger skin to reveal the human one beneath it, more wrinkled than the other but still possessing its own hidden attractions and secret delights, and he manages, finally, to achieve a satisfactory erection.

In perfect synchronization of man and machine, the Mercedes's velocity increases in tandem with its master's excitement, and with each careless turn of the steering wheel its nose peers over the abyss with suicidal abandon. After taking a curve that leaves the two left tires in midair, Nando slows down to check his speed and catch his breath, noting sadly that in doing so he has frustrated his already difficult ascent toward ejaculation.

"Sometimes it seems that you want to be down there," he says detachedly and lovingly to his automobile.

They have arrived at the highest point along the road. With the serenity of a grand gentleman accustomed to making drastic decisions without hesitation, Nando Barragán points the hood of his Mercedes toward the precipice, orders his passengers to disembark, and ejects himself with unexpected agility for a man of his size.

Colossal, powerful, and completely drunk, in the long blond wig like a Teutonic warrior, horrible and splendid, like the missing link, he pushes the vehicle toward the edge, looks at the shining sea below, swells his chest with air, and gives the final push.

The cream-colored Mercedes-Benz 500 SE falls into the abyss in a shower of sparks and crashes, offering a close-up, once-in-a-lifetime cinematographic spectacle, complete with special effects, while Nando watches in fascination as it flies gently through the limitless air. He watches it descend silently, in slow motion, striking sparks and decapitating angels along the way, bouncing softly off the black rocks, repeatedly demonstrating its Germanic solidity and unquestionable quality of craftsmanship, until at the end of its celestial journey the ocean waters receive it beneficently, cushioning the fall in their voluptuous bed, opening docilely to its triumphal passage in a happy effervescence of froth and bubbles, and swallow it whole, forever.

Above, from the edge of the precipice, Nando Barragán, the drunken yellow god, he of the magnificent blond wig and black sunglasses, with the Colt revolver in his belt, the craters in his skin, and the lame leg, contemplates the magnificent scene with his arms spread in the shape of a cross, a faraway look in his eyes, realizing that finally the moment of his ecstasy has arrived. He feels warm torrents of fluid inundating his body; he lets it flow in spurts, irrigating the planet with his seed. Then he lifts his tear-filled eyes toward the sky and, swelled with pride, shouts in a booming voice that is heard in heaven and hell:

"I'm an aaaaarrrtiiissst!"

"Is it true that there was still someone inside the car? They say that when he came back from the orgy in one of the Toyotas with his bodyguards, only Nando, the mariachis, the Mermaid, and the Tiger returned. The Peacock was never seen again."

"Since she was asleep, maybe she went over with the Mercedes and didn't wake up until she reached the bottom of the ocean. If she had been a mermaid, maybe she would have survived, but since she was only a yard bird . . ."

The musicians, who had been playing steadily the whole time in the Toyota, surround Nando, annoying him with *vallenatos*, following him wherever he goes like faithful shadows. Filled to the gills with Old Parr and exhausted after a cosmic orgasm produced by the voluntary destruction of a car worth a hundred thousand dollars, he decides to rest, like God on the seventh day of creation, and lies down to sleep in a soft patch of sand.

The musicians surround the sleeping man in adoration, softly singing boleros and other quiet songs, kneeling with their guitars and maracas, humble and solicitous, like Melchior, Gaspar, and Balthazar watching the Christ child sleep.

"Shut up, you sons of bitches! If you play one more note, I'll have you shot in a ditch!" shouts Nando, unable to sleep, cutting them off in the middle of a C-sharp. Soon after, he falls into a deep sleep, snoring like a wild beast and dreaming of Milena, the inaccessible.

"What happened to the Tiger and the Mermaid?"

"The bodyguards and musicians had their way with them while their boss slept."

The next morning in La Esquina de la Candela, in the Barragáns' garage, Ana Santana approaches one of the Toyotas, covered with vomit and stinking, and in the backseat finds a fat, half-naked woman wearing an absurd fishtail sprawled on the floor of the car, asleep.

"Give this woman some breakfast," orders Ana Santana.

"Do you want me to serve her at the dining room table?" asks one of the servant girls.

"No. Bring it to her here in the car."

"ALINA JERICÓ *had said that if she got pregnant she would leave her husband, and she got pregnant. Did she fulfill her promise? Did she leave Mani Monsalve?"*

"*The promise wasn't made exactly like that. She was a woman of character, capable of living up to her word, but she was in love with her husband, and she left him an open door. When her pregnancy was confirmed, she told Mani, 'If you're involved in one more death, I'm leaving.'* "

The lab report still on Mani's desk, Alina says it again before she leaves his office: "If you're involved in one more death, I'm leaving."

Mani remains seated, stiff and silent like a stuffed bird, not knowing what to think or say, the half-moon scar stamped on his face like a question mark.

Alina's threat looms before him like a big black frog, ready to jump in his face. Two exposed cables cross and short-circuit in his brain — he can smell the singeing: the birth of his child and the assassination of Narciso Barragán. It takes him a moment to recuperate from the cerebral paralysis and recover the use of his limbs. When he realizes that he should have hugged Alina, or congratulated her, or suggested a champagne toast, she has already walked out of the office with watery eyes and a knot in her throat, leaving behind, suspended in the frozen air, the sound of rustling silk and the memory of her Grecian goddess feet.

Mani looks at his watch. It's ten past seven, and at any moment the event may occur that could separate him from his wife and child forever. Unless he manages to turn back something that has already gone too far. He holds his head between his hands. Now he wishes for Narciso Barragán to live with the same fever with which he had wished him dead only minutes earlier.

Dully, Mani puts on his tennis shoes, ties the laces, and stands up. He's going after Alina to reassure her, to promise her that nothing will happen, but he stops — he can't lose a minute. All of a sudden he has to urinate badly, but he puts off going to the bathroom. There is no time.

He takes hold of the transparent telephone and over the internal line tells someone to send Tin Puyúa in. While Mani waits he takes a bottle of Kola Román from the refrigerator built into the bookless bookcase and downs it in one long swallow, following every curve of the cold liquid until it hits his stomach. His inflamed brain is relieved and he regains some of his courage, but now he really has to go to the bathroom.

"Do you know where to find Fernely right now?" he asks Tin.

"It wasn't right for Mani Monsalve to ask something like that. He had always been on top of everything, and now he's caught uninformed and disconnected, reliant upon his lieutenant for a life-or-death piece of information."

Tin Puyúa can smell something wrong. Mani always gives orders and answers, he never asks questions, and today all he's done is interrogate and ask opinions. The boy's ego begins to grow. He's proud to be better informed than his boss. "Yes, I know," he answers haughtily. "He's in the city at the Hotel Nancy. He said he'd be there waiting for instructions from Frepe."

"Then call him," orders Mani. The Kola Román has finished its downhill course and now further expands his bladder, heightening the pressure.

"On the telephone?"

"Yes, right now."

Tin Puyúa can't believe what he is hearing. Mani, who never makes mistakes, has just given him a foolish order. "I'm sure that Fernely didn't register under his real name," Tin says. Mani insists, as if it were nothing out of the ordinary. "I told you to call him."

Tin obeys. "The concierge says there is no one registered by the name Fernely. I told you, Mani," he says with great satisfaction. "I hope Fernely doesn't find out that we are calling him on the telephone from your house, using his name, just hours before a hit," continues Tin, emboldened.

Mani doesn't hear him. His wife and his overwhelming need to relieve himself are all that matter to him now. He is far from worrying about what Tin thinks or Fernely's security.

"Then find Fernely in the city on the shortwave radio," he orders, his distended bladder begging for release.

Tin doesn't want to. He doesn't understand what's going on, but he's willing to bet that Alina Jericó has something to do with it. He obeys against his better judgment, sulkingly. He dials the number. Mani speaks with Frepe, who has gone into the city to supervise the operation. Mani asks his older brother to find Fernely in the hotel and order him to hold off on the plan.

"I'll explain later," Mani tells him, sure that he'll have time to invent a fake reason and avoid telling him the truth.

"It can't be done," says an agitated Frepe. "The city is full of police because of an unexpected government function in a building near the hotel. I can't go over there," he warns. "It's too dangerous." Mani insists until Frepe relents, in part because his clan instinct pushes him to obey, and in part out of habit, because one word from Mani is all that was ever needed to do or not do something — without objections or questions from the other brothers. Frepe agrees to be at the Hotel Nancy in ten minutes, look for Fernely, and report immediately back to Mani.

Mani tells Tin not to move from the radio and goes to look for Alina. He takes the service elevator up two floors and walks down a wide, heavily carpeted corridor until he reaches the master bedroom. There she is, lying prone on the bed with her face buried in the down comforter, divinely tragic, like Romy Schneider in *Sissi*. Before saying anything he heads for the bathroom.

Mani Monsalve urinates. Abundant, satisfying, foamy, intense yellow. He walks back into the bedroom feeling lighter, relieved, certain that half of the drama was resolved in the bathroom. Now he only has to deal with the other half. He sits beside his wife and begins to caress her hair.

"If it's a girl we'll name her Alina," he says to make her happy, but he really hopes it's a boy. He's sure it will be.

He returns to the radio room, arriving as Frepe is calling in to report that he's at the Nancy, but he can't find Fernely. "He hasn't gotten here yet," he says. "I guess he's still on his way."

Mani orders him to do nothing but look for Fernely and to keep his men at the hotel until they find him. Mani tells Frepe that Tin Puyúa is on his way and will arrive in two hours. Frepe is to report in as soon as there is any news. Tin takes one of the cars and starts for the city under orders to help Frepe stop Fernely. "Even if it takes bullets," Mani says. Tin is sure that Mani has gone crazy, but he heads out, resolved to obey.

Mani sits by the shortwave radio and waits. He plays game after game of solitaire and empties bottle after bottle of Kola Román. An hour, an hour and a half, then two hours pass. At 9:45 P.M. Frepe calls in to say that Tin has just arrived, but still no Fernely.

"Maybe he got scared by all the police," says Frepe. "Maybe he just went on to the hit and won't be coming here at all."

Mani becomes enraged.

"Isn't anyone in charge of that son of a bitch?" he shouts. "If he said he was going to be at the Nancy, he's supposed to be there."

"He does things his own way," says Frepe in defense.

Mani begins insulting his older brother, calling him an imbecile, an idiot. He orders Frepe to stop Fernely and to tell Tin to find the model and warn her of the attack so she can intercept Narciso.

"What?" Now it's Frepe who is shouting, burning with the suspicion that his brother has sold out to the enemy. "It's too late, Mani! You want me to order Tin to get in the middle of a shoot-out? You want him to die to save a Barragán?"

Mani realizes that if he doesn't calm down he's lost the game. He breathes deeply, speaking clearly and carefully, charging each syllable with all the authority he can muster.

"Do what I tell you. Stop Fernely."

Frepe hangs up and wipes his sweat-soaked palm on his trousers. He takes a big drag on his cigarette and leaves the smoke-filled phone booth. He walks toward his car, where Tin Puyúa is waiting for him.

"What did Mani say?" asks Tin.

"Nothing," lies Frepe. "He said it's too late to do anything now."

5

NANDO BARRAGÁN is surrounded by his family in the central patio of their house, and the setting sun, peeking through the canopy of leaves from the tamarind tree, sprinkles dancing lights and shadows on his tribe of yellow people. All have religiously come to surround their leader, unconditionally at his service, as they always do when a *zeta* occurs.

They are standing, or leaning against the walls, silently inhaling cigarettes and grinding out the butts on the tiles of the corridor, ready to go and devour Monsalves at the slightest signal. Nando meditates, stretched out in a hammock in the middle of the gathering.

Except for Arcángel, who is locked in his room, Narciso, whom no one can locate, and Raca, whom no one cares about, all of the male members of the clan are present. First cousins, second cousins, uncles, fathers-in-law. The Barragán Gómezes and Gómez Barragáns, the three Gómez Araújo brothers, the two redheaded Araújo Barragáns, Simón Balas, Pajarito Pum Pum, El Tijeras, El Cachumbo.

Collapsed in the hammock, Nando smokes and thinks. No one dares break the silence of the old warrior as he reviews his strategy. Suddenly a scraggly hen climbs up on his knee and everyone thinks it's a goner. They wait for the jefe to plaster it against a wall with a mighty swat and transform it into a mass of miserable feathers. But he graciously lets it sit there, warm on his knee.

La Mona Barragán pushes her way through the masculine gathering, approaches the hammock, and whispers something in her brother's ear. Nando breaks the suspense on the patio and, with the monotone voice of a priest mechanically reciting mass, announces that he has purchased the news that the Monsalves are already in the city, at some of the downtown hotels.

"How did he buy news like that?"

"Nando had organized an infallible intelligence and espionage system. Nary a leaf moved in the city without his knowing it. He had developed a network of neighbors, taxi drivers, shoe-shine boys, lottery salesmen, prostitutes, policemen, customs agents, anyone who could deliver secret information. He paid them with money, protection, or simply in exchange for letting them live in peace."

Nando begins to bark out orders. "Women and children to the cellars. Men in the jeeps to go downtown and look for the Monsalves in the five main hotels: the Intercontinental, the Carib, the Bachué, the Diplomático, and the Nancy."

"Then it was true that there was a labyrinth of tunnels under the Barragáns' house?"

There is a subterranean refuge, humid and dark, that they call "the cellars." There are openings at street level that are guarded by men with machine guns. The Barragáns' house is really all the houses on the block combined, and the cellars connect them all underground. They are used as trenches, storerooms for weapons and merchandise, and as a hiding place. There are several secret exterior openings.

"There was talk about a tunnel that ran from La Esquina de la Candela to the outskirts of the city. Once we saw Nando Barragán enter his house and we heard that two minutes later he was twenty blocks away, without ever setting foot on the street."

"Some people said that the tunnels were just a network of sewage-filled pipes. Others thought they were the product of military engineering."

La Mona Barragán takes charge of those who stay behind. Mannish, with dark, jaundiced skin and gold-capped teeth, she had pulled her hair back in a braid, long and thick like a spike. At thirty-four years old she is as foul-mouthed as a mule driver and as evil-tempered as the devil. Her life is divided between her only two passions: weapons and *telenovelas*.

She is famous for her marksmanship and hunts rats with a slingshot. She can identify the make and caliber of a weapon from the sound of its discharge and has the quickest trigger finger.

"Around the neighborhood they said that La Mona was a woman with three balls."

Nevertheless, every day at seven-thirty in the morning and at five sharp in the afternoon she sits in front of the television to watch her favorite *telenovelas*. She cries without modesty at the sad scenes, adores the good characters, and hates the bad ones. There is nothing in the world that can pry her eyes from the screen, as was proved the day that the river overran its banks and flooded the house. While everyone else struggled to save the furniture, she lifted the television, an ancient black-and-white hulk, up in the air and placed it on top of an armoire so it wouldn't get wet and watched the rest of *Simplemente María*.

With cartridge belts diagonally across her chest, a semiautomatic rifle in her hand, wearing a long skirt and rubber boots, La Mona corrals her platoon of women and children and drives them at a trot down the dark staircase into the cellars. She illuminates the gloomy passages with torches that she sticks into the moldy clay walls and wanders about the labyrinth of puddle-filled tunnels like a general on a battlefield.

Shouting and pounding her fists she organizes her followers.

She distributes the weapons left behind by the men, an odd assortment of old relics ranging from a Chinese crossbow to a Walther P38 from a Nazi officer who fled to the tropics after the war. She orders them to gather drinking water, blankets, and provisions for the night. She puts the servant girls and the children in a dry place. Ana Santana, holding her knitting in her hands, watches silently as La Mona throws her needles and yarn into the darkness and thrusts a pistol at her.

"You better start learning how things really are around here, honey," she says.

"*What about Arcángel, the youngest brother? Did they leave him locked in his room?*"

"*No. He went down into the cellars too, with his bandaged arm, protesting timidly that he was being treated like a child and begging for a weapon.*"

"*Did La Mona insult him?*"

"*No. No one insulted Arcángel. She gave him a crooked smile with her metallic teeth and yelled three military orders in his face, which, considering the source, was a sign of affection. Then she gave him the weapon he had asked for. But she wouldn't let him follow the men, who were going out looking for more serious activity.*"

Upstairs, on the patio, the night reeks of the sweat of angry men and the air vibrates, sharp-edged and silent, with a sacred hunger for revenge. Gómez Barragáns, Araújo Barragáns, Pajarito Pum Pum, El Tijeras, they were all ready to inflict the ritual punishment on this preordained day. They divide up into groups according to Nando's orders and wait—covered in foam like horses at the racetrack, in the jeeps with the motors running—for the signal. Tense and alert, like sprinters readying for the hundred-yard dash. On your mark. . . . Get set. . . . Stop! Stop? Go back. Orders from the boss. Turn off the motors. Put away the weapons. Back to the patio.

Nando has just found out that from seven to nine this evening there is an official government function with elected officials and international guests in one of the buildings downtown. For security reasons dozens of military policemen have spread out over the area, which is already crawling with undercover agents and bodyguards.

Nando Barragán's private militia has no problem with the local police, who never interfere with their activities, thanks to an old pact respected by both sides that ensures mutual benefit and pacific coexistence. But going downtown when it's full of military personnel and patrolled by outsiders is a risk not worth taking. They'll have to wait until after nine o'clock.

"It doesn't matter," says Nando. "There's no hurry. The Monsalves are paralyzed too."

The men light up cigarettes and fall back into the melancholy lethargy of demobilized armies. At Nando's order cups of *panela*, a brown sugary drink, and chunks of fresh cheese are passed out. Some men spread out on the ground and sleep, others talk in the darkness.

At nine the vengeance seekers ready once again for battle and fill the patio with the heavy sounds of footsteps and clanking steel. The men throw water on their faces, take up their weapons, cross themselves—forehead, chest, left shoulder, right shoulder—and return to the jeeps to wait for the boss.

Nando waits a couple minutes while he commends himself to the protection of his talisman. With devotion he holds it in his hand. "Santa Cruz de Caravaca, I receive your power." And at that precise moment the telephone rings.

Severina answers it.

"It's for you, Nando," she calls out.

"Not now, Mother. Can't you see that we're set to go?"

"Wait. He says he's Mani Monsalve."

Nando Barragán tenses, like a petrified giant, when he hears the name, and the cross digs painfully into his clenched hand.

"Did the two of them ever talk personally?"

"Only once in their adult lives and it was that night."

"And how did they know about it in the barrio?"

"That's how things were. The Barragáns know everything that happened in the city, but the city also knew everything that happened in their house. Word of the telephone call seemed strange. Mortal enemies all their lives, Nando and Mani, oil and water, as they say, cat and dog, never having anything to do with each other, except over bullets, and suddenly this call. Nando thought it was a trick, or a joke, or some sort of deception, but he took the call anyway."

Nando doesn't know what Mani's voice sounds like, but as soon as he hears it, he knows it's his own flesh and blood.

"How could he recognize that voice if he had never heard it?"

"He recognized it without knowing how, by instinct or smell."

He recognizes the voice from the first "Hello?" with the same certainty that a wolf knows the howl of another wolf. A subtle ache in his wounded knee confirms that he is speaking with the man who inflicted the injury. "It's him," Nando says to Severina as he covers the mouthpiece with his bloody palm.

Mani Monsalve says five words and hangs up.

"What were those five words?"

"They say it was these five words: 'Watch out for Narciso tonight.' "

Nando Barragán sinks further into the depths of perplexity. What has just happened has no antecedent in the long history of their bloody war.

"They say he was a different man after the phone call from his cousin Mani Monsalve. His whole life fighting according to the rules, and suddenly, for the first time, his enemy appears to warn him where they're going to hit him, to tell him the secret of the next play. . . ."

Nando searches for the dimmest shimmer of light in the darkness of his understanding and finds only doubts and more questions. If they are going to kill Narciso, why would Mani warn us? Or are they going to do something else, and the call was meant to confuse us? Why would Mani Monsalve call personally? Just to play a trick? Nando looks at Severina, who is still standing beside him. He doesn't tell her what Mani has just said, but asks her, "Should I believe him or not?"

"Believe him."

"Then we've got to find Narciso."

Narciso could be at any bar or restaurant in the city at this exact moment, unsuspecting and enchanting, already in range of an enemy weapon. How can we get to him before the assassin's bullet does? Severina has the answer. "San Antonio. I'm going to stand San Antonio on his head."

"It's an old custom in the barrio. Whenever someone is looking for something, from work or a lover to a lost key, he puts an image of San Antonio upside down, and rights the saint only when he's found what he was looking for."

"Did it work that time?"

"Yes, San Antonio performed the miracle. Within a half hour Narciso appeared at the house of his own free will, without anyone having found him or called him, all perfumed and dressed up because he was going to a party at the house of his girlfriend, the model."

Narciso Barragán, the one they call El Lírico, comes in through the front door wearing a white smoking jacket with a gardenia in his buttonhole, radiant and smiling. He's just come from a Turkish bath and a Japanese massage, innocent and ignorant of any war. His lavender Lincoln is full of champagne and flowers to help celebrate the birthday of a beautiful girl he wants to fall in love with him.

"Happy New Year!" he shouts, though it's August, to his brother's armed soldiers, and he dances a smooth *cumbia* as he passes them.

"Didn't he know it was a zeta?"

"Yes, he knew, but he never paid any attention to zetas."

He goes up to Severina, crouches down to give her a noisy kiss on her forehead, and asks her in a soft, sweet voice to fix him a plate of rice pudding. He can finish only two more steps of his *cumbia* before Nando Barragán's enormous bulk falls on him and immobilizes him.

Narciso struggles to escape, shouting and swearing, throwing golden sparks from his beautiful eyes, losing his loafers. His smoking jacket is wrinkled from his useless resistance, all the petals on the gardenia blossom fall off and the Gardel hairdo is totally destroyed. But Nando holds him and drags him to the cellars without any explanation and delivers him to La Mona with a single order:

"Don't let him out of here until tomorrow."

La Mona pushes his face against the wall, knees him in the kidneys, presses her San Cristobal rifle tight against his neck, and yells in his ear in her worst ogre tone. "You heard him. You're not going anywhere until tomorrow!"

"Mani's telephone call caused Nando Barragán to change his strategy. They were no longer going to hunt down their enemies in the downtown hotels. Now the primary objective was to forge all their strength into defending the house, or rather Narciso, who was now within the house. When the Monsalves came for him they would have to break into the fortress and seize it. If they could. It was going to be a tremendous battle, the most spectacular ever, and we, the youth of the barrio, also wanted to take part. So we joined the cause and helped build trenches along the surrounding streets with paving stones, boxes, rocks, old pieces of furniture, and bags of sand."

Nando Barragán is preparing the most impressive defense that has ever been known in the country since the time of the pirates. He serves as chief commandant of the united forces of La Esquina de la

Candela and is everywhere at once, like the Holy Spirit, organizing barricades, placing snipers, forming committees, suicide commands, front lines, and rear guards. No detail escapes the grand old warlord.

"EVERY TIME *a zeta fell there was a commotion in La Esquina de la Candela. The Barragáns knew how to protect and defend themselves. Their women and children took refuge in the cellars, under La Mona's command, and the men went out to face the Monsalves. But in the rest of the barrio there was chaos. We had nowhere to go and no one to run to, so we spent the night praying, fearing the worst.*

"Our longest night was when word spread that the Monsalves were coming into the barrio for Narciso Barragán. The children ran from their parents to join the battle, while the old folks locked themselves in their kitchens to wait. Some of the really devout Catholics wandered about like prophets of the apocalypse, saying that if we didn't give up Narciso, the Monsalves would go from house to house like exterminating angels, decapitating our firstborn. We believed them and agreed. But how were we going to give up Narciso if we didn't have him? The most fervent believers said we should attack the Barragáns' house, capture Narciso, and give his head to the Monsalves to calm them. But at the moment of truth no one dared lift a finger against the Barragáns. If we were afraid of the Monsalves, the enemy, we were terrified of our friends, the Barragáns. El Bacán was the only person in the barrio who remained calm. He looked around without seeing anything, closed his clairvoyant eyes, and continued playing his never-ending game of dominoes. His friends, the combo, passed the night with him without batting an eye.

"Around midnight word spread that the Monsalves had arrived, more than sixty men in twelve jeeps. We hid behind our doors armed

with rocks, sticks, and pots of boiling oil, and waited for the worst to happen. We waited for a long time, but they never came."

"FOR THE PEOPLE *of the desert, the* zeta—*the day established for avenging a death—was the culminating point in a chain of blood, like a knockout in boxing, a home run in baseball, a flamboyant flip of the cape in a bullfight. Without the zetas the game had no meaning. A zeta lasts one night, not one minute more or less, according to a strict tradition that the Barragáns and Monsalves had respected for over twenty years. They had lived through two decades of sacrosanct observance of those anniversaries that regulated their lives in cycles of death and vengeance, as natural as the summer rains, Lent, Passover, Holy Week, and Christmas. That night, however, the hours passed without incident. Ever since the call from Mani around nine o'clock the Barragáns had remained in La Esquina de la Candela to watch out for Narciso. But twelve o'clock came and went and nothing happened. Nothing happened at one, or two, or four o'clock."*

At five o'clock in the morning Nando abandons his position and goes to Severina's kitchen to rest awhile.

"Nothing?" she asks.

"Nothing," he answers, perplexed.

He has given orders to be told if anything happens. At six the fresh light of a new day awakens the chickens on their roosts, the songbirds, the dogs, the tamed monkey—still no sign of the Monsalves.

Severina has never seen her son so nervous. The potato broth with parsley she prepared to calm him didn't help at all, nor did her patient massaging of his hairy neck. Nando has taken off his Ray-Bans, and his tiny myopic eyes, clouded with uncertainty, dance out of control. He's not worried that the enemy will attack, but rather that they haven't. He can't stand anyone disrupting his plans. The mere idea that a *zeta* may pass in peace throws him out of equilibrium and his anxiety mounts by the minute, like a fever.

Now it's six-thirty and the chickens are eating corn, the servant girls are washing the laundry, everyone is doing what he or she has to do, except the Monsalves, who still have not appeared.

"What if they don't attack?" Nando asks his mother dully. "What if this time there is no death?"

"And what if there is no death next time?" responds Severina.

It's almost seven, the final hour of the *zeta*, and Nando is almost overcome with malaise and rapid heartbeat. The Barragáns surround him, alarmed.

"He's gonna get sick," predicts someone.

"He's just tired," says someone else.

"It's stress."

"No," says Severina. "It's suspicion."

"Suspicion?"

"Suspicion that life could be different."

MANI MONSALVE has had a tiny Sanyo radio, small but powerful, glued to his ear all night, the volume so low it's barely audible. Alina, lying beside him, asks why he doesn't turn it off, and he answers that he wants to listen to music. But the truth is he's listening to the news bulletins.

They spend the night half asleep, half awake, drugged by fitful sleep and the humming of the radio, hugging and lost in the perfect universe of their king-size bed, soft and smooth, pale violet and pink, limitless satin and pillows.

"By seven o'clock in the morning there had been no mention of the news that Mani had been dreading, Narciso's assassination. That meant that the zeta *was over and Narciso had survived."*

Yela, the old maid, brings them breakfast in bed and Mani, who usually only drinks black coffee, asks for eggs, toast, ham, milk, and fruit, and surprises Yela and Alina by eating with an appetite they have never seen in him before. Then he tells Yela not to bother them for any reason, because they are going to sleep for the rest of the morning.

Finally he turns off the Sanyo, embraces Alina Jericó as a child holds his mother, and falls heavily into the deepest region of tranquil dreams, a place he hasn't visited in a long time. When he arrives he removes his clothing and bathes in a cold, clear waterfall running noiselessly among the rocks until it reaches the sea.

"It was the waterfall at La Virgen del Viento."

THE BARRAGÁNS' house becomes peaceful once again with the warm smell of freshly brewed coffee. The men are resting on the patio with the startled expression of people waiting for the end of the world who have just been told that it's been put off for another day. The domestic animals wander about innocently, unaware they had been so close to death. The sun falls generously on everyone, bathing them in grace and forgiveness.

Narciso Barragán climbs out of the cellar in a fury. He doesn't speak to anyone. He doesn't even answer Severina when she offers him an *arepa* with an egg and chunks of papaya.

"I told you they weren't going to come. Assholes, wasting my time with this shit," he murmurs indignantly while he brushes off his white jacket, ruined during the longest, most boring night of his life, ten hours besieged by foul tempers, claustrophobia, and a fog of fetid gases.

He walks by Nando and doesn't deign even to look at him. He only exhales angrily. He's not dancing *cumbias* now, or reciting poetry. He's kicking the dogs and growling at children. No longer radiating whiteness and elegance, he's dirty and worn out like Pajarito Pum Pum and Simón Balas.

He grabs the telephone and calls his girlfriend, the model, trying to compose his voice.

"I couldn't make it last night, darling. . . . It wasn't my fault, honey. . . . Yes, I know it was your birthday. . . . I promise that I . . . Let me explain. . . . That's right, but I . . . Wait a minute, I'll be right there."

He hangs up the phone, rushes to the bathroom, throws cold water on his face and rinses out his mouth, changes his shirt without even noticing which one he puts on, and dashes out of the house like a breath exhaled, running a comb through his hair.

"It must have been the only time Narciso Barragán left his house without looking at himself in the mirror for a long time."

"It was. He was in such a hurry and was so angry that he didn't even say good-bye to his own image."

Narciso starts out in his fine Lincoln, stamping his foot on the accelerator and making it fly like an airplane. He speeds through La Esquina de la Candela like a violet bullet, running over the sandbags that the neighbors haven't finished removing, his car devouring the road with no regard for traffic signals or stop signs.

The sun's rays heat up the Lincoln, cooking Narciso inside until he becomes nauseated by the concentrated smell of his own cologne. He opens all four windows and welcomes the wind that gusts in and disperses the fatigue and foul taste of a sleepless night.

Finally he arrives at a residential neighborhood on the outskirts of town. There is very little traffic. The streets are shaded by *gualanday* trees and the fences are covered with orange and fuchsia bougainvilleas, but Narciso doesn't see any of this. He is not thinking of anything but the words he will use to save himself and vanquish the resistance of the girl he stood up last night.

If he tells her the truth she won't believe it. If he lies she won't forgive him. How can he explain to this beautiful, cultured woman that he left her waiting because he couldn't get away from his beast of a sister, who stood over him with a rifle?

As Narciso drives past the large, identical houses with well-tended yards and expensive automobiles parked in the driveways, he decides it would be better to tell her he was in a business meeting that continued until early morning. Or that his mother suddenly became ill: an asthma attack, a serious fall, a false alarm.

He goes by a park with swings where children are playing and nannies are chatting. What if he doesn't even try to explain anything and tells her to leave if she doesn't like it? There are plenty of others. No, he could never do that. He doesn't want to lose her. There are plenty more, but his pride won't let him lose even one, especially this one.

Now he passes a shopping center with a supermarket, a drugstore, clothing stores, post office, flower shop. Maybe if he stops and buys her roses. No, the backseat is full of wilted flowers, the ones he was going to give her last night.

Bakery, laundry, jewelry store. He could buy her an emerald. But it's too early; it's not open yet. He continues past the shopping center, turns right, then left, another left, and arrives at her street.

In the middle of the crumbling and filthy city, this neighborhood is a rarity, no piles of trash on the sidewalk, no potholes in the streets. A couple of workers from the public-works department, in new yellow uniforms, are repairing the streetlights, and their gray truck is blocking the end of the street.

A quiet, tranquil neighborhood. A couple of kids are playing soccer in the road. Narciso blows the horn so they'll get out of the way.

He sees her, at the third house on the right, standing on the porch, with large sunglasses, barefoot, wearing a loose T-shirt and shorts that show off her long legs. She's making signals with her hand. Is she waving hello? Maybe she's not mad. But the soccer players aren't moving out of the way and Narciso becomes impatient. He hits the horn again and sticks his head out the window to yell at them to get out of the way. She looks radiant, beautiful — maybe she's already forgiven him. Now he's sorry he didn't stop to buy her a gift. Maybe he should give her the bottles of champagne. At this hour of the morning? Absurd. He'll give her a kiss and nothing more.

But the kids playing soccer still won't get out of the way. One of them, tall, blond, ugly, too grown-up to be playing with adolescents, approaches the car.

Narciso doesn't pay attention to the man; he's only got eyes for her, waiting at her door for him, and he's pleased to see her welcoming him with a luminous smile, without reproach.

The blond soccer player comes even closer, right up to the car door, as if he wanted to ask Narciso something. Suddenly Narciso perceives something horrible in the man's expression. In the ugly face he detects the intent to kill. Then, finally, in the last fraction of an instant El Lírico's glorious eyes open to the truth and watch impotently as the ugly man removes the pin from a hand grenade with his mouth and tosses it through the open window into the interior of the violet Lincoln — the sacrificial color, the color of the altar on Good Friday, the day of passion and crucifixion.

NARCISO, OR what's left of his destroyed body, lies naked in the darkness of the family chapel.

The dead are dressed by those who love them most. Nando Barragán takes a shirt off its hanger, white organza, freshly starched, clean-smelling. He leans over his beloved brother and with some difficulty covers the remains of the body, clumsily, like a slow child arranging his broken, destroyed doll.

He covers Narciso's face with a silk handkerchief and places him facedown in the coffin, on top of several layers of lace.

"That handkerchief held the imprint of Narciso's beautiful face, features intact as they were before the grenade attack. Now, still imbued with powder and perfume, it remains in the cathedral, where people who suffer facial malformations and others who have undergone plastic surgery go to pray. The priest takes the handkerchief from an urn and places it on the faces of the devout, who wake up the next morning cured of their deformity and free of scars."

Church bells all over the city peal deafeningly, darkening the skies like a flock of crows. Nando Barragán is carrying the coffin on his back; he takes it into the street feetfirst and presents it to the women, who follow it on foot to the cemetery in a stagnant, black procession, like a river of dead water.

Nando returns alone to his house, crazy from the ringing bells. He closes himself up in his office, chewing a piece of wood with his huge carnivorous teeth and giving free rein to his anger and pain. Each pealing of bells causes him to pound his forehead against the wall, cracking the cement with his powerful cranium. He tears his clothing into shreds and makes objects in the room fly without touching them, with just the magnetism of his anguish.

"He tried to stanch the pain in his soul with physical suffering, because he had learned to bear the latter, but not the former."

"His immense despair was understandable. They had killed Narciso, his adored brother, outside the rules, after the zeta was over. And with a grenade. Never before in their war had anyone been assassinated in such a cruel and irregular manner. Explosives had never been used before."

"That didn't matter to Fernely. He killed any way he chose. But Nando didn't know that. He didn't even know Fernely existed."

Severina returns from the cemetery and listens from the other side of the locked door to her son's self-inflicted punishment, but out of respect she doesn't interrupt his mourning. She brings a stool to the door and sits outside to be near him, and to wait.

"The bells are making him crazy," she says. "They'll stop soon."

The bells finally stop ringing and their throbbing echoes fade. Now Severina can hear him breathe. An agonizing inhalation, cut by the sobs of a destroyed man, a wounded beast, its fangs broken and its soul crushed.

For three days and nights Nando remains locked in fasting and penitence. On the fourth day he opens the door and comes back to life, a survivor, but emaciated, exhausted, and covered with bruises. He drinks a bottle of water, puts his battered head in the pool, falls into a hammock, and orders his men: "Find out who killed Narciso."

He consults Severina about a doubt that is burning inside him and that only she can help him resolve, because she is the only one who can decipher the enigmas of their blood.

"Mother, why did Mani deceive me?"

"It wasn't him."

"HAVE YOU *ever seen how heat can make things look blurry, as if a thin veil had been placed in front of them? Heat waves make the images wavy, as gasoline vapors do. And the overabundance of light fades the colors. That's how we saw the Barragáns appear in the cemetery on the broiling day when Narciso died, like vapor. Like a procession of stains on a mourned photograph.*

"The press was at the cemetery. Reporters and photographers from the newspapers, because news of Narciso Barragán's assassination had spread wide. But they say none of the photographs turned out clear. They captured only a blinding light that was not of this world."

The group of neighbors and curious onlookers has been waiting for a while for the Barragáns to appear. While they wait, they protect their ears from the ringing bells by stuffing them with wads of cotton and protect their bodies from the ravaging sun by huddling under the extended wings of a plaster angel, which offer the only bit of shade on the sacred ground.

The Barragán family pavilion occupies the entire northeast section of the cemetery. There are many white marble headstones with engraved names, slowly disintegrating into lime. Some have epitaphs: "Hectór Barragán, The Righteous," "Diomedes G. Barragán, His hand repaid the debt," "Wilmar H. Barragán, Avenger of his race by the will of God." Those that were Barragán on their mother's side had their paternal surname reduced to a capitalized initial and a period, so that the clan remains unified and labeled in the next life too. Barragáns and more Barragáns, all dead from unnatural deaths, awaiting the final judgment in graves heated like ovens under the huge white star.

"At those temperatures, how did the dead ever manage to find eternal rest?"

"They didn't. They turn in their graves pursued by guilt, cooking in their own gases and swelling until they explode."

Before the neighbors actually see the Barragáns they hear them approaching and become terrified. The women's cries are sharper than the highest bells and sound as if they come from beyond the grave. But they are human voices, coming closer, and now the neighbors can make out what they are saying.

"Poor Narciso, what a shame, your beauty destroyed!"

"Your black eyes, the earth will swallow them!"

"Oh, Narciso Barragán, your gorgeous eyes won't see anything down there, they won't find anything beautiful to look at!"

"They killed Narciso, El Lírico! The enemies did it! They took no mercy on his body. They even destroyed his soul!"

Only Severina shouts in a low hoarse voice, drowning in anger. She murmurs a pagan litany that does not include pardon or pity or eternal rest.

"My son's blood was spilled. Now it will be avenged."

"Did they put an epitaph on Narciso's headstone?"

"Yes. A strange epitaph, different from the others; but like them, it was dictated by Nando. It read then, and should still, if time and the heat haven't erased it, 'Narciso Barragán, He lies here assassinated, though he killed no one.'"

MÉNDEZ, THE lawyer, rides with his eyes closed in a rented car through the city streets. Tin Puyúa, Mani Monsalve's right-hand man, is driving and orders the lawyer to keep his eyes closed so that he doesn't know where he's being taken.

"Put him in the back and tell him to lie down on the seat, close his eyes, and try to sleep," Mani has told Tin.

"Sir, Mani doesn't want you to know where I am taking you and it's to your advantage not to know, so, please, just follow the instructions," Tin says to Méndez.

The lawyer tries to sleep during the ride, but he can't. He wishes he could, because it's not easy to keep his eyelids involuntarily closed for such a long time. They start to tremble and threaten to open. Then he begins to get nauseous. Since the car's darkened windows are closed, he's hot and has trouble breathing, but he prefers to leave it that way. It would be worse to lower the windows and run the risk of Nando Barragán's men seeing him.

The healthy pink glow in his cheeks and his usual fresh appearance are gone, and his pulse is accelerated. Méndez didn't get into the car of his own free will. He was pressured by Tin Puyúa, who caught him as he was leaving his office downtown and told him that Mani Monsalve wanted to see him and that he, Tin, had been sent to get him. Tin spoke to Méndez in a polite but firm manner. At first the lawyer tried to decline, arguing that he didn't have time at that moment to travel to the port to see Mani.

"Mani's not in the port," answered Tin. "He's here in the city. He made the trip just to see you, sir, and he's returning as soon as the meeting is over."

The lawyer got into the car without asking anything more, because he knows the Monsalves well and knows when not to say no. Besides that, he felt intuitively that the matter was urgent, or Mani would not have come into the city two weeks after Narciso Barragán's assassination, possibly exposing himself to Nando's wrath.

So he's lying in the backseat and his nausea grows steadily with each turn Tin makes to ensure no one is following. The boy stops suddenly, honks the horn brusquely, and for a brief moment the lawyer has the impression that the car is going against the traffic, dodging oncoming vehicles. Before getting in the car, Méndez had noticed, by a sticker on the windshield, that the car was rented. That calms him a little, since it diminishes the possibility of being caught by the Barragáns, who are hunting the Monsalves with the intensity of starving dogs.

After a half hour of winding around the busy streets, Tin stops the car and tells the lawyer to get out. "But don't open your eyes until I tell you to," he says.

Méndez walks blindly, with his head bent, holding Tin Puyúa's arm. They go down a corridor that smells clean and new. They rise several floors in a fast, quiet elevator. He feels hands checking him head to toe for weapons. Then he hears a door open and he is led into a carpeted room. He can feel the artificial cold of the air-conditioning. Finally, the lawyer is seated in a comfortable chair and told to open his eyes. He does so, but after having them closed for so long, now he can see only points of light against a black background.

Little by little he regains his vision until he can see Mani Monsalve seated across from him in a chair identical to the one he is occupying. Mani has recently bathed. His hair is still dripping and he's wearing a terry-cloth robe. Through the partly open robe Méndez sees the handle of the revolver Mani has in a holster under his arm. He has a frosty Kola Román in his hand and he asks if Méndez wants one. His voice is different, more opaque. The few words he speaks are hammered out. The lawyer accepts the soft drink and looks around while Mani gets it. We are in a suite in a first-class hotel and they have left us alone, he thinks, trying to orient himself.

On other occasions the conversation between Méndez and Mani has been fluid, brotherly, without tension or prefaces. Not today. It's a while before Mani speaks again. Méndez remains quiet. He prefers to wait. The seconds drop one by one, fat and slow, clogged in the watery clock.

Buried in his seat, Mani intentionally stretches the silence until it becomes unbearable, without giving any indication of wanting to break the ice, as if testing the lawyer. Méndez notices and fights to maintain his calm. He breathes deeply and sips his drink. Mani also drinks his soda. Finally Méndez decides to speak.

"Tell me what this is about," he says. "You asked me to come here."

"It's about Alina Jericó," responds Mani, and the lawyer's heart misses a beat, because his suspicions have been confirmed. The situation is delicate, he thinks to himself. One wrong word and he's a dead man.

"Alina Jericó is fine," he manages to say, his voice sounding almost normal.

"Maybe she is fine, but she's not with me. She left our house the day of Narciso Barragán's death and she took my unborn child. She rented an apartment and moved out. Do you know, sir, who helped her rent that apartment?"

"Yes, I know, and you yourself know, because you have ordered your men to follow her day and night. I helped her get it. And the furniture, the curtains, the dishes. I did it because she asked me to.

Because she told me that she wanted to get away from you, to protect her child."

"A week ago Alina gave a dinner in that apartment. Do you know, sir, who was invited?"

"Her sisters and their husbands and me. She served roasted chicken, mashed potatoes, salad, and beer. Have I told you anything you didn't already know?"

"Three days ago, sir, you traveled in an airplane from the port to the capital. You were wearing a wool suit."

"Yes. And earlier in the day I had worn cotton clothing. I changed in Alina's apartment. I went to help her sign the rental agreement and then didn't have time to go back to my hotel before the flight. Mani, I'm not involved with your wife. Don't imagine things. She didn't leave you for me. If that were the case, it would be easy for you to get me out of the way. The issue is more serious than that, and you know it. Much more serious."

Silence invades the room again, frozen like the frost on the red soda bottles.

Dealing with the Barragáns' and Monsalves' temperaments has never been easy for Méndez, especially when they are irritated. And jealous, as Mani is now.

I may never see daylight again, thinks Méndez, and he tries to look out the window, but he can't; the curtains are drawn. Instead he looks at a large painting with blues and pale greens, the same colors as the carpet and the fabric on the furniture. In the painting he sees a sailboat that is too stable on the waves and thinks it is poorly painted. He looks at Mani Monsalve's eyes, which are fixed on a spot on the carpet, as if he were waiting to watch the wool grow. He sees the drops of water still running down Mani's chest and dripping onto the wooden pistol handle. Maybe he'll pull out the gun and get it all over with, Méndez thinks. It wouldn't surprise him. The surprising thing is that it hasn't happened yet.

Méndez is from the same region as the Barragáns and the Monsalves, although his ancestors were white and theirs were Indians. His friendship with the two families predates the war between them. After they began dealing in funny business and started getting involved with the law, Méndez felt obligated to help them, each family on its own, because of those old ties. Every day their profits grew and so did their legal cases, and the lawyer became more and more involved in their defense. There were many times when he wanted to give up and couldn't, because without realizing it he had gotten on a train without a return ticket. He was married, without divorce options, as much to the Barragáns as to the Monsalves, and he had invested his youth and the better part of his maturity in the delicate exercise of keeping himself alive in the midst of a perfect equilibrium and a meticulous impartiality between the two clans.

He knows his physical integrity is protected, to a certain degree, by the ancestral laws of the two families, which obligate them to respect the lives of the lawyers of the other side, as well as their women, their elderly, and their children. The lawyer of your enemy—the symbol of protection not against you but against the rest of the world—is untouchable according to the internal rules of war. The bad thing is that there is not a rule about a family wiping out its own lawyers. For betrayal, for example. And that is what is about to happen. For a man from the desert the worst betrayal is for someone to touch his woman.

When Alina Jericó asked for help to separate from Mani Monsalve, Méndez foresaw with great clarity today's events—a conversation exactly like this one and this same feeling of resignation before death, which ultimately is nothing more than a sudden realization that he is tired of living. It's as if he had seen it on the television news.

The idea of another man coming near his wife without taking her to bed is not one that would naturally occur to a man like Mani. And besides, he's angry, destroyed and humiliated by the recent separation. The lawyer had all that clear from the very beginning. But it wasn't in his character to refuse to help Alina and her future child escape the curse of an incomprehensible war. He had no other alternative.

And now there is nothing else to do. It's been written, he thinks as he settles into his chair, straightens his tie, and recaptures a sense of stability. He is at peace with his conscience. He has not touched a hair on Alina Jericó's head. He has not made a single insinuation.

Although, why should he lie to himself at the moment of truth? It hasn't been from lack of desire; rather she hasn't given him a chance. And also out of respect for her pregnancy. But mostly out of fear of Mani Monsalve. It's true, his relationship with Alina has not gone beyond friendship based on professional courtesy. But mostly because she planned it that way. The lawyer smiles. I'm going to pay for a few naughty thoughts with my life, he muses. The idea strikes him as funny and he turns it over in his mind. Capital punishment for desiring another man's wife. It sounds like a tabloid headline.

Mani, who has also been submerged in a tortured and conflicting meditation, moves uncomfortably in his chair. In the depths of his soul he knows what the lawyer has said is true, that his problem is not about another man. He wishes it were. It would be easy to wipe out the bastard. But no, it's deeper than that, more difficult. On the one hand it's a relief not to have to kill a lifelong friend; on the other, he's having a hard time convincing himself that the solution to his pain is not as simple as shooting a man in the head. He debates the issue, mentally tossing a coin in his mind, throwing it into the air to look first at tails, then heads, tails again, heads again.

A long while passes, and when the only thing Méndez expects to hear is the sound of a bullet going through his head, he hears a change in Mani's voice.

"I believe you, Méndez. I believe what you have told me." His tone is not so cold now, but defenseless and childlike, despite his struggle to make his words come out right. "I congratulate you. You just saved a life. Yours. You can go when you want—Tin will drop you off where he picked you up."

Méndez has no desire to respond, nor the strength to stand up. He remains seated, silent, lights a cigarette even though he knows Mani hates smoke, and takes his time finishing the Kola Román, as if he had nothing better to do that afternoon. Mani stands, opens the curtains, and looks out on the avenue below, full of vendors with their merchandise spread out on the sidewalk, under the miserly shade of the almond trees. From his seat Méndez can see the street and he is surprised to note that despite Tin Puyúa's many turns to confuse any followers, they are only a few blocks from his office.

"Alina doesn't want to talk to me, not even on the telephone," says Mani, still looking out the window, with his back to his lawyer. "I've sent her dozens of roses and they were all refused."

Méndez notices something strange in Mani's voice. Could he be crying? he asks himself. Yes. His voice is breaking from the tears. A minute ago he was going to execute me and now he's crying on my shoulder, thinks Méndez, smiling to himself.

"Give her some time, Mani," says the lawyer. "Look for a real solution to the problem. You're not going to get anywhere with roses and desperate actions."

"So what is the solution?"

"There are three parts and we've already discussed them. One, end the fighting with the Barragáns; two, buy some respectability; and three, launder your money through real estate and legitimate businesses."

"I've been trying to do that for years, but it's not easy."

"There are some special circumstances now. The National Bank is going to open a special window that will accept dollars without any questions about origins, names, ID numbers, nothing. The only condition is that you can exchange only a thousand dollars per person. So you send a hundred people with a thousand dollars and in one day you can clear a hundred thousand dollars."

"Will you help me, Méndez? I mean, with the three steps?" Mani's voice is full of gratitude and remorse, almost servile before this man he was about to assassinate and now sees as the only way to reach his wife.

"Of course."

Méndez stands up, straightens his jacket, runs his hand over his hair, caressing his miraculously unscathed head, and prepares to leave.

"Wait, Méndez," Mani says. "I'm indebted to you."

"Forget it."

"No. I want to repay you somehow," insists Mani. "Tell me who your enemies are."

Méndez understands what Mani means. It's an old way of showing gratitude among the people of the desert, something like "Your enemies are my enemies."

"It's not worth your killing them," Méndez answers with a quick grin, and says good-bye with genuine affection for Mani.

"WAS MANI Monsalve tormented with the thought that he had betrayed Nando Barragán with the telephone call?"

"A little, but not as much as Nando. They were different. Nando was a man of principles and vague dreams. Mani was pragmatic and had only one dream, Alina Jericó. Nando was a child of the desert. Mani had left the desert when he was too young, before the sand from the dunes had gotten into his nose and worked its way into his brain."

NANDO BARRAGÁN spends hours locked in his office doing something he has never done before. He devotes himself to analysis, reading and thinking, to try to decipher the undecipherable. He doesn't bathe and smells like a caged tiger. He doesn't waste time with women, doesn't drink or eat. He survives on black coffee and Pielroja cigarettes. He pays no attention to financial matters. The business secrets went to the grave with Narciso, and Nando shows no interest in retrieving them, because when he needs money he asks the cross of Caravaca. And he has completely forgotten his wife, Ana Santana.

"You can only forget what you once remembered, and Ana hadn't even gotten that far yet."

In Nando's eyes Ana is just a silhouette sitting at the sewing machine all day and then at night a more or less desirable feminine presence in a round bed in which he never sleeps, because he prefers a hammock and because he distrusts beds, especially that one — it's more carnival attraction than bed.

When he was a child he marveled at the City of Steel, which came through town every year, rustier and creakier, and left a trail of nuts and bolts in towns across the desert. But he never rode the roller coaster, the Ferris wheel, or the bumper cars, he only watched them. He climbs into the bed Narciso gave him as a wedding gift only occasionally, for barely a few minutes, just enough to mount his wife, in silence and without getting involved, more from a sense of responsibility than for pleasure.

And now not even that. He has ordered Arcángel to come out of his room and he keeps the boy by his side. With the same absolute resolve that he kept him locked up before, Nando suddenly decided to permit him conditional freedom in order to make him his constant companion.

"What obsession did Nando and Arcángel share that made them forget about the rest of the world?"

A name. The name Holman Fernely.

When his spies brought Nando the first bits of information relating to Narciso's assassination, there was one that stood out. The night before, the Hotel Nancy had a record of a telephone call from Mani Monsalve's house to the reception desk for Holman Fernely.

It was the first time that Nando had heard the name. They gave it to him written on a piece of paper and he read it aloud.

"Is it pronounced 'Olman' or 'Holeman'?" he asked.

The second time he heard it was in a bloodcurdling scream from the cellars that reverberated all over the house. Pajarito Pum Pum had extracted it from an associate of the Monsalves that he had captured alive, an old man called Mosca Muerta. They had surprised him in his underwear in some woman's house, grabbed him by the balls, locked him in the cellars, and tortured him until he sang.

"He revealed Fernely as the principal perpetrator, and said that he had done it against Mani's will."

"Then Mosca Muerta confirmed Severina's intuition?"

"Yes. They say that Nando Barragán himself went down to hear the confession with his own ears. And his huge pain was reduced by half. He still mourned Narciso's death, but he no longer felt betrayed by Mani. His anger remained intact, but was now focused on one person, Holman Fernely."

Who is Fernely? Nando and Arcángel dedicate themselves to investigating this man's life. They gather information from high officials in exchange for whiskey. They scan and rescan photographs and bits of information but can't figure out this strange character.

"For the first time in this war, a Barragán was killed by someone other than a Monsalve. By a Fernely. An unknown. Nando found it impossible to understand. He resisted believing it, as if the broken rules of the zeta and the explosion of the grenade weren't already stamped with the signature — first and last name — of a stranger. An outsider."

Fernely's judicial files mention desertion from the army, involvement with guerrilla factions, war adviser. Through his black glasses, Nando Barragán sees pictures of him — behind bars, saluting a swastika, singing hymns beneath the hammer and sickle; receiving medals, winning bicycle races. In some his hair is light colored, in others he's got dark hair, or hair curly or long. Sometimes he's fatter or thinner. His physical appearance changes like a chameleon's; only his ugliness remains constant. No matter what disguise he uses, it's still unpleasant to look at him.

Arcángel, absorbed as if he were playing solitaire, arranges the photos in piles on the table and looks over them with his smooth, peaceful gaze, which is better suited to contemplating sunsets.

"This man is blond, left-handed, speaks very little, has a broken nose, he's five feet eleven inches and has something wrong with his eyes," he says after a while in a low voice. Nando and the others ignore him, confusing his unaffected certainty with innocence.

Fernely is accused by intelligence sources of being an agent of the CIA or KGB, a syndicate leader, a strikebreaker. The files say he is an expert trained in explosives by the ultraright in Israel, and that he graduated from an artillery school for subversives in Havana. Old newspaper clippings implicate him in assaults on military headquarters, bank robberies, kidnappings of millionaires. In his private correspondence he signs as Holman, Alirio, Jimmy, Handsome, or Skinny.

Who is this man, Holman Fernely? Nando Barragán is beginning to have a clear picture. "Holman Fernely is a sorry son of a bitch," he announces.

The jumble of contradictory information makes Nando's head spin like a carousel. Nando has never traveled outside his own country, is afraid to get on an airplane, and doesn't even speak his own language correctly. He doesn't care about weird crosses, or hammers and sickles. He's a natural leader, a common criminal, the head of a cannibal tribe. In order to begin hunting for his brother's assassin he needs to know the important details about his life. What does he like to eat? Who does he sleep with? Who's he afraid of? But there's no one to tell him, because no one knows.

Close to dawn, when the men have gone to rest and Arcángel has fallen asleep in a chair, Nando hears the first birdcalls on the patio and Severina's light footsteps as she goes from cage to cage with seeds and pieces of banana and orange. Nando scratches his enormous head and recalls with fondness the times when the war against the Monsalves was limited to scandalous shooting matches between boys, with a lot of firing and not much injury. He misses those crazy bohemian days, when the fighting was narrated in couplets. Narciso, El Lírico, used to compose songs about the Monsalves, and they, having no real inspiration of their own, hired musicians to answer the insults with worse ones.

"The whole city knew about their musical duels. The songs were played at parties and serenades. A record company even released an LP of the best ones."

Nando thinks back to the first day of the war, when he killed his cousin Adriano Monsalve because of the widow of Marco Bracho. Then he returns to the present and tries to guess how much money Fernely charged to kill Narciso. He asks himself if it's the same sin to kill for love as for money.

"A lot of water must have passed under the bridge for the Barragáns and Monsalves to go from fighting over women and songs to the cold professionalism of someone like Holman Fernely."

"A lot of blood passed under the bridge, and what had to happen happened."

Nando and his men exhaust themselves discussing whether it would be easier to find Fernely in the city or in the mountains, confront him during the day or at night, with a knife or a gun, by ambush or one on one. They come up with strategies to destroy him and hatch plans to make him eat dirt. They go on and on about psychology and his habits and weak points. Until Nando gets bored.

"Enough," he says. "I'm going to kill him my way."

6

A MAN IS fishing in a lazy brown river. He is standing on the porch of his house, a wooden shack built on poles over the water, like a long-legged mosquito, cousin to the malarial insects buzzing around his head that he doesn't even bother to swat away. He moves as little as possible, only to pull back his cane pole and throw the nylon string and fishhook farther into the murky water. Little by little the cane bends with the pull of some aquatic plant and the vibration stirs the viscous air. It's almost noon and the fisherman still hasn't caught a single fish.

"The poor river has died," he says to himself. "Now it only drags shit along."

"What was the man's name?"

"Nobody knows. He was just a fisherman."

The man's wife pokes her head out the door of the shack. "Are there any fish to fry up for lunch?" she asks.

"No."

"All right, then I'll roast some plantains," she says.

The man takes up his pole and empty bucket and he gets into a little boat, which he rows to the mouth of an arroyo fed by a waterfall coming down from the mountain. At dawn he had tied a net and now he's checking to see if it's caught any fish. From a distance he can see that something is blocking the flow of the water, forcing it to jump over the net. He doesn't get excited, thinking it's probably just some branches that the waterfall has pulled into the stream.

As he gets closer to the net, he puts his hand in the water. No, it's not branches. It looks like leaves. He pulls out a fistful. No, not leaves either.

"*What was it?*"

It's money. He pulls out a fistful of money. He puts his hand in again and pulls out more.

"*What was all that money doing there?*"

He asks himself the same question, frightened and amazed at the same time. He doesn't know the answer. He's stunned. He doesn't dare move because he's afraid the treasure will disappear. His brain is paralyzed, but his pockets react. He stops wondering and decides to gather up the booty. He looks around to see if the owner is around. Nothing, no one. Only a couple of small lizards with childlike hands are watching him. The fisherman's heart is beating violently and his mouth is dry. Furtively looking over his shoulder, terrified that he'll be discovered, he pulls in the net and tries to gather up the trapped bills. Many escape and sink to the bottom of the stream, but the net is still full. He drops them into his bucket, soaked, compressed. When the bucket is filled, he dumps the rest on the bottom of his boat.

"Look what I've brought you," he says to his wife upon his return to the shack.

They look at the gray-and-green paper, brilliant and tranquil like dead sardines.

"This money is not from around here," he says.

"They are dollars," she says. "They are dollar bills."

"What can you buy with them?"

"A new radio. And a television set. Even a boat with a motor."

"What if they're not real? Besides, the owner must be looking . . . "

The woman grabs a bill and looks at it against the light, then she bites off a corner and rubs it with her index finger.

"They are more real than the seven sorrows of María Dolorosa," she declares. "And now they are ours."

She puts them in baskets and runs to dry them in the sun, hanging them from the wire fence with clothespins.

A MILE UPSTREAM from the waterfall where the fisherman found his treasure is one of the Monsalves' extensive haciendas. The overseer and the workers had received orders from Mani Monsalve himself to dig up all the dollars that had been buried on the hacienda. They uncovered holes, rolled stones away from caves and grottoes, and removed barrels of money, which they then loaded on a truck. Some of the bills were rotten, eaten by humidity, mold, and moths. One of the barrels got loose and rolled into the stream, where it broke open against the rocks and the bills poured out and were swept down the river, freed at last.

"That was the money the fisherman found later."

"The very same."

On the Monsalves' other haciendas the workers are doing the same, digging up fortunes on Mani's orders and loading them onto trucks. And, back in the port, in several houses and apartments, walls are torn down and dollars are rescued from sealed bathrooms and garages. Floorboards are lifted, ceilings are ripped open, and stuffed suitcases are pulled down. Hermetically sealed plastic bags full of bills are extracted from water tanks.

Meanwhile, the yellow stone building that houses the National Bank, in the center of the port, gives birth to a line of people five blocks long, like a theater queue. Hundreds of pairs of feet wait, lined up one behind the other, and they advance step by step, inch by inch, to get closer to the window. They are dressed in a wide assortment of shoes. Black patent leather high heels with open toes. Suede boots with rubber soles and laces past the ankles. Brand-new high-top Adidas sneakers with air-cushioned soles. Worn-out tennis shoes with holes in the canvas. Rubber espadrilles. Authentic Swiss Bally loafers. Bare feet, browned by walking on dirt roads and hardened by asphalt streets. Interesting specimens of exotic men's shoes, red and blue velvet ones with fake diamond-encrusted heels. The owners of the various shoes have appearances as dissimilar as the shoes. But they all share one characteristic; they each have in their pocket a wad of a thousand dollars that belongs to the Monsalves.

They are all connected to the family one way or another. There are secretaries from their offices, workers from their farms, gunfighters from their squad of bodyguards, cooks, gardeners, and an army of second cousins, great-uncles, brothers-in-law, mothers-in-law, godmothers and godfathers and just plain poor folks depending on those who have so much and always hanging around, eager to do what they can to earn a few bucks.

They have been recruited to collaborate in the monumental task of laundering the money. Their job consists of taking the thousand dollars assigned to each of them, standing in line, stepping up to the special window, and changing the dollars for pesos, keeping five percent for themselves and returning the rest. Then Mani's men deposit the pesos in fake checking accounts in local banks. The rules are explained and fully understood in two minutes. There is no need for questions. The recruits are ready to perform their duties to perfection.

Around the line, a fair of sorts begins to assemble, with three separate bands playing different kinds of music, and the air begins to fill with a cloud smelling of armpits and fried pork rinds. Strolling vendors offer peanuts, puff pastries, oatmeal in pots, slices of pineapple, and ice cones with colored syrups. Eager greengrocers set up tables with blenders to make guayaba, sapote, and guanábana juices. A dubious doctor promotes iguana eggs in spring water to improve lovemaking.

Mani's men, their weapons concealed, walk up and down beside the line, keeping an eye out for anyone who may decide to take off with the money.

"They say a few managed to get away with it."

"Yes. There was a young woman in the line who began to complain of an unbearable urge to urinate. Mani's thugs ordered her to hold it, but she made a big fuss, bent over double holding her kidneys, and insisted that she was going to burst. Finally they allowed her to relieve herself behind some trash barrels in an alley. But the sneaky girl didn't just want to pee, she started to poop, and the guard who was responsible for watching her had to look away, because it was so disagreeable and because it's bad luck to watch a stranger shit. The young woman took advantage of the moment. She stuffed the money in her bra and took off running with the last fart, like an inflatable doll stuck with a pin. When the gunman turned around to see what had happened, all he found was her fresh mound with a rolled-up dollar bill stuck on top like a flag. He chased the fugitive for several blocks, firing angrily to punish her for being so dirty and impudent, until he got tired and let her go. They say the guard turned gay after that and was haunted by the echoes of her laughter for the rest of his life. And they say that the young woman went to the black market and spent the thousand dollars on French lace underwear and Oil of Olay and got herself pregnant by her mechanic boyfriend."

"HE'S A SON of a bitch," says Nando Barragán about Holman Fernely.

His words do not go unnoticed by anyone within earshot, because no one has ever heard him talk like that about his enemies before.

"To a Barragán there was nothing in the world more sacred than his mother, and Nando's mother was the sister of the Monsalves' mother. And vice versa. So to insult the enemy's mother was to insult his own."

Everyone in La Esquina de la Candela hears what Nando said and they all think the same thing. "If he murders the sons of his own aunt, what would he do to a son of a bitch?"

Since he first heard about Fernely's existence, Nando Barragán has been incapable of thinking of anyone or anything else. The desire to kill the ugly man has a grip on him like a bull's fury at the red cape. Since he heard that name he has ignored his businesses. His pain over Narciso's death has become a lustful passion of vengeance, and his melancholy love for Milena has lost its potency. Even Nando's obsession with Mani has weakened.

Nando, in his black Ray-Bans, remains cloistered in the semi-darkness of his smoke-filled office during the mourning period following Narciso's death. It's now common to see him with Arcángel, his constant companion in his new, singular fixation, to plan the avenging of his brother's death. Nando hadn't known that the soulful and peaceful Arcángel held a fascination with war. But since they joined forces to find Fernely, he has discovered that the boy has the supernatural and apocalyptic predisposition of a biblical exterminator, and he wonders if he hadn't made a mistake in keeping him away from weapons for so long.

The sky darkens, but neither one turns on the bare lightbulb hanging idly from the ceiling at the end of a single wire. The two brothers are so absorbed that they haven't even touched the now-cold plates of beans that Severina brought them.

"Severina fed Nando, her firstborn, beans, and at the same time she fed his anger with constant references to Narciso's honor, with the subtle reminders she makes, as if unintentionally, each time she enters the room with a tray of food."

"It was often said that Severina was the real engine behind the war, with her forceful mother's love that gave no quarter to forgiveness. People also said that Nando was a war machine, but that the iron will that kept him going was in her, because there is no thirst for vengeance in the world like that of a mother for her murdered children."

Nando and Arcángel are joined together in a filial union that they have never enjoyed before. When they tire of dreaming up inventive forms of vengeance they exchange memories, like schoolchildren swapping stickers for their notebooks.

Arcángel talks about the capital, which Nando is not familiar with, a freezing city where the burros are woolly, the inhabitants are heavily clothed in their own homes, and even the flowers are hairy. With the tremulous voice of a tango singer Nando conjures up images of the desert, the land of his forefathers, where Arcángel was born but left at an early age. He talks about naked Indians kicking a rag ball in the sand, of sleepy little pueblos anchored to the earth and hospitable to any traveler from another land with stories to tell of his journey. Nando speaks of *contrabandistas*, men who traded in the black market, crossing the border at night loaded with merchandise and spending their days betting their profits on dog fights.

The eldest and the youngest let the memories fly, stretching the hours while Severina's beans get cold, unaware of a melancholy presence spying on them from the doorway.

"A third person was there? Who was it?"

"I can't say his name. It's bad luck and always will be."

"Raca Barragán, El Tinieblo! The third surviving brother . . ."

Nando and Arcángel are still talking. The only one of their nine brothers still alive, El Tinieblo lurks behind them, leaning against the doorway, but neither of them hears his irregular breathing or the pounding of his racing heart. They can't see the needle marks in his collapsed veins, or feel the cold sweat beneath the damp leather jacket that he always wears. They're unaware of his icy heart beating beneath the medallion of the Virgen del Carmen, sewn to the skin on his chest over his left nipple.

Older than Arcángel, younger than Narciso, Raca Barragán has spent twenty-four tortured years doing evil things to himself and to everyone else. He would be as tall as Nando if he weren't hunched over. He would be handsome like Narciso if the light in his eyes weren't extinguished. He would be sweet like Arcángel if his blood didn't flow with so much heroin and ice.

Severina knew that she had an ill-fated son from the minute of his birth, when, in the midst of extraordinary pain, she saw the opaque stain at the back of his open eyes. "This is a child to fear," she said. Nando understood the twisted nature of his brother when he saw the fervor with which Raca tortured a cat when he was two years old.

By the age of six he had still not learned to speak, and at twelve Nando adopted him as a mascot, teaching him the art of violence and involving him in all of his adventures.

"He trained Raca to succeed him."

Nando took his younger brother by the hand to the precipices of crime and war, and transmitted to the boy all his wisdom gained from years of fighting. But he never loved Raca. Nando never felt for Raca the fascination that Narciso inspired in him, nor the tender protectiveness he harbored for Arcángel. Although Raca became the best strategist and the most skilled gunman, the coldness with which he killed and viewed death awakened in Nando a thinly veiled disdain that manifested as harsh treatment and angry words.

"Nando Barragán, king of the criminals, disdained his equals and admired people who were peaceful, stylish, and reasonable. And the man whose name I can't mention was a barbarian, worse even than Nando."

Raca became a master killer because he was pulled by instinct, but also by a need to please his older brother, whose disdain was eating away at him. His devotion to Nando was like a dog's: the more he was beaten down, the more abject he became. And since he didn't understand the reason for his brother's scorn, he tried even harder to perfect himself as a criminal and bloodied himself even further in cruelty. To such an extent that, at age fifteen, with the lives of several Monsalves already weighing on his conscience, he had become a young prince of horror.

But at sixteen the worst happened. For the first and only time in his life Raca was caught by the police, something that never happened to the Barragáns, immune as they were to the arm of the law. He was detained during a roundup one night, like a common vandal. They didn't know who he was and he remained locked up for three days and nights in a makeshift cell with twelve other prisoners, twelve sewer rats, male prostitutes, murderers, hustlers, older and craftier than he was. They made him do whatever they wanted. They drugged him and kissed his body. Then they dressed him like a woman and raped him. When he was released Raca wouldn't speak to his brothers or look them in the eye. Nando Barragán found out what had happened and personally tracked down and killed each of the twelve men who had been in the cell. But his disgust with Raca grew to the point of nausea.

That's when Raca started getting tired of putting up with the shame and bitterness. He left the house and since then has wandered around on his own, preying on others to compensate for his own misery. He robs those who have nothing. He kills for no reason. He strikes the defenseless. He arranges orgies where minors of both sexes are corrupted.

"The neighbors in La Esquina de la Candela had to put up with his perverted activities. They were dark years for the barrio. Everything that Raca touched died, everyone that got close to him suffered. Since then no one has wanted to mention his name, and we all put special herbs and brooms behind our doors to keep his evil presence away.

Sleepless, Raca Barragán rides his motorcycle through hells and nightmares that his brain, fried by hallucinogenic drugs, can't fully take in. He never speaks to his family, except La Mona, who worships him. They don't care about him and he doesn't care about them. He sleeps during the day on spoiled beaches and at night he hangs around empty lots, garbage dumps, and seedy joints in the company of a band of nameless and faceless thieves who follow him like shadows wherever he goes. His only friends are a G3 rifle called Tres Gatos and a fist that responds to the name Friday. His lovers are Señora, an M60 machine gun, Black Beauty, a set of brass knuckles that crushes bones, and Ballerina, his switchblade.

"The boy became a black legend. He did every evil thing he could, and even if he didn't do it, he was blamed for it. Whatever the calamity, floods, sicknesses, and droughts, they were all his fault. Children were more afraid of him than the bogeyman and the devil. The adults prayed to God to be free of Raca."

Sitting side by side, Nando, yellow, and Arcángel, golden, conspire confidently until a slight creak in Raca's leather jacket makes them turn their heads. That black jacket, so absurd and hostile in the hot city, he never takes off, as if it's a second skin. They look at him and he looks at them, trying to get out the words that are trapped in his frozen mouth.

"Beat it, Raca," orders Nando coldly. "You're drugged up."

He tries to balance himself on his wobbly legs, waiting meekly like a dog, searching in vain in the mixed-up archives of his damaged brain for a word to bridge the abyss, to grant him a pardon.

"Go on," Nando says again without raising his voice.

Raca obeys silently and goes off down the corridor toward the street, giving off a sad, dark shadow as he passes that frightens the animals on the patio and darkens the corners.

"Raca and I are no help to you," says Arcángel to Nando. "He's too bad and I'm too good."

"I pushed him and stopped you. I was wrong. I shouldn't have interfered."

"Let me call him," begs Arcángel. "We're going to lose him."

"Let him go. We lost him a long time ago."

THAT NIGHT, after spending the day in quasi-legitimate business meetings, Mani Monsalve returns alone to his huge house on the tranquil bay.

Yela, the old cook, left with his wife and he doesn't even know the names of the new maids. Without Alina's firm presence, the bodyguards have taken over the residence, which has gone from perfectly organized, like a luxury hotel in Miami Beach, to a foul-smelling bachelor pad. There are women's stockings on the lamp shades, ashtrays full of cigarette butts, newspapers and plates of food on the dining room table, rifles leaning against the overstuffed sofas, muddy boot marks on the white carpet, and radios and television sets blaring at all hours. The enormous vases, previously filled with roses, are empty; Nelson Ned no longer croons on the stereo; the windows and the marble tabletops are dirty and sticky from the sea air. Every trace of Alina Jericó's presence has been obliterated.

The only place where Mani can still find it is in her closet, an interior room measuring twelve feet square, filled with shelves and mirrors illuminated with an overabundance of lightbulbs, like the dressing room of a Hollywood star. Her smells, secrets, memories, anguish, wasted hours, and vanities remain closed up and distilled in that room, as if absorbed into every shoe and picture she left behind, into the underwear that remains in the back of the drawers.

Most of all in the boxes. In the little boxes where she kept things, small cases of different styles and materials—chests, jewelry boxes, sewing boxes. Some are made of wood, others of straw, mother-of-pearl, or Chinese lacquer. Mani has never ventured into them before and now he spends long sleepless nights perusing their contents.

Back from work—which is each day more legitimate, more insipid and fastidious—Mani Monsalve locks himself in his bedroom with strict orders not to be bothered, meticulously washes his hands, and removes the cases from Alina's closet.

He opens them with devotion, as if handling sacred objects, and dumps the contents on the bed. They are full of tiny treasures, incomplete, useless, haphazardly thrown together. There are medals, notes, newspaper clippings, buckles, all things that remind Mani of his wife's solitary, intimate moments, those that held no interest for him when he lived with her, but that now he's desperate to recover.

He holds each button as if it were a unique creation, trying to guess which dress it belongs to, each mateless earring, trying to remember when he last saw her wear it, each shard of broken porcelain, looking for the rest to piece them together, in a vain attempt to mend the item. That's how he spends his nights, pawing through boxes filled with a past that he was only dimly aware of.

The next day he returns, drowsy and disappointed, to a reality that interests him less and less. While he waits for his dinner to cool he looks at a list of possible figureheads that Méndez has given him. They are men with respectable names, practicing Catholics, fathers of good families and members of exclusive clubs, to whom he proposes business ventures in which he will invest money and they will contribute their names and faces. He has hired to run his businesses an energetic and youthful group of sons of wealthy families freshly graduated from foreign universities who speak English and use fax machines, telexes, and computers.

To begin his new life with a clean face, Mani has agreed to forgo wearing blue jeans and tennis shoes and has exchanged them for bright suits, showy shoes, black shirts, and iridescent ties, which, far from improving his appearance, only highlight his street fighter's scar, his playboy manners, and his crassness. "Money equals educa-tion," he repeats to himself each time he deals with distinguished individuals. He contributes and donates generously, always picks up the tab, and squanders money on gifts.

He puts his hand in his pocket and passes out money as quickly as he used to pull out his weapon and spray lead. Following his lawyer's advice, he has sent each business associate a brand-new Renault 12 as a gesture of goodwill.

When he studies the new strategy, he has to admit that it has paid off. His bourgeois partners are more susceptible than he thought to easy money and the magical multiplication of profits. Legitimate businesses owned by Mani sprout up everywhere: impor-tation of automobiles, cattle farming, leasing and factoring compa-nies, stockbroking firms, insurance companies, loan offices, real estate, and many others, all equally unknown and boring to him and all of which produce profitable income statements.

But when he looks at it from a personal angle, his conclusion is the opposite. For the most important society benefit of the year, Mani bought half of the tickets and paid for the orchestras, the flower arrangements, the fireworks, and the seafood and champagne buffet. The event was a huge success and raised a lot of money for a rehabilitation center for drug addicts. At the close of the evening, a group of distinguished matrons presented Mani with a bouquet of roses accompanied by a great deal of applause and general gratitude.

Méndez advised him, "This is your chance. Submit your appli-cation to join." So he did. Admission was decided by the club's board of directors, who were already his business partners. The entire board met and voted.

The next day they informed him of the results—several black-balls. Application denied. The people he had supported, leeches on his fortune, had voted against him.

"They love my money," Mani said laconically to his lawyer. "But they detest me."

There was no anger in his voice, or disillusion, just apathy and fatigue.

"If Alina Jericó was the only thing that really mattered to Mani, why didn't he leave everything, the war, his businesses, all of it, and just go away with her?"

"Because he couldn't. Because men don't do those things."

Where is Alina Jericó? She's nowhere to be found, as if the black mare had carried her off into the darkness of one of her nightmares, or as if she'd faded away in her beauty-queen daydreams and was acting in another *telenovela*, or gone into hiding with her unborn child in a secret refuge.

It's clear that Alina does not want to see Mani; she doesn't listen to his messages, open his letters, or take his phone calls. That's why he spends his day running around dressed like a tropical dandy, carrying out his financial plans and fulfilling his social responsibilities. But his real life happens at night, closed up in his bedroom, where at least he can find his wife in her boxes, and now and then, for an instant, he thinks he's found her in the bill for a broken necklace, or in a stray key separated from its lock.

TWO HORSES are galloping along a serpentine trail over the mountain, scratching their loins on the undergrowth and inflaming their noses as they rub against stinging nettles. The riders' legs are protected by suede chaps and their faces by the wide brims of the black-and-white hats of the desert.

They reach a clearing and look down toward the broad valley lit with the last rays of the afternoon sun. Turning their heads slowly in a semicircle, they see the extensive plain beneath them, dotted with zebu cattle wandering peacefully over an infinite sea of slopes planted with marijuana.

One of the riders, the younger one with the dark scar cutting across his face, is Mani Monsalve. The other, the graying one smoking a cigarette, is his older brother, Frepe.

"It looks good," says Mani, and lets his horse chew grass.

They head back, with the reins held loosely, letting the animals find their own way. Mani takes his feet out of the stirrups and lets them hang, relaxing his leg muscles, closing his eyes and pushing his hat forward. His unbuttoned shirt flaps in the breeze. He lets inertia hold him on the saddle and is lulled by the animal's gait. Worn out by the ride, which began at dawn, he naps.

"You're getting soft from hanging around white folks so much," goads Frepe, who has noted how tired his brother is.

Mani opens his eyes, tense again for a moment, but he lets the provocation pass. He answers with a bored "Hmmm" and relaxes back into his stupor to watch the continuous projection on his mind's screen of his only memory, Alina Jericó.

Frepe rides tranquilly behind his brother with a cigarette hanging from his lower lip, cleaning his fingernails with the tip of a knife. No one would guess that not long ago a showdown over Narciso Barragán's death nearly culminated in violence between the two brothers. But gradually the heat was lowered, thanks to an agreement between all the brothers that allowed Mani to take control of all the urban, legitimate businesses and Frepe of all the rural, clandestine ones.

In reality it was the division in two of Mani's previous position as jefe. But Mani willfully agreed to lose power in exchange for getting rid of the problems and gaining freedom to pursue his path to legitimacy. Now each of the brothers takes care of his own business without stepping on any toes, and from time to time — like now — Mani visits the haciendas to make superficial inspections, which he uses to give a little relief to his soul, still crushed from the abandonment by his wife.

Night falls clear and fresh, and they've almost reached the ranch house when they hear the sharp echo of laughter from the mountain. Mani sits up straight in his saddle, electrified. "It was probably just an owl," lies Frepe. Mani pricks up his ears. That wasn't an owl. It was a man's laugh, loud like a crow's caw. Mani spurs his horse into a gallop in the direction of the noise. Frepe follows him. They ride into the thick vegetation and take a trail up the side of the mountain, into the darkness, until they are stopped by a voice close off to the left. "Who goes there?"

"Patience until the pig's trial!" Frepe shouts the password.

Mani hears an invisible man communicating by radio, then shouting back, "Proceed."

The trail rises sharply and the animals climb loudly up to a forest of poplars, silvery and silent under the bright moon. In the middle of a small clearing is a building lit by a single gas lamp. Another invisible voice calls out from the darkness, "Who goes there?" Frepe repeats the password, "Patience until the pig's trial," and again they hear a radio squawk, then are cleared to pass.

The building is large, without walls, and appears to be a soldiers' barracks, but it's disorderly, filthy, steeped in the rancid air of dirty, lonely men. To one side of it they have made a clearing and set up a firing range. Inside there are hammocks and weapons, boots and military clothing. At the entrance, roughly drawn on the wall, is a picture of a skull wearing a red beret with a snake entering one eye socket and exiting the other; printed below are the words "Happiness is a dead enemy."

There's no one around. Mani enters the building and counts the hammocks. Twenty-three. He is surprised by the variety and caliber of the equipment he sees—Madsen machine guns, M1 semiautomatic rifles, .357 Magnum revolvers, combat knives, binoculars, a telescope, a new high-precision crossbow, and a manual lathe to drill grooves in bullets to make dummies.

The remains of a meal are on a table, empty aguardiente bottles, maps, a lantern, and some pamphlets in English—*Combat Techniques, Survival Manual, The Soldier's Weapons.*

Mani takes the lantern and looks around the back of the building. On the high mud wall that protects the back of the building, the barbarian graffiti artists have drawn more skulls clenching daggers between their teeth and there are more quotes: "Clean boots, dirty hands." "Travel to faraway lands, meet interesting people . . . and kill them." Mani turns off the lantern.

"What is all this?" he asks Frepe, though he has already guessed. "Fernely's camp?"

Frepe doesn't answer; he just exhales smoke through his mouth and nose. Mani asks him again.

"Are you keeping that man here, training *sicarios?*"

"They aren't *sicarios.* It's a self-defense group, trained to protect the haciendas against seizure by the army or guerrilla attacks, or cattle thieves or kidnappers. It's very dangerous out here."

Mani knows he's lying, but he doesn't say anything. Frepe knows that Mani knows that he's lying and notices that he keeps quiet.

"Maybe Mani was happy with the new roles. I mean, it wasn't so bad for him to worry about laws and negotiations, while behind the scenes Frepe, Fernely, and his sicarios *took care of the rest."*

"But the fight between Mani and Frepe was real. They squared off in a battle over control of the family. They both had their pride and their ideas of how things should be managed. In the weeks following Narciso's death, the people around the Monsalves began to fear that the battle would end in the death of one of the brothers. Then it cooled off."

"Maybe because Mani already knew that by the straight and narrow he could go only so far. At any rate, when he discovered Fernely's clandestine camp, Mani didn't say anything."

"Because he couldn't, or didn't want to. Who knows? With those people it was impossible to know."

From not too far off, footsteps and voices are heard, male crows cawing, shouting, shooting bullets into the air. Mani looks out and sees them coming, descending the mountain like a gang of puppets, wearing camouflage uniforms with their faces painted black and green, a hybrid of soldier, bandit, and hooligan. Pushing and laughing, they play around, throwing their knives at the feet of the man in front of them.

Behind the others, silent and gaunt, his ash-blond hair plastered under a beret as red as his infected eyes, comes Holman Fernely, dragging his feet. Mani recognizes him and hurries to leave. He has nothing to say to him. He gets on his horse and heads in the opposite direction. He's barely begun to descend the slope before he hears Fernely's nasal voice throwing him a taunting farewell.

"Adiós, jefe."

"MANI AND Frepe had become two different faces of the same person. Frepe was the black face, Mani the white face."

"That's right. They repelled each other like water and oil and were afraid of each other, but they depended upon each other like Siamese twins. As much as Mani wanted to walk in the sun, he would always have a shadow."

"Frepe. Frepe was his evil shadow."

PALE AND golden, as if bathed in the light of a cathedral, Arcángel Barragán lies stretched out on his messy bed. Earlier that day, La Muda, barefoot and shrouded in her mourning clothes, had come into his room to bring his breakfast and change the bandage on his arm. Although months have passed and the wound has healed, the ritual is performed ritualistically day after day, and she dedicates as much time and care to the nearly dry scar as she did when it was fresh.

It's almost noon and Arcángel doesn't want to get up, weakened by a series of nights spent with Nando and by the terrible inner struggle he faces each morning against his monstrous love for his aunt, La Muda.

He is destroyed by his guilty desire for the forbidden woman. His tender mind and his adolescent body can't bear the weight of this huge, atrocious sin. He recites the Lord's Prayer and other prayers, one after another, always interrupted by thoughts of her. He sanctifies and blesses her salty odor, her mare's rump, the bulk of her large breasts, the tinkling of her secret metalwork, the rosy color of her mute tongue. He begs the saints to let her look at him, approach him, accept him. Father, let her fulfill my desires that are not a child's but a man's, have pity on my soul that is not a man's but a child's. Let me open her steel belt, enter her cave, and hide inside forever, amen. And God forgive me for I know not what I do; do not punish me for such evil, for such pleasure.

WEARING comfortable sport clothes, Méndez, the lawyer, gets out of a taxi in front of a new condominium building in the port. It's a glorious Sunday morning; brightly colored flowers are sprouting everywhere and a warm wind shakes the guayacan trees, showering the ground with yellow petals.

"Was the lawyer handsome?"

"No, handsome he was not. He was a tall man, large, pink, and protective. He had a serious, agreeable voice, and the peculiar quality of always seeming fragrant, as if he had just stepped out of the shower. All these things combined to inspire confidence in women."

The lawyer tells the doorman he has come to see Alina Jericó and he is allowed to go up. He takes the elevator in Tower C and rings the bell on a door on the eighth floor. A different Alina greets him at the door. Her face, now fuller, isn't tanned or made up as usual, but she appears serene. Her hair is shorter and somehow shinier. The pregnancy has transformed her perfect 36-28-36 to a comfortably round 36-36-36, and her beautiful bare feet are swollen.

"What do you think, Señor Méndez? My shoes don't even fit anymore."

She lets him in. The apartment is modest in comparison to the ostentatious luxury of Mani's house, but it's comfortable and well ventilated. There is good light and Alina has decorated it subtly and enthusiastically with wicker tables, white slipcovers, bowls of fruit, and large vases of flowers. They sit on a small terrace under a canvas umbrella and her old maid Yela brings them cold *lulo* juice. They talk about health, the weather, little things, and then move on to more substantial topics. The lawyer has brought a briefcase full of papers for her to sign: tax declarations and the separations of property.

Méndez spreads the documents on the small round table and begins to explain accounting principles and show her invoices. He takes out a calculator and adds, subtracts, and multiplies before Alina's sad gray eyes, in which the numbers pile up incomprehensibly, unprocessed facts, figures, and dates.

"Do you understand, Alina?"

She responds that she does but the only thing that is clear are her beautiful gray eyes that turn green and fill with tears every time Mani Monsalve's name is mentioned. The lawyer tries to remain objective, concentrating on the numbers, and keeps trying to explain them. But the wind that keeps blowing the papers off the table doesn't help much, nor does Alina's disinterest, nor do the sad, lonely clouds in her head. Finally Méndez realizes that it's useless. This is not the right time for facts and figures, losses and gains.

"We'll do this another time," he says as he gathers up the documents, his voice sounding warmer, more personal. "Now, tell me how you're feeling."

As if given permission she has long been awaiting, Alina gives free rein to a long, uncontainable sobbing, a serpentine fit that, once it starts, can't be stopped until the last kink is unfurled. Accompanied by hiccups and huge tears, it flows like a river, a tumult of words and memories, a chaotic stream populated by Mani Monsalve, the Barragáns, her unborn child, the distant past, the present perfect, the uncertain future, frustrated dreams, recurring nightmares, imaginary gardens, and the blossom of hope.

Now it is Méndez who doesn't understand anything, except his own repressed desire to embrace this desolate, pregnant, beautiful woman, to protect her, to help her come out on the other side, to feel her near, to blow her little red nose with a handkerchief, to caress her shiny, silky hair, which shakes with each sob in such an irresistible, tantalizing manner.

And maybe he would have, ignoring the final timid warnings of his conservative instinct nearly destroyed by the attractiveness of Mani Monsalve's wife, if the old maid Yela hadn't appeared on the terrace with a bucket in one hand and a mop in the other, yelling that the kitchen was flooding.

Switching seamlessly from tragedy to comedy, Alina and Méndez follow quickly behind the old woman, making their way through great puddles to the dishwasher, which is spewing water like a lawn sprinkler. The lawyer removes his shoes, rolls up his pants legs, looks for the water valve, closes it, and emerges from the disaster soaked, smiling, and triumphant.

Grateful, dripping water, and momentarily free of worry, Alina apologizes to Méndez for so much bother and offers him a good hot bath and a robe while Yela puts his clothes in the dryer. The lawyer accepts and thinks to himself that the only thing missing now is for Mani to come in and find him in his underwear. Alina goes to her bedroom to change clothes and thirty minutes later they meet again on the terrace. They decide that the only way to save a wet Sunday is to go to an exposition of exotic flowers that she has wanted to see for days but hasn't had the energy for.

He drives her car. They arrive at the exposition and walk through the greenhouses, Alina amazed by the extravagant orchids and irises and Méndez paranoid, but unable to admit it, and constantly looking over his shoulder for Mani's men.

When they pass an orchid with carnivorous cavities, of the genus *Odontoglossum*, Alina becomes dizzy from the lack of oxygen and the concentrated organic smells. She takes the lawyer's arm and asks to go outside for some air. They find a breezy patio with a stone fountain and sit on a bench until she recovers and says she's starving.

They agree upon Italian food and walk to a festive restaurant, decorated in green, red, and white, where they order lasagna, white wine, and gelato. The lawyer, a man with a big appetite, would have felt completely happy if he were not seized every now and then by the fear of Mani's reaction when he finds out about the separation of property, the orchids, and the lasagna. And he will find out, there is no doubt of that, and it will be sooner rather than later.

In a small open-air café, they have espresso to shake off the drowsiness that the wine caused. Then they visit a shopping center, walking slowing, not in a hurry to be anywhere. Alina is happy to look in the windows and Méndez is jumpy, imagining a spy on every corner.

In a toy store Alina buys the baby a windup monkey and a music box, and Méndez, who manages for a few moments to forget about Mani and to enjoy the presence of this woman whose company he is beginning to like more than is healthy for him, asks her to look at albums with him. They talk about their musical tastes and laugh happily when they coincide.

They stop in front of a movie theater to look at the marquee and he can't resist asking her if she wants to go in. But he's relieved when she says no, that she's too tired and needs to put her feet up. Good, I'll drop her off at her house and maybe save myself, he thinks to himself, but is suddenly seized by the desire to be with her a while longer. He is trying to think of something to propose that won't sound disrespectful or indiscreet when he hears her say, "Why don't we go home and watch a video." Méndez visualizes Mani breaking into the apartment with a machine gun, spraying bullets, but he says, "Excellent idea," feeling that it's worth risking his life for a few more hours with Alina Jericó.

They make themselves comfortable in front of the television in the living room, Méndez in a chair and Alina lying on the sofa, with her feet raised on cushions. There are two movies to choose from, a drama and a war film. She wants to see the drama and he wants to see the war film, so they toss a coin and he wins, but says they should watch the drama. Yela brings them some fresh fruit and the film turns out to be wonderful. It's *West Side Story* with Natalie Wood, and tells the story of young love between members of rival gangs. Alina is fascinated by the music and the dancing, but is disappointed by the tragic ending.

"Why is it that everything, even in movies, has to end in death?" she asks.

"No, Alina," says Méndez, "not everything has to be that way. To dedicate oneself to killing and dying is one option, but there are men who choose other things."

"Well, show me one, because I don't know any."

Méndez looks at his watch. It's eight o'clock, and he jumps up when he realizes how late it is. That morning when he entered Alina Jericó's building, he promised himself he would not stay more than

an hour, only as long as it took to help her with the papers. And he
has ended up spending the whole day with her, first in public, then
behind closed doors in her apartment. He has strolled around with
Mani's wife in Monsalve territory, under their noses. I don't think I'll
live to explain this, he thinks.

For years Méndez has handled his relationship with the Monsalves with white gloves, never making a mistake. And now, he has
suddenly gone crazy, irresponsibly playing with fire. To top it off he
has a meeting with Mani the next day, to advise him about some
business matters. He's already had to reassure Mani about his relationship with Alina, and he barely scraped through. Tomorrow he'll
have to do it again. Will he be able to do it again? And what if Tin
Puyúa is down in the street right now waiting to take him to his jealous boss?

No, no more, thinks Méndez. It's suicide to challenge Mani.
He firmly decides not to see Alina again for at least two or three
months. He will continue to help her, but through third parties.
Never personally. The decision is final. His life is at stake. There's
no going back. He calls a taxi and she walks him to the door.

"Thank you for such a wonderful time. It's the only peaceful
day I've had in years."

"Peaceful?"

"With family, that is."

"Oh, I see. Well, good-bye."

She stands in front of him with her hands on her hips and her
large belly sticking out. Then she pushes a lock of blond hair
from her face. She looks at him with liquid eyes and asks in a voice
already soft with sleepiness, "When are you coming back, Mr.
Méndez?"

"What?"

"I asked you when you are coming back."

"Uh, next week."

"Do you promise?"

Méndez hesitates before he responds.

"Yes, I promise," he answers, completely beaten, knowing that unless Mani physically prevents it, he will be there the next Sunday, knocking on this very door.

A POOR, OLD man, missing a hand, approaches the assassins guarding La Esquina de la Candela and asks for Nando. If it weren't for the stubby arm, a rather distinguishing feature, the tiny man would have been invisible. Insignificant and poor like all the others.

"Tell Nando that it's his compadre Mocho Gómez, of the Gómezes from the desert."

After being searched, the old man arrives in front of the head of the Barragán clan. Intimidated, he removes his hat and sits on the edge of a chair, drinking the coffee offered to him with tiny, indecisive, noisy sips, as if it were burning his lips, holding the cup by the handle with his only hand and supporting it underneath with his stub. He respectfully asks to be left alone with Nando, then speaks nervously.

"Nando Barragán, I have come to sell you a secret."

"It probably wouldn't interest me."

"It will interest you. I know where you can find Holman Fernely."

"I will buy your secret. If your information is true, I will make you rich. If it's a trick, I'll kill you."

ONE-TWO, ONE-TWO, one-two, one-two, Corporal Guillermo Willy jogs, lifts weights, jumps rope, flexes his muscles. Inhales and exhales, in and out. His T-shirt is soaked with sweat. He takes command of the space with brusque, aggressively juvenile movements. Arcángel follows him, concentrating quietly, standing on the tips of his toes. They are working out together on the back patio. They used to do it inside, closed up in Arcángel's room, but then Nando lifted the quarantine. At first Arcángel didn't want to come out, clinging to the security of his four walls. But the corporal was able to persuade him, insisting that being closed up would weaken his lungs.

Although the two boys are the same age, Guillermo Willy is already an adult while Arcángel is still a child. He still has a sweet voice, a cowlick, and skin like peach fuzz. He moves weightlessly, as if ready to take flight at any moment. The corporal's body, on the other hand, has matured under the harsh life in the barracks. His dark skin is weathered like calfskin and his closely cropped hair looks like a horsehair brush. He has grown strong and massive, though he is still short.

Worn out from their morning exercises, they throw towels around their necks and head for the cistern to get rid of the heat and exhaustion with cold water. Arcángel plunges the bucket into the tank, fills it, lifts it over his head, and lets a stream of cold water pour over his shining body. Shivering, he rubs himself with a bar of soap, then pours more water. The suds run down his legs, over the tiles, and disappear down the drain.

The boy takes a mouthful of water and sprays it out, happily looking at the rainbow he's made. He sees that his friend is distracted, talking to the parrots, and takes another mouthful of water and sprays him. Guillermo Willy twirls his towel, making a whip to snap at Arcángel, who laughs and dodges it. They wrestle in the soapy water, pushing and sliding, and suddenly stop when Severina sticks her head out and yells for them not to get the corridor wet.

"They loved each other like brothers."

"The corporal was Arcángel's best friend. His only friend."

They are lying in hammocks on the back patio, among the freshly hung laundry on the clotheslines, watching the servant girls, dark skinned and barefoot, with blue ribbons in their hair. Guillermo Willy plugs in his tape player and they listen to *The Wall* by Pink Floyd. La Muda brings them roasted chicken and sodas for lunch. Arcángel hardly touches his plate. His friend devours his and then finishes the other plate too.

"You haven't shown me your pistol," Guillermo Willy says to Arcángel when they finish eating.

"Nando doesn't like me to take it out."

"How long has it been since you cleaned it?"

"A couple days."

They get out of the hammocks and walk to Arcángel's bedroom. It's siesta time on a Sunday afternoon and the silent house seems deserted. The animals are still out in the heat. The servant girls are no longer heard on the back patio. Tijeras and Cachumbo are lying down in the shade, asleep.

Arcángel takes the pistol from under his bed. It's a Walther P38, German. The one La Mona gave him in the cellars the night of the false alarm.

"Let me hold it," says Guillermo Willy.

"No one could enter the Barragáns' house with a weapon. Even though La Muda had said that Corporal Guillermo Willy could be trusted, Nando's men, always suspicious, still searched him when he entered the house."

"Was there never a traitor among the bodyguards?"

"No, because they were all family members. All Barragáns. Second cousins, poor uncles, cousins, sons-in-law. Nando never hired anyone who didn't have the same blood he did. Simón Balas, El Tijeras, Cachumbo, and the rest were all Barragán Gómez or Gómez Barragán, Gómez Araújo or Araújo Barragán. There were a pair of twins, good marksmen, who were Barragán Monsalve. But they had sworn loyalty to Nando and they never turned on him. The only man with foreign blood who entered that house, except for Méndez, the lawyer, was Quiñones. That's why the men distrusted him so much."

"And Arcángel gave him his gun?"

Guillermo Willy holds the pistol in his hands. He feels the cold weight of the black steel and caresses it lovingly, as if it were a woman's skin. He removes the bullet in the chamber, takes off the safety, and opens the carriage. Arcángel hands him a brush and Guillermo Willy cleans the barrel. He raises it to eye level and looks carefully to make sure no lead remains. Arcángel passes him a rag and Guillermo Willy rubs the grooves to remove powder residue. Then Arcángel gives him a bottle of three-in-one oil and the corporal lubricates the sights, the carriage, the trigger, and the hammer.

"*And nothing happened?*"

"*Nothing happened.*"

"*If he had wanted, Corporal Guillermo Willy could have killed Arcángel.*"

"*If he had wanted, but he didn't want to.*"

MANI MONSALVE slowly climbs the great stone staircase. As he advances he is enveloped in an old, tranquil air, which he tries to swat away from his nose with his hand. He balances himself unsteadily in his Austrian chamois shoes, not trusting the slippery stairs, polished and worn by two centuries of footsteps.

He has always detested the smell of old things. Every time he buys an automobile, a piece of furniture, or a rug, he is comforted by the reassuring smell of its newness, of the wealth and happiness it symbolizes for him. He has moved into a newly acquired residence, yet everything in it smells secondhand. It stinks like a museum, he thinks. He aims his nostrils upward, toward the high ceiling supported by wooden beams, and smells dampness. Before he moved in, he sent an army of workmen to fix leaks and broken pipes, to repair the general deterioration of the place.

"We did what we could," the foreman told him as he gave him the bill. "But there's no real fixing these old houses. You don't finish patching a hole before another appears."

Mani reaches the second floor and walks through a half dozen enormous rooms, full of dark furniture and red carpets with lightly frayed edges. From the ceiling hang fans so lazy that their blades don't make the air flow, but just stir it around a bit. Heavy curtains block the afternoon sun, and in the darkness he hears the arrhythmic ticking of pendulum clocks whose hands mark odd hours, probably several years behind.

A few servants are quietly dusting.

"Open the windows to let a little light in this cave," orders Mani without looking at them.

The invisible servants dare to tell him that if the light enters, so will the heat, but he keeps on walking, without paying attention to an explanation that doesn't interest him.

Mani has contracted the services of an image consultant and public-relations expert, Miss Melba Foucon, who was born in the capital and educated in London. She tells him how to dress, how to use his utensils at table, which cologne to wear, and which words to eliminate from his vocabulary. Miss Foucon's instructions were thorough. He must immediately vacate the ostentatious nouveau riche house on the bay and move to another that is more in accord with his new personality.

Mani Monsalve agreed, going against his personal tastes and natural instincts for the sake of legitimacy, respectability, and Alina Jericó. After carefully studying the possibilities, Melba Foucon opted for a colonial mansion in an old, exclusive neighborhood of the port; it had belonged to a distinguished family that was willing to give up their ancestral home to begin a new life in Pompano Beach, Florida.

"They were fleeing precisely to get away from people like Mani."

"But they sold everything to people like Mani because that's who had the money, and there were a lot of others like them."

With the help of his attorney, Méndez, and the advice of Miss Foucon, Mani Monsalve made them an offer to buy the house and everything in it: commodes, armoires, and chiffoniers, oil paintings, Rosenthal china, Christofle silver, pianos, bronzes, lace table linens, Limoges porcelain, urns, Baccarat crystal, a complete library with two thousand volumes in French, carved inlaid secretaries, a genealogical tree, a pair of Afghan dogs, a bald, homosexual majordomo, and three trained housemaids.

When Melba Foucon took Mani to see the property that was going to be his new home, he looked desolately at the benches carved from Nazarene wood, the gilded picture frames, the colonial santos that the passing of the centuries had left without limbs or heads.

"This place is perfect for an archbishop" was his only comment, before he ordered his men to give him the suitcase full of dollars, which he presented to the intermediary in exchange for the keys. That's how he became the owner of what appeared to him to be a ruin, barely fit to be bulldozed over and made into a parking lot or an eight-story building.

Mani left all of his belongings in the house he had shared with Alina, everything that until then he had considered elegant, beautiful, and pleasurable. His glacial air-conditioning, his ultramodern stereo systems, his Jacuzzis, his giant-screen television and Betamax player, his electronic devices, and his collection of telephones.

He had to give up his comfortable king-size bed and satin sheets for a tall, hard, narrow bed with a high headboard, mosquito netting, and a porcelain basin beneath it, in which Simón Bolívar, the national hero, the liberator of the country, had slept one night on his way to Jamaica. It is a historical relic, a museum piece, but when Mani sleeps in it he feels as if he is suffocating from a lack of oxygen and dreams that he is dead and buried in a sarcophagus. To make matters worse, the bed is made up with starched linen sheets monogrammed H.C. de R. During the sleepless nights Mani spends in it, which is every night, he asks himself who H.C. de R. could have been.

What the hell am I doing in the liberator's bed? The only thing I need now is for the spirit of H.C. de R. to come lie down beside me, he says to himself.

Miss Foucon threw out her boss's old clothes and completely updated his wardrobe, from handkerchiefs to umbrellas. She didn't let him bring any of his former furniture, not even the paintings by Obregón and Botero that Mani had hated so much while he lived with them. But now he misses them when he looks at the unbearable collection of oil paintings of pale priests, bearded ancestors, and distinguished-looking matrons, all unknown, who fill the ancient walls from top to bottom.

Only the little boxes. Alina Jericó's boxes are the only thing Mani can't replace and that he won't agree to part with. Everything else, really, is just something to be taken off or put on, bought or sold. But not the boxes. He packed them himself and arranged them in his new bedroom on a commode, next to his bed. Sometimes, at night, when he feels asphyxiated by sadness, he opens them and pours their contents onto the mattress, reviving the ritual that he initiated in the house on the bay. But they have lost their magic from so much handling. Before, each time he opened one, Alina flowed out like a genie from a lamp. Not anymore. The energy imprisoned within has dried up, like rancid perfume in a bottle. Mani still caresses each button, each earring, each pin. And, though he doesn't realize it, even those sacred gestures have become routine. He clings to the ritual, but has forgotten its significance.

Mani arrives at the double doors of the main salon and opens them. Inside, a perpetual darkness, only barely relieved by the shining furniture, hovers and a musty silence rings, accumulated from countless social calls conducted in lowered voices, whispering in corners, conspiracies in the shadows, and fainthearted lovers' chats.

He walks across the shining floor—polished with wax daily by the three housemaids until the wood gleams like metal—listening to his footsteps and their echoes, and watching his solitary image infinitely reflected in the mirrors on the walls. Mani steps into the center of the room and sits in a formal carved oak throne. Uncomfortable, restless, tense, he, too, appears to be carved out of oak. He's not hungry but waits, without anything better to do, for the majordomo to announce that dinner is served.

Without Alina Jericó, his personal and domestic life has been reduced to long sequences of dead time managed and subdivided, by the majordomo and the housemaids, into breakfasts, lunches, and dinners — served with an excess of trays, dishes, glasses, and protocol — which he leaves almost untouched on the table.

Each day at dawn, when he opens his eyes and sees that his wife is not at his side, he's shaken by a sharp pain that leaves him distraught on his inhospitable ancestral bed. It's the same sensation that one feels when awakened from anesthesia after an organ has been removed. As with any convalescence from major surgery, the unbearable pain gradually diminishes in the face of a dull lack of motivation of body and soul, a lucky laziness that acts as a sedative for the tortured soul.

In general terms, except for the moment he awakes and other occasional vulnerable moments, he has already conquered the strident tortures of despair, jealousy, and wounded pride, and fallen into a painless, insipid limbo, in which the urgency for Alina's return is no longer felt like sharp lashes on bare flesh, but rather like a monotonous and bureaucratic obsession, constant, dull, and heavy like the steps of an obedient burro. Everything Mani does, he does so that she will return. His desire to win back Alina is the only motivation that guides his decisions and business dealings. That hasn't changed, but the difference is that now his soul is flooded by a calm void born of a sad foreknowledge, a presentiment that no matter what he does, Alina is never going to come back.

Nevertheless, there are mornings when he manages to convince himself that she will. He takes a cold shower, asks for eggs at breakfast, feels as if he has regained a tenacity that he thought he had already lost, and he starts out ready to move mountains and sky to reconquer Alina Jericó.

Such as when he agreed to give a black-tie dinner, with the apparent motive of inaugurating the new residence. The real reason was to see his wife in the new surroundings and to make her forget the killing and his barbarian past.

Miss Melba Foucon arranged everything, from the menu to the guest list, and she struggled to ensure that all the symbols of his new prestige would be shown to best advantage. The Afghan dogs were walked through the salons by a servant. The majordomo wore a new toupee to hide his bald head. The three housemaids wore new black uniforms with white lace aprons and white gloves. The fireplace was lit despite the warmth of the tropical night, and the urns were filled with salmon-colored roses. The tall regal palms in the garden were illuminated with spotlights. A row of torches guided the guests along the walkway leading to the front door.

Ruthless when creating the guest list, Melba Foucon included very few members of society from the port.

"They say she said she didn't want too many provincials, because it lowered the level."

"She didn't invite military officers or beauty queens either, the main staples of Mani's earlier parties."

"And don't even mention Mani's brothers. She was repulsed by those unsociable, evil-eyed creatures, covered with gold chains and diamond rings. So far they hadn't set foot in the new house and Melba Foucon wasn't going to let it happen on the day of Mani's first party and ruin everything."

Instead, a jet was chartered to bring guests from the capital, with hotel rooms provided. Among them was a cabinet minister, the dean of a private university, the head of a chain of radio stations, the owner of a powerful financial group, the leading television reporter, and the ingenue from the most popular *telenovela*.

Alina Jericó received an engraved invitation, and despite the RSVP notice, didn't respond as to whether she would attend or not, which made Mani burn with anticipation, because it left open the possibility that she would.

The night of the dinner, on the advice and counsel of Miss Foucon, the host received his guests in a white Yves Saint Laurent tuxedo, holding a glass of Scotch on the rocks in his hand.

"Why Scotch if he didn't drink?"

"He didn't drink anything all night, but each time he left his full glass on a table, Miss Foucon immediately brought him another, because holding the glass was part of the look. She hadn't given up on the war against Mani's bad habits and manners, and in most areas she had obtained favorable results. Except for a few noisy disasters, like her attempt to make him change his Kola Román, a plebeian national soda with a dubious color, for Coca-Cola, which was fashionable around the world."

Melba Foucon was satisfied. She observed Mani Monsalve from various angles in the salon and noticed how he had gone through a real transformation since the afternoon she had met him. He had been wearing a tasteless suit the color of Pepto-Bismol, black-and-gray shoes, and a green, geometric-patterned tie. Now, though she was scrutinizing him with a critical eye, searching for defects to correct, and despite the asexual professionalism that she used to block her feminine sensibilities, the public-relations expert and image consultant perceived the virile magnetism emanating from her strange employer, and she was surprised to see how well the French tuxedo fit his perfectly proportioned physique. Miss Foucon even confided to Mani that the beautiful looseness of his movements, stemming from his proletariat background, could pass for athletic prowess or aristocratic disdain.

"If it weren't for his nauseating green skin," sighed Melba Foucon, "and the scar that tells everything, the ugly mark of a thug stamped on the middle of his face."

Melba Foucon saw that Mani was separated from the guests and was standing alone, so she headed toward him to give him a couple of tips to improve his presentation even more.

"I advise you, Señor Monsalve," she said, in a tone somewhere between supercilious and scared shitless, which was her normal approach with him, as if she didn't know whether she was addressing a waiter or the master of the universe, "that starting tomorrow morning you take twenty minutes a day to tan in the sun, and that, please don't be offended by what I'm about to say, but I think you should have some plastic surgery to get rid of that scar."

Mani Monsalve's gaze went from his watch to the front door, back to his watch, then back to the door, as if Miss Foucon didn't even exist. She noticed he wasn't listening to her and thought it might not be a good moment to talk to him—he must be nervous among the high-caliber guests.

"Come with me," she said, changing to a topic that she thought more appropriate. "You really should speak a little with the minister, who paid us the honor of attending. We can use the opportunity to photograph you together."

"Not now. I'd rather you found my attorney, Señor Méndez."

Mani was preoccupied by a single thought. It was nine-thirty, and all the guests had arrived, except Alina. The rest, excellencies, ministers, señoras, and señors, could all fall dead where they stood on the floor of his main salon, he was so uninterested in them. Let Doña Foucon talk to them and give them the money they were looking for. He wasn't going to worry about anything but finding a way to bring Alina to his party. He thought of having his public-relations expert call her on the telephone, but he rejected that idea, as too inefficient and rash. He opted for something more practical and certain. He steeled his heart, swallowed his feelings of jealousy, and asked Méndez, who had been located among the guests, to go and convince her.

"*How were things going at the time between Mani and the lawyer?*"

"*Difficult. Méndez saw Alina frequently, and Mani, who had them watched twenty-four hours a day, knew everything they did, and sometimes even what they talked about.*"

"*So that's how he knew there was no romance between them.*"

"*Yes, and that's why he hadn't ordered his men to kill the lawyer. What's more, Méndez was his key man, not just for his plans for legitimization and social ascension, but because he was Mani's only contact with Alina. He had to trust the lawyer. But at the same time he knew he couldn't trust him blindly.*"

The lawyer agreed immediately and left for Alina's apartment in Mani's Mercedes with Tin Puyúa at the wheel. He knew that what he had been sent to do was illogical and ill-conceived, and he was sure that she would refuse. It was absurd to arrive at that hour, when she would already be in bed, to propose that she accompany him to Mani's dinner party, especially after she had expressed in a thousand ways that she wanted nothing to do with her husband.

But he agreed to go because he was being given a pretext to see her, even if only for half an hour, and because it was an intriguing situation: visit Mani's wife, on Mani's orders, driven in Mani's car, by his chauffeur. It seemed like a joke out of a cheap comedy and it probably would have made him laugh if he didn't know that once again he was treading a dangerous line, playing roulette. Nobody laughed at Mani Monsalve, and anyone who thought he could woke up in a ditch with a bullet in his head. But he can't order me to go, then shoot me for obeying his order, thought the lawyer in amusement as he rang the buzzer at Alina's door. He was about to ring a second time, feeling guilty about waking her and making her get out of bed, when she opened the door, coiffed, made up, perfumed, and dressed elegantly.

"What a surprise, Señor Méndez! I was just leaving for Mani's dinner."

"Well, I was there, and I came to get you," said Méndez hastily, realizing that he had made a grave mistake.

"How nice. Let's go! Should we take my car?"

Méndez felt bad when he told her that they didn't need to because he had Mani's Mercedes, but he didn't dare say anything about Tin Puyúa. Then she asked, with a hint of surprise, which he interpreted as disdain, if Mani had sent him to get her, and at that moment his masculinity was shattered in a million pieces. He felt like a cretin, an idiot. He saw his reflection in Alina's gray eyes and realized that he was just like all those other poor devils whose lives, dignity, and deaths depended upon Mani Monsalve's disposition.

"Alina looked spectacular, wearing a loose black silk dress that revealed her pregnancy but was sexy at the same time and showed off the perfect skin of her back and shoulders."

"What did they talk about in the car?"

"Nothing. Tin Puyúa drove at a suicidal speed. Alina was very upset. Her anxiety about seeing Mani again was obvious. The lawyer felt uneasy, angry with himself, and, at the same time, depressed and discouraged. He had thought that Mani mattered less to Alina each day, and now he saw it wasn't true."

"He had reason to be confused, because she always swore that she never wanted to see Mani, not even in a picture."

"She didn't want to see him, but at the same time she was dying to see him. That's how things are with love, unpredictable."

"*They sure are. One day you win, the next you lose. Look at the lawyer, who had just been laughing at Mani; now he's fallen apart, because the joke is on him.*"

"*Mani almost had a heart attack when he saw Alina enter his house, so beautiful, so pregnant. He had dreamed of this moment for months. He immediately took her out on the balcony to talk alone, but they were interrupted constantly, to be toasted, or thanked, or proposed business deals. Señorita Foucon also interrupted them, insisting that Mani attend to his guests.*"

"*So they didn't get to talk alone?*"

"*They did talk, but it was too little and too difficult. He tried to ask her to come back, but he got aggressive as soon as she said no, and suddenly they were fighting about who would keep the child when it was born. They said cruel, ugly things to each other, and instead of repairing the relationship, made it worse. Alina once again felt the rapid heartbeat, the anguish, and the nail biting of the first days of separation, and after being there only half an hour, she seriously regretted having come. So she asked the lawyer to take her back to her apartment.*"

"*Then the lawyer did have the last laugh. . . .*"

"*Not really, because Alina cried all the way home and he didn't even try to console her, because he felt jealous, and he was tired of being played for a fool. It was a sad night for all three.*"

The evening sun has gone behind the neighbor's house, and the liquid orange fragments of its last rays still filter through the blinds protecting the main salon. Mani is sitting in a sober oak armchair, not thinking about anything in particular. In the semidarkness he watches the Merthiolate-colored threads of light dancing on the furniture.

From below he can barely hear the sound of an automobile engine starting, men talking in loud voices, someone giving orders.

The sounds are coming from the basement, where the bodyguards and the weapon stockpile have been installed, along with a collection of motorcycles, a communications room, garages, and cells for prisoners. Now they're called offices and they are hidden underground. Mani hardly ever goes down there, and of his men, only one, Tin Puyúa, is authorized to come up to the main part of the residence. But he doesn't stick his nose there unless it's absolutely necessary, because he doesn't like the place and finds it eerie.

Every once in a while Mani feels nostalgic for the happy camaraderie that united him with his men during dangerous times. Then he'll go down to the basement and sit with Tin Puyúa in the backseat of a Land Rover, drinking Kola Román from a bottle and talking. But even that happens less and less now.

Annoyed, sad, enthroned in the middle of the immense room, Mani Monsalve lets his mind wander and just allows time to pass, bored and lonely as a king.

After a while he pulls a nail clipper from his pocket and starts trimming his fingernails. Each time the clippers click, a nail jumps irreverently into the air and falls onto the red rug along with its fellows.

On the wall in front of him, above the magnificent and useless mantel abundantly laden with heavy silver candelabra, hangs an imposing oil painting. It is the portrait of a general with white, woolly sideburns and a chest full of medals. His skin is green in places where the humidity has damaged the canvas. His stern blue eyes seem to scrutinize Mani with surprise and disapproval. But it doesn't disturb Mani. He's busy working on his cuticles with the nail clipper.

Miss Foucon told him the soldier in the picture is the family patriarch, the great-grandfather of the previous owners, hero of the civil wars a century ago.

"And what's that old buzzard got to do with me? Why do I have to put up with him in the middle of my living room?" Mani asked her.

She responded that he would get used to seeing the portrait. It was part of the process of gaining ground and creating an illustrious past.

"In a few years, Señor Monsalve," the image consultant foretold, "everyone will swear that general was your great-grandfather, and even you yourself will believe it."

7

"WHO DID *Arcángel make love to that afternoon?*"

"*A thin, dark-skinned girl that La Muda took into his room.*"

"*What was her name?*"

"*No one knew. Arcángel didn't ask her name.*"

He undresses her gently, without curiosity, and lies down naked next to her, asking about a scar below her knee. She says she got it when she was very young, on a barbed-wire fence, and she asks him about the wound on his arm.

"Does it hurt?" she asks.

Arcángel doesn't answer. He carefully loosens the girl's braids, trying not to pull her thick, wavy hair. He takes the ends and passes them over her skin, as if her hair were a brush, painting her eyelids, her eyebrows, her neck, her lips, her ears, her nipples.

"Don't laugh," he says. "If you laugh, you lose."

The girl tries to be serious, still, but the tickling gets the best of her and she twists and smiles shyly, then laughs, making sounds like the cooing of a dove. Arcángel climbs on top of her fine body and begins to make love to her, half playfully, half seriously, thinking about other things and looking around the room.

His sweet, caramel-colored eyes scan the opposite wall, which had been painted sky blue years ago and has now turned dirty gray.

They stop on a crack where a dark, shiny insect lingers. Sort of hairy, like a spider. A black, hairy spider, half-hidden in the shadows, clandestinely spinning the silky threads of a new web.

Arcángel's eyes move down along the wall, passing over the feather pillow, covered by the voracious nest of the girl's hair, and then continue until they stop again on a spot at the edge of her lip, a funny little mark placed almost in the corner of her mouth, as if a small insect that lives in the recesses of her mouth has come out to look around and now wants to return to its hiding place. But it doesn't move. It's just a mole — its mystery dispelled in an instant, and Arcángel forgets about it.

His body balances above the girl's, and the cross of Caravaca, hanging from the chain around his neck, swings like a gold pendulum. While his organ works, his eyes wander, moving down the sheet to the green-and-white tiled floor, like a checkerboard, to the corner where his breakfast tray sits, on which two coppery cockroaches have set up camp among the remnants of food, their infallible antennae ready to detect the slightest danger. Rising above the dark-skinned girl, Arcángel Barragán rocks, up and down, as if on a swing, and watches the powerful cockroaches with their hard shells that have survived La Muda's monthly fumigations and daily sweeping. But no matter how long it lives, a cockroach isn't much, and Arcángel loses interest.

Under him the nameless girl emits quiet sighs in discreet attempts to get his attention. Arcángel takes her like an automaton, not thinking about her, in the same disciplined and machinelike manner that he does his two hundred abdominal exercises each morning, or rides his stationary bicycle. He takes her, but doesn't desire her. He makes love to her, but doesn't love her. She's like all the others, and as pretty as she is, an anonymous girl still isn't much.

But that spider scratching and weaving, watching him. That dark spider haunts Arcángel. His eyes search for it again, climbing the wall until they find it buried in its hole, beneath the dust. Alive, active, vigilant, intelligent; there is something unnerving about the insect that makes Arcángel want to watch it. A magnet. A familiar intensity, a brilliance he has seen somewhere. The spider sends out weak signals that the boy understands. That he slowly recognizes. The spider is not a spider. Its legs are eyelashes, its movements are blinks, its brightness, intense and moist, is desire. The spider is a human eye. It's La Muda's eye, watching him from behind the wall. La Muda's magnetic eye, hairy and carnivorous, like a hungry spider hypnotizing and attracting her young nephew to the recesses of her cave, opening and closing to devour him alive in all the splendor of his cloistered beauty.

"Then what they say is true. La Muda took girls into his room so she could watch them make love."

Burning with secret love beneath her steel harness, his lonely aunt hides in the adjacent room and watches her idolized nephew.

"She probably caressed herself in the darkness while she watched."

"She couldn't. Not with a chastity belt with thirty-six sharp teeth in front and fifteen in back."

"Maybe there was no belt."

"Then why do they say there was?"

"First, because people like to talk. Second, because she never had a man. And, third because it's the only explanation for the metal sound that was heard when she passed, like the soft dragging of chains. There was a quiet steel sound beneath her skirts."

"What did Arcángel do when he realized his aunt was watching him?"

"He became an adult."

"Is that you, Muda? Are you there? Is this your body and your soul?" In the moment that he recognizes the presence of his aunt, he imagines that it is she whom he is embracing, and Arcángel

Barragán becomes a man. A sudden virility hardens his tender body and his cotton dreams are transformed into the quest for power and possession.

With both eyes locked on his aunt's, his mind focused on her, and his heart filled with love for her, the celestial child becomes a ravenous red demon with an engorged, excited member. Arcángel pitches upward with the force of an earthquake, lifting the poor girl in bed with him up into the air, then lets her fall and throws himself on top of her like a wild man. He squeezes her as if she were a rag doll, chokes her with his tongue, swallows her with kisses, brays at her like an animal in heat, licks and bites her eagerly like a puppy. He penetrates her and devours her, like a tiger with its prey.

"And what did the girl do?"

The surge of lust and strength is so sudden and spectacular that at first she is startled, then becomes afraid, and finally faints from pleasure, though she has the strange feeling that she has not inspired Arcángel with such extreme behavior: the playful indifference at the beginning, then the violent passion at the end.

Meanwhile, the new man, with his body on top of the girl with no name and his mind on his aunt, is infinitely regretful, infinitely grateful, thanks heaven and begs for forgiveness.

"Forgive me, Muda, as I forgive you, and receive pleasure, as I do also, while I tear off your black clothing and feel your ripe flesh. I look at you and smell you and break the steel encasing you into a thousand pieces. I destroy the locks that keep you from me and I release you from your silence. I beg you, I order you, I demand you to let your mouth speak. Open your legs so that I may enter and your eyes to see how I am nourished by you. I suckle your strength and then pull away to conquer the world, only to return again to suck your energy, and pull out again, and enter again, and pull out and enter, pull out and enter, pull out and enter, and this terrible love that is killing me bursts into a blinding light, and finally I rest, holding you close to me. I close my eyes and the windows. I lock the doors and erase all memories, forget the deaths, remove myself forever from any danger. Your words comfort me and I sleep on your breast, holding your hand, and may God, who is all-powerful, forgive us both."

THE ADDRESS of a garage. That's the secret that Nando Barragán has bought. A garage in the city. Any minute now he will have Holman Fernely in his hands. All he has to do is sit and wait for him to come by to pick up a truck that he left here. Nothing more. So many nights spent poring over information, guessing at psychological profiles, racking his brain to find a clue, setting up and canceling operations, and now it turns out that he'll fall all by himself, like ripe fruit. Sold out by a mutilated man from the desert who slips away to bring the information in exchange for a little money.

Mocho tells Nando Barragán that Fernely stashed a red-and-white Ford in the garage three months ago. He should be coming for it anytime now. Maybe at midnight, or in the morning, to bring it back the next day, or maybe not to come back for a few weeks.

Nando pales. His cratered face is transformed into a lunar surface. Before Mocho has finished speaking Nando throws his chair back and stands up, forceful and slow like a robot that has just been switched on. Mocho shrinks back, terrified by the war machine that has sprung into action. Nando takes out his Colt revolver—the one he used to kill his cousin Hilario Monsalve—and loads it with silver bullets engraved with his initials.

"Let's go," he orders the incomplete little man. "Take me to Fernely."

Mocho is so afraid he can't stand up, as if in addition to missing an arm he were missing his legs, and he waits, trembling, for the giant to lift him up with one hand, but instead Nando stops, suddenly deactivated.

"Wait a minute," says Nando, and he sits down again and calmly lights a Pielroja.

His huge hands empty the bullets from the Colt, and he says, in a low voice, "Give me a security deposit."

"In spite of his desire to get Fernely, at the last moment Nando controlled his murderous instincts and put off any immediate action. He wanted to cover his back in case it was a trick. It wouldn't be the first time the Monsalves had bought people to ambush them."

"They agreed that the security would be Mocho's father, an ancient man, and his youngest son. He was supposed to bring them from their pueblo and leave them at the Barragáns' house as hostages. If everything went well, Nando would give them some land in the desert and some cash. But if anything went wrong, the old man and the boy would die."

"And before I kill them, I'll make them suffer," threatens Nando to close the deal.

"DURING THE *time that Mani Monsalve lived in the colonial mansion he became richer than ever. Businesses were sprouting up all over. Partners were falling from the sky. Señorita Melba Foucon was a key part of this success. She arranged it so that the prejudices against Mani were relaxed. She knew how to get people to soften their morals. She sat them at her boss's table and dangled his money in front of them."*

"No, the decisive moment was the separation of labor Mani had arranged with his older brother. Frepe stayed in the shadows, making hot money, while Mani worked the front end and laundered the money. Though there was still jealousy between the two, they made a winning combination."

"On the other hand, the Barragáns became poorer and lonelier every day."

"Once Narciso died they forgot about business. They never made another dime."

"So Fernely's plan worked, first ruin them, then conquer them."

"Yes, it worked. Although the truth is that when Narciso died there was very little money left anyway."

"What about the mountains of dollars they hid in the cellars?"

"They ran out. The money was spent on parties, wars, and luxuries. Their last big extravagance was Nando and Ana Santana's wedding. In better days, Nando Barragán had new cars driven off precipices for the pleasure of watching them smash into pieces. He ostentatiously lit cigarettes with hundred-dollar bills, and he liked to throw money in the street to watch the boys in the barrio scramble for it. It was his way of buying faithfulness and making himself popular, and at the same time he enjoyed seeing how men would kill each other to grab a few dollars, how they kicked and punched in the crazy scramble for money. Another of his favorite pastimes was the greased pole. On Sundays and holidays he had a twenty-foot pole, coated with lard and topped with a bag of money, set up in the plaza. We went crazy trying to climb that pole to get at the prize, and Nando, feeling like a king, loved watching us turn into greasy, eager monkeys. No one ever reached the top. The highest anyone ever got was nine or ten feet, only to fall back down. One Sunday a quiet, redheaded boy named Fosforito climbed all the way to the top. The whole barrio yelled and applauded. "Bravo, Fosforito!" "Good job, Red!" But he didn't reach for the bag. Instead he stood on top of the pole and looked at us sadly and disdainfully for a moment, then spread his arms as if to fly and leapt into the air. He fell headfirst and splattered on the ground. That afternoon at the wake we got drunk on beer and started crying about how sad and macabre our lives were. They were unsettling, difficult times. There was money everywhere. Rivers of blood flowed. Bombs went off. People didn't know who they were or what their names were, or even what they were supposed to do."

"Did everyone in La Esquina de la Candela get money from Nando Barragán?"

"No, not everyone. El Bacán and his group of domino players were proud that Nando was never able to dirty their hands. Their elegant poverty irritated some people, who considered it a challenge, and one night, amid confusing circumstances, someone shot at Bacán's house. He was in his usual place, outside in his wicker rocking chair, looking at the white nothingness and listening to his wife's lilting voice as she read to him from an old newspaper from the capital. When he heard the gunshots he didn't even flinch. Seven bullets whistled by, without touching him, and were embedded in the wall behind him. They're still there now. From then on the rumor spread that even death respected him."

"So Bacán and his group were the only ones to stand up to the Barragáns?"

"There were a few others like them. But most of the people in the barrio had grown accustomed to receiving money in exchange for protection. And when the Barragáns stopped passing out money, those same people lost their fear and respect, and turned their backs. It had already been rumored that they were running out of money and couldn't pay their bodyguards when, one day, the rumor went around the barrio that without Nando's knowledge his sisters had sold what was left of Narciso's violet limousine, which Nando had preserved like a sacred relic. They sold it because they didn't have money for food. For years they had been accustomed to Nando leaving wads of money in the kitchen drawer every morning. Whoever needed some took it. Nobody worried about accounting, or making a budget—why should they, since they had more money than they could ever spend? One day they opened the drawer and it was empty. And the next day too. They didn't dare complain to Nando, so they sold the Lincoln.

They sold it to a funeral parlor, which fixed the damage caused by the grenade and turned it into a hearse. They say that was the beginning of the end."

ANA SANTANA wanders around the Barragáns' house like a shadow. At first they hated her, but now not even that. No one seems to notice her timid presence as she walks the corridors watering the geraniums, or as she leaves the bathroom in her faded bathrobe with her wet hair wrapped in a towel, or when she sits at her Singer to mend the curtains from her bedroom window or the sheets from her round bed, which jammed and is no fun anymore. No one speaks to her and she speaks to no one. Each day adds another brick to the wall of silence enclosing her.

Because of her isolation, Nando and the other Barragáns haven't noticed that for months she has been taking in sewing, charging the neighbors for making simple outfits, mending, hemming, and updating old clothing. Her friends, who haven't seen her since the wedding, enviously imagine that she lives like a queen with all her husband's money. But the harsh reality is that she covers her own expenses with the money she earns: shampoo, tampons, panty hose, chamomile tea for nerves, and thread, buttons, and the other materials she needs for her modest life as a decent working girl. The same now as when she was single.

Ana's wrists ache. Loneliness and frustrated love have settled in her body in the form of a painful arthritis concentrated in her wrists, frequently forcing her to stop working. She lays aside the blue pleated polyester skirt that she is shortening for a cousin, leaves her bedroom and heads for the kitchen to rest awhile over a cup of coffee. Uncertainly, she looks around the room, which is filled with smoke and the smell of onions, to make sure Severina isn't there. Ana Santana can't stand the domineering and hostile presence of her mother-in-law, her eyes hardened by anger and reddened by pain. She's not there. Ana goes in, takes the pot of warm coffee with *panela* that is always on the stove, and pours a little in a cup. As she turns to leave she glimpses the silhouette of La Muda eating guayabas in the darkened pantry.

"Oh, I didn't see you," Ana says to her.

The other women in the house are afraid of her, but Ana has come to respect La Muda. Her tenacious energy and lack of ostentation inspire confidence in Ana, as does the single-minded manner in which she dedicates her life to serving others. La Mona is a killer, thinks Ana, but La Muda is strength. In contrast to Severina's voluntary silence, which hides poisonous words and criticism, La Muda's forced silence seems neutral and calming to Ana. It nurtures secrets and invites confidences.

Ana Santana isn't the only one to give in to the temptation to confide, at length and without inhibitions, in La Muda. Everyone in the house does it from time to time, aware, of course, that they won't receive an answer or any advice. Or maybe that's precisely why they consider her the ideal confessor. She's the only person who will listen attentively and keep her mouth shut.

"Last night Nando talked about that woman in his sleep again, that Milena," Ana Santana confides, as she sits on a stool next to La Muda. "He came into the room very late and was upset about something that had happened, but he didn't want to tell me about it. He slept in the hammock, as usual, and left me alone in the bed. He smoked five Pielrojas, one after another, and smashed the butts on the floor. I could tell when he fell asleep, because he started to snore. Then later he started to talk about her, like the other times. Asleep, answering his own questions. Then he turned on his side and didn't say anything more. I cried until dawn."

La Muda's fathomless eyes observe Ana, penetrating her layer by layer. First the antique doll's white skin, then the protective packaging of a poor, suburban girl, and deeper still her tortured, bleeding soul, committed, like a fakir, to lie on the sharp points of her broken pride, her dreams of love shattered, and her jealousy growing daily. For a moment Ana Santana can't bear La Muda's burning stare. She stands up, pours herself more coffee, then sits down again, rubbing her aching wrists, and continues.

"I asked him when he met her. He said many years ago, at sunset at the flamingo sanctuary. He was traveling and had gotten out of the jeep to wait for the flock of pink birds to return. As he saw them appear on the horizon, a twelve-year-old girl approached him. A miserable child, skinny, dirty, with rotten teeth. 'Take me away in your jeep,' she begged him. He laughed and asked her, 'Where do you want me to take you?' 'Far away. Where my husband can't find me.'"

La Muda already knows. Her eyes, with their hairy eyebrows and lashes, are like X rays and see too much. She has watched her nephew Nando while he sleeps, and has seen the flamingos in his dreams. There are seven dozen and they return every night to the same place where they have roosted for generations, tired, flapping their wings slowly in the fiery sky. Nando is very young and is alone on the salty, deserted beach, wearing a short-sleeved shirt, his skin like gooseflesh from the cold wind. Before him extends the ocean, and behind and on both sides, as far as his eyes can see, the hot white desert.

No humans live at the beach, except for an old Indian with a gruff voice who speaks very little and whom the government has given the bureaucratic task of counting the birds. Each evening he notes, with infantile lettering, how many birds arrive and the exact time. The next morning he writes down the time they fly away. It's his only job, aside from harassing the sporadic visitors to ask for a voluntary donation and make them sign the guest book. Nando knows the old Indian because he has come to this place many times. But now the man's not here, and the child approaches to ask for his signature. The child-wife of the old Indian.

"Was it his wife or his daughter?"

"It was his wife, and probably his daughter too."

She is a clever little girl, tricky, an expert in the art of survival, and she watches Nando closely. She waits until he is absorbed in watching the birds ease their long legs in the golden water and scurries toward the jeep, climbs in the window in a blink of an eye, swift and agile as a lizard, and steals his briefcase. Nando sees her, grabs her by the neck, lifts her up, and shakes her roughly. "Let go, you thief," he yells, and she sinks her teeth into his arm.

He smacks her rump and she drops the case.

"Do you understand, Muda?" asks Ana Santana. "That child was Milena, although she wasn't called Milena then and she wasn't blond yet. Nando couldn't forget her from that very first day, when he helped her run away from her husband. It's her fault that your nephew hasn't loved me since before he even knew me."

THE BLACK, heavy sea laps gently at Raca Barragán's feet. His stretched-out body, sprayed with droplets of water, has the dark, silent patina of bronze. Nocturnal crabs explore his naked skin. The full moon bathes his body in blue splendor as the blood flows from his open veins, drop by drop, into the absorbent sand. These are welcoming celestial signs for the night of Raca's death. Finally, there is light for Raca, El Tinieblo. Peace for his torment. Now his name can be spoken; it's no longer an evil omen or synonymous with horror.

"There will always be an ocean to cleanse the soul," his brother Narciso, El Lírico, once said to him. And now in his agony, Raca remembers those words. With his last breath of life he went to the edge of the sea and collapsed. The salty water forgave him and death returned the grace that this world had kept from him. At the end he was beautiful and holy.

"*How did they kill him?*"

"*They murdered him cruelly. They shot him, then they stabbed him.*"

"*Who did it?*"

"*Fernely and his sicarios, in an orgy of blood. They wiped out El Tinieblo (notice I say 'El Tinieblo' in order not to mention his name) and his whole gang. They killed seven of them and chopped them into pieces afterward. But Fernely didn't fare very well either, even though he caught them by surprise, approaching from behind. He hadn't counted on the ferocity of El Tinieblo; he killed four of Fernely's men before he died. Among the four were two of Mani's brothers, Hugo and Alonso Luis. They worked as thugs for Fernely because they couldn't do anything else.*

"*For the first time in a long while the Monsalves had suffered a hard reversal. In a single night the seven surviving brothers were reduced to five. If he, whose name I won't mention, had returned home, the Barragáns would have celebrated his feat with a party lasting several days. They would have composed songs about him and carried him on their shoulders. But then again, who knows, because Nando never wanted to celebrate anything about him, or recognize any of his merits. It doesn't matter now, because El Tinieblo didn't make it home. He was barely able to get to the sea to die, while his friends' bodies lay strewn along the highway among scraps of broken steel and burned motorcycles.*"

Cut and bleeding, like Christ on the cross, the unmentionable one managed to escape his tormentors. He crawled into the bushes and rolled downhill through the underbrush. His eyes could no longer see and his ears could no longer hear; his mind was unplugged and could no longer function. But an obstinate, tortoise-like instinct guided him in the direction of the sea. The desperate plea for forgiveness he had always carried deep inside and his child-like desire for affection afforded his body sufficient energy to walk, drag itself, and crawl on four appendages, like a beaten dog, a mile, and then another, until he reached the beach.

Along the way he took off his clothing. Later, near the highway, they found his leather jacket with four small, round bullet holes. The first was in the back at his right shoulder blade, the second at his left shoulder. In front there were two more at waist level.

"The next day a forensic doctor performed the autopsy on the cadaver. He put on rubber surgeon's gloves and inserted his fingers into the four bullet holes and nineteen knife wounds."

Further along they found his tall black police-issue boots with long laces, which surely must have slowed his agonizing progress. He had to stop, reach toward them, and coordinate the movement of his inert hands just to remove them. A couple of yards away they found his discarded trousers in a sad heap. But they never found his beloved weapons, which he always carried with him, the machine gun named Señora, or Tres Gatos, his rifle, or Ballerina, his switch-blade.

"Maybe they caught El Tinieblo unarmed."

"No way. How could he have killed four men otherwise? His killers must have taken the weapons. I can imagine Fernely hanging them on the wall as a trophy."

The only thing he managed to keep to the end was his medallion of the Virgen del Carmen, patron saint of difficult tasks and protector of *sicarios*, which had been sewn to the skin over his heart. He arrived innocent and naked at the still water, like a newborn baby.

The warm evening enveloped him in its mist and calmed the mortal shivers that wracked his body. The sea licked his wounds and the salt cauterized his pain. The waves soothed his thirst and put out the fires of his despair. Tiny fish entered his mouth, swam around his insides, and emptied all the cruelty that he had received and imparted. The moon's rays crowned him with pale halos, and a mermaid placed a martyr's palm branch in his hand, since he had lived like a martyr and had made martyrs out of his numerous victims. The curing waters repaired his damaged body and a swarm of snails wove his battered head back together with their slime. The zealous clams formed a mother-of-pearl shield around his aggressive member, and for his ringing ears there were soft lullabies carried on the wind.

The tide ebbs slowly and leaves his body on the damp sand, bidding him farewell as it barely grazes the bottom of his feet. Like a bronze statue, Raca Barragán has lost his life, his pain, and his guilt. He shines, solitary, invincible and eternal, like a young god. "Dark in life, luminous in death," says the epitaph that will never be placed on his grave, but that the stars have painted in the sky in his honor, and will have disappeared in an instant.

IN A TEFLON skillet, Alina Jericó is browning mushrooms in butter. She had never been interested in cooking, or never had to be, because Yela is a master chef. But recently she has become interested in cookbooks and the simple recipes in her women's magazines.

Today, like every Tuesday, she is cooking dinner. She opens the refrigerator and pours herself a glass of Coca-Cola with ice, goes back to the pan and seasons the mushrooms with salt, pepper, and lime juice. She tenderizes the beef loin that will go into the oven later and carefully washes the fresh lettuce leaves. She enjoys feeling them in her hands as the cold water runs over them. Her pregnancy is quite advanced now, and the curve of her belly fills the gap between the rest of her body and the dishwasher. She slices tomatoes, carrots, and radishes, then sets the table, choosing two white hand-embroidered place mats with matching napkins and two sets of silver utensils. In the center of the round dining room table, she places a vase filled with freesias. She adds a pair of wineglasses, a basket of bread, and her white plates with gold borders. She adds a candelabra and then takes it away; too romantic, she says to herself.

"Who had she invited to dinner that night?"

She walks barefoot from the kitchen to the dining room, because the doctor hasn't been able to reduce the swelling of her feet and she can't bear to wear shoes. She tires quickly and has limited her daily routine to knitting, preparing the nursery, watching *telenovelas* in the afternoon and movies on video at night, taking short walks, caring for the plants that now cover her terrace, decorating the apartment, listening to records, and looking at magazines.

Three times a week she goes to a childbirthing class. Alina doesn't have any friends and only sees her sisters every now and then. She became accustomed to isolation imposed by illegitimacy during her marriage to Mani Monsalve; it effectively prevented her from making new friends and separated her from her old ones.

"Who was coming to dinner that night when Alina set two places at the table?"

Her only company was the old maid, Yela, who takes care of her and watches over her night and day, and Méndez, the lawyer, who resolves her problems, from a blown socket to her taxes, and who has become her confidant and adviser. His is a fun, protective, and tranquil presence in the midst of a loneliness that, if not for him, would have driven her back to Mani long ago. She has almost gone back many times. She has had the telephone in her hand, at three o'clock in the morning, at six o'clock in the evening, ready to dial his number and surrender.

"When you are about to call Mani, call me first," Méndez has told her, "so we can discuss it calmly. Don't let desperation or sadness force you to take a step that you will regret for the rest of your life."

Alina has gained such confidence in him that she asked if she could wake him up when she has the nightmare about the black mare, which continues to haunt her dreams, foaming and twitching, catapulting her into an abyss of anguish and fear.

"Anytime," said the lawyer. "Call me and we'll scare the beast away."

Although he lives in another city, Méndez travels twice a week to the port. He has business reasons, but mostly he goes to spend time with her. He religiously spends Sundays and Tuesday evenings with her.

"So Méndez was her dinner guest."

At eight o'clock sharp Méndez rings the doorbell, freshly bathed and smelling of cologne. He is wearing a new shirt, and Alina notices and makes a big deal about it. Beautiful as a porcelain doll, wearing a rose-colored dress and a ribbon of the same color holding her hair back, she lets him in.

"Despite her pregnancy, she was still a beauty queen."

Eydie Gorme and los Panchos are playing on the stereo. They sit at the table and eat. The meat is dry, but he says it's delicious, eating everything on his plate and asking for more. They laugh and talk.

Later, while drinking coffee in the living room, Alina shows Méndez a new sweater she has knitted for the baby. But the lawyer is nervous; his mind is on something else. He doesn't see the little sweater in front of his eyes and mutters unintelligibly when she asks if he thinks the minty color of the yarn is too bright. He doesn't even know what the film they're watching is about.

The cause of his worry is inside his briefcase. It holds what could turn out to be the key to his happiness, the final piece of the puzzle that destiny has been building little by little. Life continues to push Alina Jericó further from Mani Monsalve and closer to him, and he has worked the wind to his favor to tighten the invisible ties with infinite doses of patience and affection, all the while trying not to force her hand and spoil everything before it's ready. He has never behaved as a suitor. His meticulously documented role has been that of unconditional, disinterested friend to a lonely, pregnant woman. Until the precise moment arrives, Alina must never even suspect his desperate love and carnal desire. She must never know that he wants to marry her and take her far away, to adopt the child she is expecting, to love it and raise it as if it were his own, to adore her and care for her until death separates them, which could happen soon, if Mani finds out. But Méndez doesn't care; he's willing to run the risk.

"Méndez couldn't rush things, but he couldn't let too much time pass either."

Waiting is as dangerous as rushing things, and if he didn't stir things up a little, the current situation could go on indefinitely and he'd be stuck in the role of Good Samaritan forever.

"Or cuckold. He'd have to take care of her and watch over her until someone more eager takes her away. So what was in the brief-case?"

He has the latest issue of *Cromos* magazine in his briefcase. It features a section entitled "The Barragáns' War Against Their Cousins, the Monsalves," which describes in great detail the massacre of El Tinieblo and his friends, complete with photographs of mutilated bodies lying in the highway. Horror spread out in full color. A brutal reminder for Alina, in case she has forgotten the bloody taste of the world of the man she loves and doesn't want to leave.

But that's not all. There's more in the magazine, as if it were a dossier prepared especially for Méndez to make the final push in his laborious campaign of convincing and seducing. In the social pages there is a graphic report of a birthday party in the capital.

"*What did the party have to do with Alina Jericó?*"

The person being feted was Miss Melba Foucon, who was turning thirty-four, and next to her in all the pictures was "the prosperous coastal impresario" Mani Monsalve. Méndez doesn't know whether they published the two articles simultaneously for any special reason, or whether it was coincidence or editorial carelessness. In the first photograph Melba and Mani are dancing. Then they appear together with other guests; in the third she is blowing out the candles, and in another he is presenting her a gift. In the last two they are embracing.

According to their Tuesday evening custom, once the movie is over, around midnight, the lawyer stands up and says good night. This time he doesn't. He prolongs his visit, buying time to make up his mind. Should I give Alina the magazine, or would it be a selfish act of cruelty? He's leaning toward giving it to her, and asks for another cup of coffee. Then he thinks maybe not, and talks about soccer. Then yes again, as he leans back in his chair and says he's tired. Then no, and he stands to leave.

At the last minute he risks it, taking the magazine out of his briefcase with a gesture that he had meant to be discreet, but which ends up being very theatrical. "Have you seen this?" he asks.

She takes the magazine, flips through it, coming across first the photos of the killing, then the ones from the birthday party, and her gray eyes flood with tears. First she cries timidly, then she lets go.

"Why are you showing me this?" asks Alina. "Now you're going and leaving me torn apart."

"I won't go if you don't want me to," Méndez says hurriedly, embracing her.

They sit together on the linen sofa. She pours her burning tears on his shoulder, soaking his new shirt. He hesitantly caresses her hair with devotion disguised as paternal, then dries her face with his handkerchief and hands it to her to blow her nose. He pulls her against him and murmurs sweetly to her and the baby, as rivers of honey flood his heart.

"*His little game worked.*"

Caramel and sugar flow in Méndez's veins as he feels the warm, soft body pressed against his. Little by little the torrential crying subsides and stabilizes into prolonged sobbing, which descends to a soft trembling cut by sighs, and then finally settles in a melancholy drowsiness, which returns a peaceful gray tone to her reddened eyes.

Alina dozes on the lawyer's shoulder, and it's like a miracle to him that the minutes pass and she doesn't pull away. It's as if she had decided to build a little nest against his large, middle-aged body.

"They offered me a very good position in Mexico." He lets the statement fall into the air. "Do you like Mexico?"

"Now you're leaving for good?!" she says, about to start crying again.

"But I'll take you with me, if you want to go," Méndez is about to say, but he stops. It would sound repugnantly opportunistic. He'd better wait until tomorrow, or the next day. For now he should only shelter her in his arms, idolize her silently, and caress her chestnut-blond hair without passion or lust until she says she's tired and wants to go to bed.

"*At two o'clock Méndez left the apartment, sure of his triumph. Finally, after so much sewing, he had made the last stitch. Now all he needed was to tie it off with a good knot, but he still thought it best to leave it for another day.*"

"*Down in the street he hailed a taxi and asked to be taken to his hotel. He was so happy that he gave the driver double the cost of the ride.*"

At four o'clock the lawyer is twisting and turning in his bed, unable to sleep. His forehead is warm from excitement. He replays the scene he has just experienced over and over in his mind, to make sure it happened, to lock it into his memory. His fingers remember the texture of Alina's hair; his nostrils can still smell the scent of strawberries from her shampoo; his neck is still damp from the warmth of her breath; his back still feels the pressure of her long, beautiful hands.

All of a sudden, he is startled by the ringing telephone. "It's Alina," he thinks.

"Was it Alina?"

"Yes, it was."

Méndez lifts the receiver and says *"Hola"* with a loving voice from the depths of his soul, expressing pure adoration, infinite gratitude, and the promise of eternal happiness.

"I just called Mani," she tells him, "because I want to go back to him."

"What?!"

Alina repeats what she has just said.

"Are you crazy? Do you want your child to grow up among assassins and end up murdered?" The lawyer says in a loud, uncontrolled voice. He doesn't understand. He uses language he has never used before. There's a horrible pain in his chest, as if a heart attack were lurking nearby. He tries to regain his composure and adds, "Wait, don't do anything. I'll come over if you want."

"There's nothing to do." Her voice echoes in his ear like a funeral bell. "I already called him. I hope you'll still be my friend."

"You'll still be my friend." The words whistle through the telephone wires and stick in his brain like poisoned needles.

"Why did you do it?" he is barely able to whisper.

"El Tinieblo's murder was atrocious, that and the other things, but Mani didn't do it. He hasn't killed anyone in a long time. He's changed. Do you understand? He changed for me."

"POOR LAWYER. *He got shot in the ass. The magazine worked, but in reverse.*"

"When Méndez left the apartment, Alina lay down on her bed with the magazine. She looked at the photographs for hours, not the ones of the killing, but the ones from the birthday party. She saw how handsome, rich, and elegant Mani looked. Completely different from the thug she had been married to. She saw distinguished people around him. No weapons. No gunmen, not even Tin Puyúa. She saw Mani as she had always dreamed, except for one detail: he was with another woman. She must have thought, 'I put up with the painful years so she could have the fruitful ones.'"

"Jealousy is stronger than fear."

"Jealousy was the final straw. And since the infamous party in Mani's colonial mansion, she had been seduced by the idea that he had become good and honorable, that he had abandoned the war and the Barragáns had forgiven him."

"NANDO BARRAGÁN'S anger, when he learned of El Tinieblo's assassination, was terrifying, but completely internalized. He made no fuss or demonstration. He had spent several days and nights sitting in front of the garage waiting for Fernely to appear, and meanwhile Fernely went and wiped out his brother. It was like a cruel joke."

"Did Nando kill Mocho and his father and his son? Did he torture them before he killed them, as he promised?"

"No. His men wanted to, but he wouldn't let them. His anger didn't blind him. He thought to himself, What has happened is not due to human betrayal; it is fate. So he kept waiting for Fernely in the same place, more eager and diligent than before. He didn't even go to the burial. La Mona bathed Raca's body, dressed it, and put it in the coffin. Only she could have done it, because no one else loved him."

"Did his death hurt Nando?"

"It made him angry, but it didn't cause him any pain."

Nando has swallowed whole the idea of erasing Fernely from the map, and he doesn't allow himself the luxury of thinking about anything else. He doesn't leave the Silverado, which is well camouflaged and parked two blocks from the garage. A network of lookouts has been set up to alert him the moment the victim appears. He smokes, eats, and sleeps in the Silverado. But he sleeps poorly, slouched in the seat, tense and alert, wearing his weapons, with his Ray-Bans perched on his boxer's nose. His head hangs to one side and his mouth is wide open. Nightmares make him call out in a hoarse voice, while his pupils dance beneath his dark glasses and closed eyelids. In some he sees his blond Milena walking away; those are the most common. The most interesting feature Tío, desert wise man, spiritual adviser of the Barragáns and Monsalves, an old man crazed at times by the ravages of arteriosclerosis and so emaciated that he's almost a whisper, a little bit of nothing wrapped in rags.

"Who is Holman Fernely and how do I approach him?" Nando asks him in his sleep.

"He is no one and he has no manners. You are Nando Barragán, the Great, and the world expects elegant feats from you," Tío answers with otherworldly wisdom, his breath foul and ghastly.

Zero hour arrives and the alarm sounds. Radiophones and walkie-talkies cross signals, messages come and go from corner to corner and car to car. The air is electric. Nando gets out of the Silverado and shakes away the vestiges of drowsiness. He's still wearing the Colt with the silver bullets. His muscular mass hardens; his emotions freeze and his heartbeat is paralyzed. He becomes solid nerve and metal, the impenetrable warrior.

A slow, tired shuffling is heard, like the sound of an old woman out to buy bread and vegetables. The flip-flops cross the corner and Fernely appears, tall and ungainly, his filthy hair glued to his skull. He's wearing a faded T-shirt and his waxy skin is a ghoulish white.

His inflamed eyes look from side to side; he looks behind him to see if anyone is following. He scans the unpaved street leading to the garage. It's empty except for the mosquitoes buzzing around the puddles and the yellow dog that always comes out when he goes by. Now it's following him, barking at his heels, and he scares it off with a rock.

For months he has used this place to hide a vehicle and hasn't had any problems. He likes it because it is discreetly hidden in a proletariat barrio of the city, on a deserted street, with no nosy neighbors. The truck, old and rusted, goes unnoticed. It's not a war vehicle, but it helps him get around without being seen. He gave a false name and doesn't think the caretaker suspects anything. There's no reason to suspect. The caretaker has no way of recognizing him. He's never seen Fernely before. Everything is the same today as always. Nothing happening. Fernely makes a rhyme, "Nothing's doing, cow is mooing."

This time he is mistaken. He's already in the high-precision sights of Nando's men, who hide behind windows and whose gazes follow him down the street toward the garage. Despite all the time he has spent in wars, guerrilla operations, and *sicario* activities, and surviving in prisons, mountains, and underworlds, nothing has alerted his old fox's instincts at the precise moment he is about to step into the lion's den, alone, as defenseless and innocent as a child at his first communion.

They watch him, but they don't shoot. Boss's orders. They all know that one clean shot, entering his chest and exiting through his back, would put an end to the whole matter without bothering anybody. Or they could just put a bomb in the truck to send Fernely flying into the sky. But Nando doesn't want that.

"*To Nando killing was an art and a vocation, like bullfighting to a toreador, or performing mass to a priest.*"

"*That's how the Barragáns were. People with old-fashioned ideas.*"

"Three times that day Nando spared the life of Fernely, his brother's assassin. Three times that became famous in La Esquina de la Candela, like the three falls of Christ or the three hairs of the devil. We knew them by heart, the first, the second, and the third, and yet we never tired of telling or hearing about them."

"What was the first?"

Hidden behind a wall, still as stone, Nando observes the tall gray man enter the garage. Is it really Fernely? Yes, it's him, just as he had imagined during his deliriums of vengeance, except for the hair. It's thinner, and he seems more embittered. It's him, there's no doubt. The tattoo of God and Mother marks his arm as a brand marks a slave. He's so close that Nando can hear his raspy breathing and smell the acid stench of his two-day-old sweat. He examines Fernely with a professional eye, noticing every detail, his monklike thinness, the cruelty in his knotted hands, his chronically infected eyes. He detects the weapon hidden in his belt, beneath the soiled T-shirt.

Without realizing he's being watched, Fernely approaches the garage attendant. "What's up, ketchup?" he says, exchanging a couple of bills for the keys to the truck. Then, rubbing a handkerchief over his red, swollen eyes, he gets into the Ford and opens the window. He warms up the engine, puts it in reverse, and backs up. "See you later, alligator," he says as he aims for the exit.

"It took Holman Fernely seven long minutes from when he entered the garage until he drove out. Nando Barragán didn't kill him out of respect for the old belief that you don't lay traps for your enemies. You must warn them before you shoot. That was the first time Nando spared Fernely's life."

"What was the second?"

Holman Fernely starts down the road in his red-and-white Ford. Nando Barragán follows him, alone, in his metallic gray Silverado. He has forbidden Pajarito Pum Pum, Simón Balas, and El Cachumbo to interfere. War must be fought man to man, one on one, he says.

For a block and a half Fernely doesn't notice anything. He moves along slowly, stopping at intersections, not taking his usual precautions, exposing his scrawny neck, as if inviting them to shoot him from behind.

"*But Nando didn't, because he doesn't shoot people in the back. That was the second time he spared Fernely's life.*"

"*What was the third time?*"

Fernely looks in the rearview mirror and realizes a car is following him. He recognizes Nando Barragán and initiates a chase right out of a movie, complete with sharp turns to the right, then to the left, screeching brakes, burning tires, sparks, roaring engines, suicidal speeds, and shooting from car to car. Fernely manages to get on the coast highway, but he can't shake Nando, who's stuck to him like a leech. The powerful Silverado catches up to the Ford, pulls beside it on a curve, and tries to force the smaller truck off the road. On the fifth try, Nando does it. The Ford veers into the ditch and rolls over, wheels still spinning.

Nando looks down disdainfully from the Silverado, disgusted by his lack of emotion at this turn of events. Now he has a new reason to hate Fernely. The man has turned out to be such a lousy adversary that Nando is underwhelmed by his victory. Yawning and disillusioned, he waits, with the ivory handle of the Colt in his fist, for the varmint he's cornered to show signs of life.

The driver's door of the Ford opens and Fernely, scratched and bruised, his clothing torn, falls out in a cloud of dust. He's unarmed and raises his hands above his head.

"I give up, buttercup," he calls out innocently.

"*Nando Barragán didn't shoot, because he doesn't shoot conquered enemies. That was the third time he spared Fernely's life.*"

Fernely draws nearer, his hands still in the air, and climbs up through the underbrush. Still moving forward, he takes advantage of a bush that partially obscures his body to pull out a grenade he's hidden in his pocket. He removes the pin with his teeth and is about to throw it when a silver bullet with the initials N.B. is shot from the Colt. The bullet hits Fernely in the middle of the forehead, killing him before he can say a word or witness the phenomenal explosion that pulverizes his eardrums, his burning eyes, his parched tongue, and the rest of his body. He never heard the powerful boom of the grenade he held in his hand.

"You blew yourself up, like what you did to Narciso," says Nando blankly, looking disgustedly at Fernely's sad, blackened remains.

He gets back in the Silverado and returns to the city, thinking as he drives that it's too easy to kill people.

"Word of the latest killing reached La Esquina de la Candela before Nando did. 'Nando Barragán killed Holman Fernely!' the children shouted in the streets. People began to tell the story, and they're still telling it, of how Nando, a living legend, had converted Fernely into a dead one. That afternoon we stood on the sidewalks to watch the conqueror pass. The Silverado was covered with bullet holes and dents from the chase, and dust and mud from the crime scene, but we never saw Nando; he was hidden by the polarized windows."

With the weary step of an old warrior, Nando walks into his house and heads straight for the kitchen to look for his mother, to tell her what he has done. He has avenged his brothers' deaths and is expecting a hero's welcome, with tears of gratitude from Severina, lots of commotion and admiration from the rest of the family, music, rum, fireworks, a party lasting several days, the usual when a Monsalve is liquidated. But no one comes out to greet him.

Down the silent, tiled corridor comes his welcoming chorus — the cacophony of the nursing pig, the caged jays, the parrots on their perches, and the pet monkey as they settle down for the night. Nando Barragán, the great Goliath who has slain the dwarf, enters the kitchen and slumps onto a stool, which miraculously supports the weight of his body. He removes his black glasses and turns his myopic, suddenly meek eyes to his mother. Severina pours him a cup of coffee and gives it to him without a word. Then she stands behind him and rubs his hairy neck with her fingertips. Nando closes his heavy eyelids and begins to relax. He surrenders to his mother's touch and is transformed into a little boy.

"Isn't there going to be a party for me? All I get is coffee?" he asks Severina, his voice heavy with fatigue.

"What more do you want? You didn't kill a Monsalve, only their dog."

Nando is stunned. He is crushed by the duality that has puzzled him since he was a child—the harshness of his mother's words that wound his heart so deeply, and the peaceful magic of her caresses that heal him.

OUTSIDE THE glass dome, in the close heat of the night, the crickets are chirping and the orange trees impregnate the air with their cloying sweetness. A tiger runs along a mountain path, making the parrots shriek. Far from shore a lone fisherman's lantern draws a circle of light on the black surface of the sea.

Beneath the dome, the blue, translucent water in the Olympic-size pool emits soft, wavy reflections of light and the warm scent of chlorine. In the moist air a woman's echoing laugh, the pattering of bare feet on cement, and the sound of a body plunging into the water seem far away.

"Why was there a covered pool in the middle of the warm jungle?"

"Mani liked it because it cost more."

An invisible servant has left two dry towels near the edge of the pool, along with a pitcher of Kola Román with ice, two glasses, and a tray of fresh fruit—watermelon, mango, papaya, pitahaya, *níspero*, pineapple. In the pool, sitting on the steps at the shallow end, Alina Jericó looks toward the other end, where Mani Monsalve is diving headfirst from the high board.

She applauds his effort and laughs. Her hair is tied back so it won't get wet. Her polka-dot bikini shows off her large belly, but despite the extra weight her legs are still spectacular. Mani's head bobs up out of the water and he swims toward her. His stroke is enthusiastic, but sloppy. It's obvious he learned to swim in a river, and that only as an adult has he swum in a pool. Halfway across the pool he stops, spitting out water and rubbing his eyes, to look at his wife. She's beautiful. Her face may be fuller and her breasts heavier, but she's as gorgeous as always.

"*La Virgen del Viento had been abandoned and swallowed by the jungle, but Mani ordered an army of carpenters, gardeners, and maids to make it ready in four days. He wanted it to look as though Alina had been there the day before. They rebuilt, repaired, painted, rearranged, and cleaned. Furniture, tennis courts, swimming pool, horse barns, gardens, beaches, walkways, and fences. Everything was spruced up to perfection.*"

"*Alina called him on a Tuesday night to ask him to pick her up on Saturday—she wanted to talk to him. They agreed to spend a week together and had barely hung up, at four o'clock in the morning, when Mani called Tin Puyúa and ordered him to leave immediately for La Virgen del Viento with the cleaning and repair crew. The next morning he called the state governor and asked him to have the access road fixed, because he was afraid that the potholes would upset his wife's delicate condition. The governor sent out twelve asphalt trucks. No one ignored Mani's orders.*"

"*When Melba Foucon heard about the plans, she asked Mani if he wanted her to oversee the organization of the house. He told her that he didn't want any changes. Everything was to remain just as Alina had planned it months ago. He did want one new thing, though: a nursery for the baby, in blue, completely outfitted and filled to the ceiling with toys.*"

"*Had Melba Foucon and Mani become lovers?*"

"*No. She dreamed of it, but he never considered it for an instant. His loyalty to Alina Jericó was rigorous and obsessive, like a soldier's to his country. Not only had Miss Foucon approached him, but many others had as well, and he was cold to all of them.*"

At La Virgen del Viento, Alina has at her feet, like Eve, an earthly paradise with every imaginable pleasure. Green snakes and wild monkeys observe her from a distance as she and Mani stroll arm in arm through humid tunnels of orchids and ferns. Silently, as if the months of separation were a rending too painful to mention, they climb each dawn to a misty forest through which six waterfalls cascade. Under the canopy of jungle trees, they eat a breakfast of fruit picked along the way. Deer and birds, docile as house pets, approach to eat from their hands. They take their siesta at the edge of a river covered by the oversized leaves of a victoria regia vine, and they awaken to hear the salamanders singing and to see birds hunting insects in the sky. They spend their afternoons with their horses. Alina exercises them on a line, then she brushes them and rewards them with pieces of sugar. At night, when the cold fog descends from the mountains, they warm their hands over a fire on the beach fueled by wood scavenged from old shipwrecks.

They've spent six days away from it all with no disturbances. Invisible hands fill the cupboards, leave meals on the table, clean the house, and saddle the horses. Alina no longer wakes up at night startled by men shouting or dogs barking. The sound of machine guns doesn't interrupt the long card games she and her husband play on the shiny electronic game table.

"*They didn't talk about the past? Or the future?*"

"*Only a little, and with trepidation. On the telephone the night of the reconciliation, Alina told Mani that she would spend a week with him, as a test. The week was almost over and he wanted to propose an extension, to suggest that she not return to her apartment. But he didn't dare. He was afraid she would say no.*"

From the middle of the pool, Mani looks at Alina. She's beautiful and happy. He's not afraid anymore. He knows she won't leave him.

"Let's call the boy Enrique," he calls to her, with something like enthusiasm resonating in his carefree voice.

She approaches him slowly, dog-paddling to keep her head above water, and extends her arms to embrace his neck.

"Why Enrique?" she asks. "No one in your family has that name."

"That's why."

Behind her the sound of smashing glass echoes under the dome, shattering the silence and leaving them breathless. They turn toward the noise. Someone has broken one of the windows in the glass wall. Seven men enter through the newly formed hole. Mani recognizes the dirty, gray hair of his brother Frepe.

"Don't worry," he says to Alina, "it's only Frepe and his men."

She already knows who it is. The unmistakable stench of her brother-in-law's cheap tobacco has already reached her nostrils. She asks in a low voice, trembling with fear and indignation, "Why did they come in like that, breaking the glass?"

"*What happened to Mani's bodyguards? Why didn't they stop Frepe?*"

"*Because it was the boss's brother, part of the same clan. They suggested that he not go in, but they would never have dared to forcibly block his way, and especially now after Mani had given them explicit orders to maintain peace and quiet. 'I want you to act like ghosts,' he told them. 'I don't want to see you, hear you, or even detect your presence.' But they came running with their weapons pulled when they heard the glass breaking. Mani said it was nothing and told them to go away.*"

"*So Frepe's* sicarios *and Mani's men were on the verge of battle that day?*"

"That's right. If Mani hadn't stopped them, no one would have survived."

"That's how their life was. At any moment anything could happen, and anything could spark a battle."

Frepe's killers have their faces painted in camouflage colors and are wearing camouflage pants and brightly colored shirts like tourists in Florida. Some have bandannas tied around their foreheads, others wear baseball hats. They enter threateningly through the mist, crazed, like clowns thrown out of a circus, like mercenaries coming out of the swamp.

"They killed Fernely yesterday," Frepe shouts at Mani from the edge of the pool, "and we couldn't tell you because you ordered your men not to disturb you on your honeymoon. Two days ago they killed two of our brothers and you didn't go to the funeral. Are you trying to forget about us?"

"Stay here," Mani orders Alina, and he gets out of the water slowly, seeming undisturbed, with the boredom of an emperor interrupted during his bath by servants. Only Alina has noticed the change in him. She sees that his scar is more pronounced, darker, like a pale thunderbolt.

"Why are you here? Why did you come in like a bunch of thieves?" he asks Frepe as he puts on a robe over his bathing suit, unhurriedly, allowing his athletic body to be seen, flaunting his youth, which is in itself a small victory over his brother, who is old and clumsy.

"I came to talk to you, but they wouldn't let us in. You're so elegant now, you don't want to hear about death, but that's how life is, brother, a pile of shit."

"Who killed Fernely?" Mani asks as if he didn't already know.

"Nando Barragán, and by now he's celebrating, proud as a peacock and drunk as a skunk."

While the brothers talk, the seven painted men take over the place. Noisy, powerful buffoons, they horse around as Alina treads water to stay afloat. One of them is eating the fruit on the tray, spitting seeds into the pool, burping and laughing. Another is drinking aguardiente, swearing and grabbing his balls. A third plays *The Broken Glass* by Alci Acosta at full volume on the record player behind the bar. Still another is amusing himself by slashing the canvas on an umbrella. Another two bounce noisily on the diving board, then jump into the pool fully clothed.

As the riffraff approaches, Alina swims to the edge of the pool, upset, as if fleeing the plague, and calls to her husband, "Mani, help me out. Mani, hand me a towel, please," but he doesn't hear her. She screams hysterically, trying to raise her voice above Alci Acosta, who, from the record player, is toasting the woman that betrayed him. Frepe motions to Mani with a finger. "Give her a towel," he says. "The queen doesn't want us to see her big belly."

Mani helps Alina out of the water, wraps her in a towel, and asks her to wait in the house.

"No, let her stay," says Frepe. "It's better if she stays, so we can chat, like nice people."

"We're not going to talk at all if you don't tell your men to get out," says Mani, oozing tranquillity.

"But why, when they're having such a good time? Are they bothering the queen?"

"Get them out, Frepe"—Mani bets the remainder of his authority—"and make them shut up. My head is splitting."

Frepe regards his brother challengingly, his black-striped face looking very much like a bitter old zebra. But he doesn't dare disobey. To his dismay, his brother's air of superiority still intimidates him. He puts two fingers in his mouth, whistles, and orders the rabble to wait for him outside.

"You can sit down," Mani says to him with the sober tone of a boss, indicating a seat. Then he says to Alina in a tone that leaves no room for argument, "Go wait for me in the house. Take a hot bath and get dressed."

"No," she says, still shaken by the commotion and the cold air, and she stands next to her husband. "I'd rather stay here with you."

Frepe's lit cigarette saturates the air with rancid smoke. Watermelon rinds and seeds float grotesquely on the illuminated surface of the pool. Struggling to retain control of the situation, Mani goes to the bar to turn off the song about the ingrate who left her man, and as he does he realizes that Frepe and his men played the song on purpose, to stir him up. But he won't let himself be provoked. He offers his brother a glass of aguardiente.

"I just came to tell you not to worry." The old zebra blows smoke into the air as he speaks. "I have no problem taking care of business while you hang out with actors and government officials. Fernely and my other men were killed so you can pose as a grand gentleman. But that's okay, it's part of our deal. I'm not upset that you won't let me in your house. I'll even forgive you if you don't go to my funeral. It doesn't matter. To each his own. But what does bother me is the thirty percent you're giving me."

"Go take a bath, Alina," insists Mani authoritatively.

"The cigarette," she murmurs in a weak voice, as the horrible smoke surrounds her, completely draining her energy. Her legs become weak, her eyes cloud over, and the pinkness of her cheeks is frightened away, altering the color of her skin. "I'll be right back," she tries to say, and walks away with her last ounce of strength, balancing herself like a tightrope walker, struggling to keep anyone from noticing her weakened condition. She makes it through the sliding glass doors separating the pool from the living room and collapses onto a tall armchair a second before the world goes black, her senses disconnected, abandoned to the soft pillow of unconsciousness.

"*How long did she lie there?*"

"*No one knows, because no one noticed, not even Mani. He couldn't see her because she was hidden by the back of the chair; he thought she had gone to take a bath. It must have been only a few minutes. When she came to, she heard the brothers' tense voices floating toward her from the pool. They were still talking, not quite fighting, but almost. She heard enough to know that they were plotting Nando Barragán's assassination, but she didn't want to know the details. She heard the word 'cocaine' several times, and that's how she knew the Monsalves had started a new business. As soon as she could she stood, went into the kitchen, and drank a Coca-Cola, which restored her strength, then she went to her room. When she returned to the pool she was dressed and had regained her natural color.*"

"You should be happy, little queen," Frepe says when he sees her reappear. "Your husband is going to be ten times richer than he is now. A hundred times richer. Maybe one of these days he'll be president of the republic, and you'll be the first lady. Well, that's all, I'll go now. Good-bye, little queen. It was a pleasure. Take care, and the baby too. This is going to get very ugly; don't say I didn't warn you. The stuff with the Barragáns was child's play, just a little family thing. Now the real war is starting, with real enemies. The more money, the more blood, you know? Okay, bye then. Fifty percent, right, Mani?"

"DID MOCHO *Gómez ever collect the land and money that Nando had promised him in exchange for telling him where to find Fernely?*"

"*Mocho Gómez collected double. Nando paid him without ever knowing that Mani was also paying him.*"

"*Mani Monsalve? Why?*"

"*Isn't it obvious? It was Mani who gave Mocho the information about the garage, and gave him money to go, as if it were his own doing, and tell Nando Barragán. He made a bank shot—he managed to get Fernely off his back without pulling the trigger and starting a battle with his brother Frepe, who had handpicked the sick character. Mani had to put up with his infrequent, rhyming sentences, the sound of his dragging flip-flops, and his perpetually teary eyes. But not for long. The 'Adiós, jefe' that Fernely spit at him one day kept ringing in his ears, half jokingly, half threateningly, and he couldn't rest until he found a clean, untraceable way to get rid of the nuisance."*

"So that night by the pool, did Mani give Frepe the go-ahead to assassinate Nando Barragán? Hadn't Mani given up his criminal ways?"

"He wanted to, but the past isn't easy to shed. The harder you push it away, the more it comes back to you, like a faithful dog."

"And his desire to win back Alina? Didn't he want, at any cost, to be good so she would stay with him?"

"I told you, it was his nature. The same thing happened to Mani that happens to a lot of people: he wanted to be good, but he just couldn't do it. Evil and tricky, much more than Frepe, that's how he was. After all, he was the jefe."

SEVERINA IS chopping onions at the kitchen table. Years of practice have taught her right hand to handle the knife at a whistling speed that the eye can't even register, and the fingers of her left hand to withdraw the necessary fraction of an inch at the exact instant that the knife glides along her fingernails and falls on the onions, slicing them mercilessly.

Sitting across from her, Nando watches her work, letting the acrid smell of the onion pull tears from his meek, porcine eyes.

"I saw Soledad Bracho today," he says, and two decades of cruel memories flash before his eyes. "I ran into her in a church."

"What were you doing there?"

"I went in to pray for Adriano, because it's been exactly twenty-one years since I killed him. She was lighting candles for Marco Bracho, who's been dead twenty-two years now."

"Then it wasn't an accident that you saw her. Nothing happens by chance, nothing."

It happened at about noon. The city was nobly enduring a sunny, ninety-degree day, but inside the empty temple, under the old stone arches, it was dark as night and the temperature was hovering around fifty degrees. Milky clouds of incense, cold and supernatural like mist inside a refrigerator, enshrouded the faithful. On his knees, his hands folded in prayer, humble before the Almighty, Nando Barragán, the Terrible, was struggling to remember fragments of the Lord's Prayer when an old woman, dressed in black with a white lily in her hand, approached him, interrupting his praying.

A sickly old woman, with gray hair and weathered skin. She wants money, thought Nando, and he took some coins from his pocket to get rid of her. Cachumbo and Simón Balas, who were watching from behind, came closer, alert, in case the old woman with the lily turned out to be a *sicario*. She proudly pushed away the coins and said, "It's me, Soledad Bracho, Marco's widow."

Nando took off his Ray-Bans and rubbed his eyes, at first incredulous, then stunned by the evidence. He recognized her behind the mask of wrinkles and bitterness.

"What happened to you, Soledad?"

"You can see for yourself. After you killed Adriano, the Monsalves burned my house. I rescued a few things and wandered around, struggling with life. It was very hard, but with the years things got a little better, and now I've reached old age, early but peacefully."

In the half light of the kitchen Nando can see the sparks of anger shining in Severina's eyes. She lays down the knife and says to her oldest son, "Peaceful, Soledad Bracho? Didn't you remind her of the deaths she has caused?"

"It wasn't her fault; it wasn't anybody's. On the first anniversary of Marco Bracho's death, what had to happen happened, and we all got screwed, generation after generation."

"What if something else had happened?"

"Be quiet, Mother. Remember Uncle Ito Monsalve, who started to think about it and ended up plunging a screwdriver in his forehead. Wondering about things like that can make you crazy."

"NO ONE WOULD *ever have found out about Guillermo Willy Quiñones's secret if he hadn't fallen asleep in the Barragáns' house one afternoon.*"

"*What happened?*"

"*It was noon during the middle of the week on a humid, sticky day. He had eaten a lunch of two bowls of a hot, hearty soup, which left him sound asleep in one of the rocking chairs on the corridor of the back patio. A while later he awoke suffocating and couldn't remember what he had dreamed. He had the sensation that someone had erased the blackboard of his memory, where all his dreams had been written in chalk, leaving only a cloudy vagueness. He couldn't figure out what had happened. La Muda had sat down beside him while he slept, and contemplated his dreams, silent and in black and white, like an old movie. She was so horrified by what she saw that her first instinct was to have him killed right there, in his sleep, to send him from his dreams straight to hell, without giving him a chance to repent or beg forgiveness.*"

"*What did she see?*"

"*A betrayal.*"

"And she condemned him to death?"

"No. She thought of something better."

"THE DAY OF *Arcángel Barragán's burial strange and contradictory things happened. Some below ground, others above."*

"Nobody knew what was going on in the cellars of the Barragáns' house during the burial, at the same time they were shoveling dirt onto the child's coffin. Everything was common knowledge in La Esquina de la Candela, but this secret was kept for many years, and even today many people doubt its veracity."

A mournful pealing of bells shrouds the city. Severina marches before the funeral caravan wrapped in a black shawl, and her perpetual mourning, stained with blood for the tenth time, shakes the buildings to their very foundations.

The paid mourners part to make way for the grieving woman as she passes, wailing loudly in the cemetery's burned air.

"Compassion for her pain! They killed her youngest child!"

She advances slowly, lady of pain, orphan of ten children, alongside her youngest child's body. Her face holds a dark expression and her ill-omened lips murmur an evil curse. "My child's blood has been spilled. His death shall be avenged."

The onlookers are subdued and speak in low voices, murmuring in indignation. "His best friend betrayed and killed him." The killer's name passes from mouth to mouth: "Corporal Guillermo Willy Quiñones, may the devil take him."

"How did Quiñones kill him?"

"With the dead boy's own weapon, a Walther P38 passed down with a curse from his ancestors, because it had been used by a war criminal to massacre Jews."

Nothing else is talked about in the city, the whole country. The newspapers cover the bloody details on the front page. Magazines feature essays, interviews, reports. The tabloid headlines ask: "Where is the assassin?" "What happened to Corporal Quiñones?"

No one knows where he's hiding. He fled after the crime. As usual, the authorities have no clues, witnesses, or proof. They don't even show an interest in the case. But everyone knows. It's the same old thing. Quiñones never escaped; he was wiped out by the Barragáns, as revenge.

"What happened to his body? Did it ever show up?"

"They threw it to the dogs, who devoured it. No one should even bother looking for it. It'll never be found. No vestige or memory of him will remain. Maybe a bare bone will remain, on the back patio."

"No one saw La Muda during the burial."

"No one saw her because she didn't go. But what nobody knew, and still very few know, was that Arcángel Barragán, the dead boy, wasn't there either."

"That can't be. We all saw his coffin."

"He wasn't inside. He wasn't even dead. Severina had buried an empty coffin."

"So everything was staged?"

"Yes."

"Then where was Arcángel?"

"Hidden somewhere in the cellars with La Muda. And with his friend Guillermo Willy, who was also alive."

The afternoon that Guillermo Willy fell asleep in the Barragáns' house, La Muda, who observed his disloyal dreams, grabbed him by the arm, digging in her nails until she drew blood. She dragged him to the back of the house and locked him in the tool room with her and smacked his face, again and again. He didn't dare defend himself; then he collapsed, crying like a child, and told everything.

"What did he tell her?"

He confessed that the Monsalves had given him money to win Arcángel's friendship and confidence and then kill him. He also confessed that he had had several opportunities.

"But I didn't want to, because Arcángel had really become my friend, almost like a brother."

The Monsalves became alarmed because so much time had passed and he hadn't complied with their orders, so they began threatening him. They had given him a week. The week had passed.

"Now Frepe Monsalve doesn't trust me. My days are numbered," Corporal Guillermo Willy told La Muda, who looked deeply into his thoughts and scrutinized his feelings, until she knew for certain that he was telling the truth.

That's when she came up with a plan and started it in action. She brought Arcángel and, using hand signals, made Guillermo Willy tell his story again. She made Severina, La Mona, and Ana Santana her only accomplices under a sacred pledge of eternal silence, and, writing everything on paper, she dreamed up the assassination, hid the two boys in the cellars, spread the word of the deaths, and organized the fictitious funeral.

"Did they tell Nando the truth?"

"They told him that Arcángel's death was a lie, to prevent his heart from breaking in two. But they didn't tell him about the escape, or where the two boys were hidden. They were afraid that Nando would kill the corporal in his anger, because he didn't know how to forgive traitors, even ones who had repented."

La Muda digs up her savings, carefully hoarded during the family's better days, and gives the money to Arcángel. It is an amount large enough for them to travel far away and live without worry anywhere they choose. She packs suitcases of clothing and outfits a jeep with a couple of weapons, extra gasoline, bottles of water, and a basket of food.

When the others depart for the cemetery, leaving the house and the whole block deserted, and while the novelty of the crime and the commotion of the burial claim the neighborhood's full attention, La Muda guides her nephew and his friend through the dark, secret passages of the cellars, taking them, underground, outside the confines of the compound. Following the path of the sewers, they flee through the intestines of the city.

They are buried alive in the underworld of underground caves and sewers like zombies behind a glowing lantern. Hot, earthy gases envelop them, and invisible bats' wings brush their faces as the creatures fly past. Above, they hear a river of footsteps and somber prayers running parallel with their path. Arcángel, perplexed, recognizes the sounds of his own funeral.

On tiptoe, the boy follows his aunt. Silently and docilely he obeys, even though he knows that the tunnel they are following, which is time itself, distances him step by step from the past shared with her. His heart is galloping wildly, unbridled, at two opposite speeds. With each contraction his heart shrinks in agony at the thought of leaving her; then, during the dilation, his emotions are expanded with excitement about his new freedom, terrified and fascinated at the same time about the world he is about to enter.

"They arrived at the end of the subterranean labyrinth at the same instant that shovelfuls of earth fell onto Arcángel's coffin."

Before them is a ladder with thirteen steps climbing toward a door, at the foot of which is a white line of daylight that shines in their faces. With rapid gestures, without fuss or delay, La Muda makes sure that Arcángel still has the cross of Caravaca around his neck and gives him the keys to the jeep parked outside the door. She opens the heavy locks, pulls back the bar from across the door, removes the chains, and pushes the heavy portal, which creaks and finally opens. A rectangle of light suddenly falls on them, bathing their entire bodies, blinding them for an instant, causing them to lose a few seconds while their eyes adjust.

Arcángel embraces La Muda. He says nothing; she can feel the pair of bongo drums beating inside his chest. Then she says, effortlessly and clearly, the only words she's ever spoken in her life.

"Go far away, and forget us."

The two boys run down the dirt road toward the jeep, and La Muda stays behind, leaning against the door frame. As she listens to the last echoes of the funeral procession fading in the distance, she puts her hands in the pockets of her black skirt and watches dry-eyed as her adored nephew leaves her forever. In the gold light she sees her glorious Arcángel freshly arisen from his false death.

8

ONCE AGAIN Nando Barragán's world is green and hallucinating. Mint green, optical green, surgeon's-scrub-suit green. Painful surges of lucidity alternated with numb waves of lethargy stir the murky lake in his head. The anesthesia is wearing off, leaving him alone with a burning sensation in his chest.

"Why was he back in the hospital? Did they wound him again?"

"No. Well, yes and no. He ended up in the hospital as a result of a chain of unforeseen events that was unleashed at nine o'clock in the morning on an ordinary day."

At nine sharp the national army, for the first time ever, interfered in Nando Barragán's affairs and broke into his house. They arrived in eight jeeps, three motorcycles, and a tank. There were sixty-three soldiers under the command of a Colonel Pinilla and they searched everywhere for weapons, explosives, drugs, fingerprints, suspicious books, foreign money, subversive pamphlets, maps of Cuba, anything that might implicate Nando Barragán.

"They thought they had searched everywhere, but they were wrong. The weapons had been stashed in the cellars where they would never be found. But it didn't matter. They detained Nando anyway."

"Why, if they didn't find anything?"

"*They said they had found five bullets beneath his bed, so they handcuffed him and took him away. Pajarito Pum Pum, Tijeras, and the others couldn't do anything. There was no time. They had never confronted a platoon of men before, or even a tank, for that matter. Even Nando didn't protest, so great was his surprise. He would have expected disloyalty from anyone except the authorities. They had never interfered before.*"

"So for five bullets they took him prisoner?"

"*That's right. They locked him in a cell in a state of total confusion that preceded the explosion of his powerful anger, like a recently captured tiger drugged in the jungle and taken to a zoo. That was his condition when he received a visit from Méndez, his lawyer, who arrived pale and unkempt, a far cry from his usual perfect appearance. His agitated preoccupation was so evident that Nando noticed it immediately.*"

"What's going on?" he asked the lawyer.

"The Monsalves bribed Pinilla, the colonel who brought you in. They've locked you up here so they can kill you."

"*They were going to finish Nando off right there, in the cell?*"

"*That was the plan. But Méndez had moved quickly and had a medical certificate, with all the necessary seals and signatures, according to which Nando urgently had to be transferred to a hospital.*"

"We're getting out of here," he said, "because they're going to operate on you."

"They're going to operate on me? Are you going to tell me why?"

Méndez is already pulling him by the arm toward the door when he answers, "Whatever, it's not important, but it has to be now."

"*What did they operate on?*"

"*They transferred Nando to a hospital and a friend who was a surgeon agreed to diagnose a fake cardiac problem. He put Nando under anesthesia, opened his chest along an old scar, and then reclosed the wound without having touched anything inside.*"

In the green hospital room Nando Barragán comes back into reality, like an astronaut returning from outer space. His first contact with earth is the pain in his chest; his second, with his eyes still closed, is the presence of a woman.

"Milena, is that you?" he asks, still doped up on Pentothal.

"No. It's Ana Santana."

"Come closer, don't leave me. Give me some water, Ana. The last time I came out of anesthesia Milena was at my side. She was at my side when Mani Monsalve got me in the knee. I didn't feel any pain, but I knew it was badly damaged. I fell down, in a pool of my own blood, unable to defend myself. Then Milena lifted me up, and helped me stand so I could shoot, protecting my body with hers while she supported me. She's a strong woman. It wasn't the only time she risked her life for me."

"So that's why you love her."

"Come here, Ana. Come closer."

Ana Santana takes a step closer and stands next to the bed.

"Take off your clothes," Nando says, and a look of complete surprise covers her face.

"I told you to take off your clothes."

Ana Santana looks around to make sure there are no witnesses. There are no doctors or nurses in sight and the bodyguards are on the other side of the door. Ana is alone with her husband in the recovery room. She meekly begins to obey. She unfastens her blouse, button by button, indecisively. She closes her eyes and holds her breath, as if preparing to receive an injection. Impulsively, she takes it off all at once and stands there in her bra, rigid and heroic, like Joan of Arc being burned at the stake.

"Naked," says Nando.

The bra is so wide and reinforced that it looks bulletproof; its elastic straps are so tight that it cuts into her chaste, white skin. Her hands move to her back and work blindly at the evasive fastenings until they are released. The brassiere springs away to reveal Ana's breasts, bathed in green light among the antiquated cream-colored surgical apparatus. Nando looks at her for a moment, then he tells her to take off the rest of her clothes and get into the bed with him.

"*Two nurses passing by saw them, and went to tell the others. They said Ana Santana was completely naked, straddling Nando, making love to him.*"

"*How could he, with the fresh wound on his chest?*"

"*He couldn't. He was weak and in pain, and his thing didn't respond. It wouldn't stand up, and at that moment the prophecy was fulfilled.*"

"*What prophecy?*"

"*Roberta Caracola's first prophecy.*"

As Ana Santana leaves the recovery room, straightening her blouse, her hair mussed and her cheeks flushed, she passes Méndez, the lawyer, who is going in to see Nando with Pajarito Pum Pum, Simón Balas, and Cachumbo. Méndez tells him that a few minutes after they left the prison, a bomb exploded in the corridor, obliterating the eleven inmates in the neighboring cells. Pajarito Pum Pum and the others were witnesses to the explosion, which is already being reported on the radio.

"You saved my life," says the fake patient to his lawyer. "How did you know they were going to kill me?"

"From Alina Jericó."

"Another favor I owe you. Are you going to let me repay you this time?"

"Yes, Nando. This time I will."

"ISN'T IT *curious how coincidences happen? At the same time Nando was in the hospital in the city, the most prestigious plastic surgeon in the port was performing surgery on Mani to get rid of the scar on his face.*"

"*Yes. But look at the difference. On Nando they were opening a new wound, while on Mani they were erasing one forever.*"

"*Did anyone visit Nando during his recovery?*"

"*Yes. Ana Santana went to the hospital every day. She arrived each dawn bringing Pielroja cigarettes and home-cooked beans. He treated her sweetly, like never before, but he called her Milena, not Ana. The confusion with the names became permanent, to the point that Nando Barragán completely forgot his wife's real name.*"

"*Didn't Ana complain?*"

"*No. She calmly assumed her new name and identity, and gratefully accepted the tenderness she had long ago stopped hoping for. One day she even dared to complain to him about his mother. She told him that Severina had sold their bed, the one Narciso had given them as a wedding gift, to a luxury hotel that bought it to promote its bridal suite for honeymooners.*

"*'It doesn't matter,' said Nando. 'It's better this way. It was ridiculous anyway.'*

"*'But what am I going to sleep on now?' Ana protested.*

"*'You'll sleep with me, Milena, in the hammock.'*"

THE GENERAL with the imposing mustache and the moldy stains on his skin looks down from the canvas as Mani Monsalve converses confidentially with Tin Puyúa in front of the cold fireplace in the grand salon of his house.

"*Mani, whose scar was now gone, had begun to look a little like the green general in the portrait. At least that was the story that Melba Foucon proudly spread, attributing the similarity to her handiwork.*"

But today Mani's face is dark with an almost animal-like expression that would have scared Señorita Foucon. Tin Puyúa, on the other hand, is thrilled, on high voltage, feeling like his old self for the first time in months. Overnight he has reassumed the place he had lost in his boss's heart. They are whispering to each other, even though they are the only ones in the room, and sit so close that their arms are touching.

"Didn't Mani hate physical contact with other people?"

"Yes, but that day he needed to feel Tin's support."

There is an almost filial intimacy uniting the two men, like in the old, dangerous days. Once again they see and smell things identically, say the same words. They are blood brothers, partners to the end through good and, more important, through bad times.

"What brought them back together like that?"

"A piece of information that someone had given them."

They go over the latest events, they ponder the information and always arrive at the only possible conclusion, which makes Mani see stars in front of his eyes. Alina Jericó told Nando Barragán that they were going to kill him. She's the only one who could have done it. She must have heard when Frepe was planning his death by the pool at La Virgen del Viento. She told a little bird, who took flight and saved him. Méndez must have told him in jail, then arranged a special permit and taken him to the hospital just before the explosion. The only reasonable explanation is that Méndez found out from Alina, though the thought of betrayal by his own wife is the sharpest pain that Mani Monsalve has ever known in his rough life.

Tin, however, is licking his lips, savoring the satisfaction of seeing his wildest dreams coming true. He was always jealous of Alina and could never hide his hatred of her; the only reason he doesn't point out Mani's realization with an "I told you so" is that he doesn't want to throw salt on the wound. It's enough to know that he has recaptured his position as the only person close to Mani and has gotten rid of the competition without having to lift a finger.

"Alina had committed high treason by giving key information to the Barragáns, but that wasn't all, because she was a step away from a second betrayal, much worse than the first."

"What was that?"

"A policeman had alerted Mani Monsalve about Avianca flight 716, leaving at two-fifteen in the morning for Mexico City. Alina Jericó and Méndez would be traveling together on that flight."

Mani Monsalve listens in silence to the information. He throws the poisonous bone into a pot in his soul and cooks it over a low flame into a thick stew of jealousy, rage, and pain, seasoned with the salt of dementia, the sour drops of disgust, and the bittersweet taste of the leaves of hope. Tin Puyúa lowers the flame, stirs the concoction, and treats himself to a spicy, delicious whiff of revenge. Then he serves it in two deep bowls and sits with Mani to eat it with a spoon, still steaming, letting it burn his intestines.

"That guy is trying to take my wife and child," says Mani, drunk from the fermented soup, with the voice of a caveman challenging the hostile universe in a desperate attempt to preserve his race.

Alina is a sly traitor, Tin reminds him, knowing that Mani can no longer deny it. He wants to prevent at any cost his master's forgiving the sinner and trying to bring her back. He dares to go a step further. "The punishment should be for all three," he declares.

"No, not the child," brays the father-to-be. "He is innocent. I'm warning you. Whatever happens, the child must not be harmed."

They agree to keep the matter strictly between the two of them, not to tell the rest of the family, and to act on their own, with no plan other than last-minute inspiration and instinct.

Throwing back a lock of loose hair and trembling with excitement, Tin goes down to the garage to prepare the jeep and the weapons. Mani goes up to his bedroom, undresses and gets into the shower. Luxuriating under the stream of water, he lets it calm the violent burning that threatens to burst his heart and skull like a volcanic eruption. He tells himself that the fever's gone. Now he must control the spewing lava. Whatever happens now must be carefully and rationally thought out. He feels the steam penetrating his

body and dividing it in two. One Mani, burning with pain, disinte-
grates and runs down the drain, while the other Mani, overcome
with desire for revenge and excited by the prospect of adventure, is
revitalized and reborn. This latter Mani gives himself over to the
strength of the water, absorbing the energy he needs for the task
ahead, staying there, in no hurry, not thinking about time, for as
long as his body and soul require.

He steps out of the shower and goes into the bedroom with the
graceful stride of a young cat on the prowl. He rejects the idea of
dressing in the elegant, discreet clothing of a social climber, as
advised by Miss Foucon. Likewise, he rejects the bright, ostentatious
colors he wore when he first started separating himself from his past.

From the bottom drawer, where he hid them from his image
consultant, he pulls out his old blue jeans, soft and flexible as a second skin, his gangster's sneakers, and his oversized faded cotton
shirt, missing buttons and frayed from years of washing. He dresses
ritualistically, caressing each item of clothing, like a warrior unpack-
ing the armor he has worn in a hundred battles.

"He became his old self again."

"Yes, but no. To be the same as before he needed one little detail,
the scar. He doesn't have it anymore. He can never be the same as
before."

Mani Monsalve grabs a revolver, goes down to the garage, and
jumps into the jeep next to Tin Puyúa, who is already at the wheel,
ready and waiting.

"To the airport, brother," he orders, slapping him on the back
conspiratorially.

MÉNDEZ, THE lawyer, counts eleven and can't believe it. He
counts again. Yes, there are eleven suitcases piled on the floor of
Alina Jericó's living room floor.

"They're my things, Yela's, and the baby's," explains Alina innocently. "We've been packing all day."

"Yela too?" he asks, his voice frozen with surprise.

"Of course. I can't go without her."

"But she can't go, Alina. I didn't get her a ticket."

"We'll buy it at the airport."

"You don't understand. What if there are no seats left?"

"The only thing I know is that I'm not going without Yela."

"What about a passport?"

"She has one from when she went to Ecuador to visit her brother who's dead now."

Méndez had twenty-seven hours, not a minute more, to prepare for the flight to Mexico. Passports, tickets, dollars, work visa, letters of recommendation for his new job, last-minute preparations, and a thousand other things. He acted with the utmost discretion so as not to draw suspicion. His plan is to leave the port secretly, discreetly, without being noticed. He is fully aware that if Mani Monsalve finds out he will kill them in the act, and he told this to Alina, though not in those exact words; he didn't want her to get any more upset than she already was.

And now it turns out that he has to carry out this high-risk, clandestine operation not only with an eight-months-pregnant woman, but also with a heart attack–prone old woman and eleven suitcases. He doesn't say a word though, because he has detected that the unpreoccupied, almost frivolous manner in which Alina speaks and acts is a thin veil masking her profound inner turbulence. He sees the coat of polish she uses to cover the fathomless desolation caused by making a decision with her mind that goes against the inclinations of her heart.

Since it is dangerous to use Alina's tapped telephone, Méndez runs to the corner to a pay phone and makes a call to try to secure a seat on the airplane for Yela. They tell him that there's no problem. Fortunately, the plane is nearly empty.

He goes back to the apartment. It's eleven o'clock at night. They have to be at the airport no later than 12:45, and it takes a half hour to get there, but Alina is still barefoot, with curlers in her hair, packing a set of dishes. She lovingly wraps each plate in newsprint before placing it in the cardboard box. At this rate, the lawyer thinks, she'll never finish.

"Alina, I'm sorry, but we don't have time."

"Help me, Mr. Méndez, and you'll see how quickly we'll finish. If I leave my things spread all over the place, when I get back they'll be ruined."

"It may be many years before you can come back."

"All the more reason to leave them well stored."

Méndez doesn't want to pressure her. He's not going to add a single twist of additional tension to her spirit, which is already taut as a guitar string. He knows that one wrong word could explode the charge of bitterness and struggle that she must be feeling to have to bury a large portion of her life, undesirable as it may be, still rabidly alive.

He kneels next to Alina and begins packing dishes with slow, deliberate motions, as if he has never done anything so important or at a more appropriate time. He knows that his only chance with her depends for now on a long and humbling chain of acts like this, which little by little will thaw out the stiff, frozen intuition of a woman who is too young to have already convinced herself that it's too late to start over.

Sweating, laden with bags and suitcases up to his ears, the lawyer takes all the luggage down in the elevator and packs it in the cars waiting in the garage. When he returns, Alina is wrapping the last coffee cups. Although the recent difficulties have made her lose weight and the eight-month pregnancy looks more like six, Méndez fears that there may be problems getting her on the plane; he has heard that airlines often refuse to transport women who are too close to giving birth.

"We have to disguise your stomach," he suggests.

"How?"

Méndez has already foreseen this and has a very large old overcoat from his days as a student in Europe. Alina is tall and the sleeves can be rolled up. She starts to protest that she'll die of heat; it's ridiculous; she doesn't like the color; but she finally agrees. It is getting dangerously late. Alina has already put on her shoes and brushed her hair. Everything seems ready and the lawyer opens the door of the apartment to leave, but she stops him. Before they leave she has to speak with him in private.

"They had already spoken when things had gotten complicated and they'd agreed that the only way to survive was to escape. Emboldened by the urgency of the situation, the lawyer had confessed his deep love for Alina, and she had listened to him with a gray, serene look that he took to mean that she had known all along. Then he invited her to live with him in Mexico, and she accepted."

Yela, wearing a hat, is moving about the living room with a pitcher of water, watering the plants for the last time, so they go into the bedroom and close the door.

"I want it to be clear, Mr. Méndez, that I am going to Mexico with you because I think very highly of you and because my child's life is at stake, but I am still in love with Mani Monsalve."

"Don't worry. I am going to love your child so much that you will have no choice but to fall in love with me."

At one o'clock in the morning Méndez makes his grand entrance at the airport with the suitcases (twelve, counting his own), an old woman in a hat, and a pregnant woman in an old overcoat. A few people are wandering around the large space, looking in store windows at things they'll never buy, moving slowly, as if waiting for indefinitely delayed flights. Alina notices the desolation in the cold glare falling from the fluorescent lights and the smell of yesterday's cigarette butts emanating from the scattered ashtrays, and suddenly realizes that this is the time when people who are not going to return travel, people who have no one to see them off.

Méndez takes care of business at the Avianca counter. He hands over the tickets and passports, then pays the airport tax and a huge sum for excess baggage, finishing each step with a sigh of relief, as if it were the final obstacle, the mortal trap that was about to make them miss the flight. They proceed immediately to the gate, an isolated, controlled area, where the lawyer thinks there is less chance of danger.

The air is too quiet; the few sounds heard are dull and distant. A few other people sit resignedly in chairs, clinging to their suitcases as if the place were crawling with thieves, disinterestedly working crossword puzzles and looking very much as if they have nowhere to live. Alina is pale, and tries to calm herself by looking at the perfumes in the duty-free shops. The lawyer watches her. Her paleness and the overcoat seem to enclose her in another place, in another time, like an actress in a forgotten movie.

"*I don't understand how Méndez and Alina got all the way to the gate alive.*"

"*It was by chance. Méndez had planned all sorts of security measures, but they all failed at the last minute. In order for Alina to leave her apartment with her luggage without raising suspicion they had to spread the word that she was moving in with one of her sisters. In the end, the sister and her husband hadn't shown up as they had agreed, because they were afraid. For the trip to the airport, Méndez had arranged with a friend in the government for a bulletproof car, in case of attack along the way. But the car was so heavy that it dragged on inclines and the driver had to back up and take a longer route in order to use flatter streets. But that wasn't all. Méndez had arranged for a security agent to meet them at the airport to help them get checked in and get to the gate as quickly as possible. The man was there; he helped them and then disappeared. What Méndez didn't know was that he was the one who had turned them in to Mani Monsalve. So the fact that they were still alive was due to Mani's decision to act personally and keep his men out of it. So we're back to the same old thing. They were alive by mere chance. It was simply that their time hadn't arrived, and no one dies a minute before, or a minute after, his time."*

A gentle breeze brushes Méndez's neck, heightening his nervousness. At first he felt everything was fine, but now he has the sensation that the enemy is behind him. He's felt this way before. It is an infallible alarm that more than once has saved his life; the familiar dull buzzing in his ears has started.

He tries to pressure the flight attendants to let them get on the plane before the others, but they refuse. "The cleaning crew is still on the aircraft," they say. "Don't worry, we're almost ready to board," they add, but Méndez only hears the alarm in his head, its volume now almost deafening. Suddenly, he grabs Alina and Yela by the arms, although they protest loudly that they have to get their carry-on bags, and makes them run, pushing them toward the passageway leading onto the airplane, despite the airline personnel trying to block their way.

The passageway is a long, dark worm, buffeted by disquieting blasts of cold air. The three run holding arms like an absurd insect with six legs clumsily fleeing a fire. The women are exhausted from the exertion, making them heavier and harder for Méndez to shepherd along. He looks ahead toward the lighted doorway waiting for them at the end of the passageway — the fifty steps that define the difference between before and after — and hopes desperately for some benevolent force to propel them toward the end of the tunnel. He prays for a miracle that will spit them onto the other side of the light.

"Suddenly, out of nowhere, Mani Monsalve and Tin Puyúa

*appear, silent and gleaming, and aim their guns at them from behind.
Yela trips and falls, pulling down Alina and Méndez, who become
entangled in a web of legs and never see how Mani Monsalve hesitates a second before shooting, then stands in front of Tin to prevent
him from shooting while he tries to find a better angle on Méndez so
he won't injure Alina."*

*"For Mani, Méndez wasn't an easy target, because he was escap-
ing with two hostages, his wife and his child."*

*"The scene froze for a fraction of a second, the pursued lying in
a knot on the floor, looking death in the face, and the pursuers losing
their only shot, allowing Pajarito Pum Pum, Tijeras, Simón Balas,
and Cachumbo to empty their pistols.*

"Where did Simón Balas and Nando's other gunmen come from?"

*"They had been there from the beginning on their boss's orders.
Nando was still in the hospital, but he had sent them. They had
escorted Méndez and Alina from the apartment to the airport and covered their backs once they were inside the airport."*

"Why did they do that?"

*"When Méndez took Nando out of jail and saved his life, Nando
offered to repay the favor and Méndez, who had thought about it for
a long time, asked him for the favor of helping him escape the country with Alina Jericó and Mani's unborn child."*

"Mani ended up giving his life to defend Alina and her child's."

"Yes, I guess it was something like that."

*"THE NIGHT that Mani Monsalve died on the black vinyl floor of a
jetway in the international wing of the airport, his son Enrique was
born during Avianca flight 716 on its way to Mexico City. The rattled
flight attendants who helped Alina Jericó with the premature birth
washed the baby, wrapped him in a blanket, and gave him to his
mother, who was resting from the commotion and exertion, looking out
the window at a flock of pink clouds grazing on the infinite plains of*

the sunrise. When they handed her the baby, Alina was surprised to see that, by some strange genetic whim, his skin wasn't green like the Monsalves', but yellow, like that of his cousins, the Barragáns."

"Enrique? The child was named Enrique?"

"Enrique Méndez, the name his natural father had chosen and his adoptive father's last name."

"AT ABOUT *three in the afternoon on a day during Carnaval, everyone in La Esquina de la Candela was asking the same thing: 'What is Nando Barragán doing, sitting alone at his front door?'"*

"For several weeks, or maybe months, he had been free, but we never heard anything about him. A period of total violence had arrived and our lives were being destroyed by death and killing. But the Barragáns were no longer the epicenter, nor the Monsalves. Overnight, like mushrooms after rain, all over the country there was a proliferation of other protagonists who were more spectacular, ferocious, and powerful. So, one day the Barragáns and Monsalves were reduced to local folklore. We started seeing them as the precursor to the real story of our violence. They had been only the beginning of the end. When Nando sat that afternoon in his doorway, he was a mere shadow of his former self. Surely even he must have noticed, because according to those who saw him, he was behaving strangely, more like a shadow than a man."

"That day, the third and last of Carnaval, Nando Barragán had hallucinated from the moment he woke up. When they noticed he didn't want to get up, the women took him coffee and strips of fried plantain. While he ate breakfast he kept thinking the absurd thought that he would like to die in peace."

"I don't know of anyone who has died of old age in his bed," he says to Ana Santana when she comes into the room to remove the tray.

It seems to Ana an odd longing in these times when death is more serpentine and showy than life, when instead of saying "So-and-so died," people say "He was killed." But she doesn't say anything. She only puts a hand on his forehead to see if he has a fever and asks if he wants more coffee.

"That morning they noticed him wandering around the house, hypnotized by the shrill music in the streets and lethargic from the smell of garbage that permeates the air during Carnaval."

At eleven he sits on the patio to drink white rum with lemon and salt. When they see that he's drunk the whole bottle, the women calm down. "He's returned to normal," they say to one another. But it isn't that simple, because the rum doesn't produce the normal reaction, the awakening of a brute force inside him that drives him into the street looking for victims, but rather it submerges him in a sleepy, melancholy mood, characteristic of the people from the desert, which is very serious when it reaches an advanced stage, when it traps someone for good and hangs on to the end.

He starts a second bottle around three in the afternoon as he sits in the doorway of his house, watching the seminaked bodies of the dancers and the beauty queens. They are powdered from head to toe with a mixture of ground coal and lard that makes them glisten pungently in the hot sun, long trails of sweat streaming down their bodies.

"Weren't the bodyguards watching to keep the filth from passing in front of his house?"

"Nobody cared anymore. Cachumbo, Simón Balas, and the others forgot about the war for a while and took advantage of the moment to enjoy themselves among the crowds, with their identities camouflaged beneath their costumes of hooded penitents. Even Nando didn't seem worried about anything. With Mani Monsalve's death, the war had ended for him, and probably life too, for that matter, because hatred had always been his greatest love."

"He never enjoyed his victory?"

"No. The final triumph over his eternal enemy left Nando with nothing more than the unpleasant taste of salt."

With childish glee Nando listens to the music, to the crazy sound of flutes and maracas. Dizzy from the alcohol, he watches, as if in a dream, while the euphoric fauna passes, rabbit costumes and alligator men, throwing flour and dancing as if possessed, and there, alone on a stone step, with his guard down and suddenly aged, he commits a huge extravagance; he lets an almost imperceptible sigh of happiness escape.

The parade keeps going, not waiting for anyone who lags behind. Nando is anchored to his step, as if he senses the arrival of a guest of honor.

A flash of light captures his attention. It comes from a golden carriage, with closed curtains concealing the passenger. It is carried on the shoulders of two pairs of lesser devils, and is followed by a band of poor musicians, covered in flour from the craziness that has exploded all over the city. As it passes in front of the Barragáns' house, the fringed curtains part, and Nando sees the Pepsodent smile of a beauty queen, seated on her throne and wearing a crown bigger than Queen Elizabeth's. She leans toward him exquisitely, batting her false eyelashes and tossing her stiffly lacquered ringlets. Nando closes his eyes and waits for the golden vision to give him a kiss, or to whisper coquettishly, but the tricky little vixen takes a handful of flour and throws it in his face. He doesn't move. He docilely receives the powder with the idiotic and grateful expression of an old drunk, calmed suddenly by senility.

"So he just sat there, with the white stuff on his face?"

"He sat there, all floured up, like a sugar cookie, because he no longer had the brains to remember the prophecy."

"He didn't remember Roberta Caracola's warning?"

"No. He couldn't think. He was beyond remembering."

The noisy, colorful Carnaval parade moves on toward the center of the city and leaves the barrio buried in a jumble of paper and trash. A dwarf Humpty-Dumpty, straggling behind his fellow revelers and weighed down by his costume, sits beside Nando and asks for a drink from his bottle. His foul breath hits Nando like escaping gas, and when he looks through the holes in the dwarf's mask he receives the dazed, bilious glare of a man crazy from beer and heat.

The dwarf zigzags off down the street, and Nando becomes absorbed in the trampled confetti and streamers, his head a whirlwind of disjointed, colorless thoughts.

Down the street dances Death, alone. It's not an impressive Death, with a powerful presence and luxurious costume, but a poorly improvised, skinny skeleton, with a bunch of sticks for ribs, a sheet for a cape, and a large animal bone in its hand. The neighbors hide in their houses so it will go on its way, peeking out from their half-open windows and commenting that they've never seen such an insignificant and grotesque Death, cursed, treacherous, and without any style, too much like the real thing. Death takes over the deserted street, swinging its oversized arms, stirring the air weakly, without rhyme or reason.

"Did it find Nando, crouched on his step?"

"No, it didn't see him, or it pretended not to see him, and began to whistle a strange, tuneless song. Nando, however, looked Death right in the face, having seen it before. He had run into Death so many times that he could immediately distinguish the real from imitations. This one isn't worth my time, he thought, and let it pass."

The sound of old African drumbeats calling slaves to rebellion vibrates up out of the earth, while above the late afternoon sky is painted with brilliant red and yellow rays, scandalously bright and ostentatious. Nando Barragán has unbuttoned his white guayabera shirt and just sits there on the step, revealing his chest, indifferent to the spectacular sky, removed from himself, his legs numb, wasted on alcohol. Night falls, sheltering and befriending him, and throws a couple of violet shadows across his shoulders. Nando wraps himself in them and becomes one with the darkness, a quiet hulk, invisible, with no name or personality.

"So Nando was invisible when the treacherous band of Marimondas came down his street?"

At first sight the blackness is complete. Looking closer, his white face, like a fresh round cheese, can be distinguished, innocent and absurd beneath the flour, contemplating happy dreams that aren't his and puzzled by the uncertain, barely comprehensible message that his inebriated heart is trying to send him, the disquieting suggestion that his life could have been better.

"Weren't the embers from his cigarette visible?"

"Yes, they were. In the darkness, the red, betraying tip of his cigarette glowed intensely, like a tiny neon sign blinking on and off, saying, 'Here I am, here I am.' "

"What time did the Marimondas pass Nando's house?"

"It was very late, when the rest of the revelers were far away and the Carnaval was celebrating its last cumbias of the final night of celebration. Everything was strange about those Marimondas, despite the fact that their costumes were the ones traditionally worn, the masks of male monkeys, the disguised bodies of women. But they weren't dancing or having fun. It was obvious that they were in a hurry. The only one who didn't see anything out of the ordinary was Nando himself; he didn't feel anything when they surrounded him and stabbed him, maybe because he was already dead when they killed him."

"What do you mean?"

"According to the doctor who performed the autopsy, Nando Barragán had been dead since early that morning."

"So the rough sadness they saw drawn on his face all day was really death?"

"It was death, and no one had been able to recognize it. What happened later, during the night, was terrible and profane. The false

Marimondas weren't happy with just killing him; they dragged his body through the streets of the barrio to teach a lesson and celebrate Nando's death. Everyone ran to see the body. They touched it, tearing the clothing off, and then they recognized him. There was no doubt, it was definitely him, and the realization of his death was heavy and naked like the body itself."

"Didn't anyone have compassion for the dead man?"

"No one took his side, or even felt sorry for him. If anyone felt badly for him he just kept quiet so as not to further upset the angry group of neighbors, who were finally able to take their revenge. A collective vengeance had unconsciously built up over the many nights we had to stay hidden in our houses, behind locks and bolts, our children awake and terrified, while outside in the street the Barragáns went crazy, shooting all over the place. That's why his death was a sort of vengeance, the fulfillment of the old law of an eye for an eye. The fear we had for him was reversed and transformed into aggression in a proportional quantity. The most downtrodden before were the most vengeful now. We wanted to remove a hair from his head for each time he had made us afraid, a tooth for each night of anguish, a finger for each death, his eyes for all the blood he spilled, his head for the loss of peace, his intestines for the shame he had made us swallow. We wanted to take away the life that he no longer had in exchange for the screwed-up future that was upon us. We cursed him forever, because he had affixed the stamp of death on our faces."

"There really was no one who pitied him?"

"Just the opposite; everyone took advantage of the situation. A man dressed up like Mandrake the Magician saw the cross of Caravaca, tore it off the body, and made off with his prize. The gold Rolex with its forty-two diamonds was saved, more or less, because the Barragáns had sold it while Nando was being operated on in the hospital. The watch's new owner turned out to be none other than Elías

Manso, the same man who during the wedding was ready to eat his own shit to own it."

"How could Manso have bought it if he was such a poor man?"

"He wasn't poor anymore. He had become a millionaire through illegal businesses."

Seeing the old tyrant fallen prompts much merriment and unleashes anew the excitement of the Carnaval. The Marimondas, savage and triumphant, drag the naked body around like a hunting trophy. When they get tired of boasting, they take his last possession, the black Ray-Bans, throw them in a corner, and disappear in the crowd, unmolested, with their monkey masks, fake breasts, and ridiculous hyena laughter. "There go the Monsalves!" yells everyone, pointing at them and letting them go.

"How did you know who they were?"

"We never saw their faces, but we were sure it was them. Them or their sicarios. It was all the same."

The Marimondas leave and the crowd takes possession of the body, jiggling it like a rag doll and dancing behind it, in an orgy of horror and happiness, the most animated and atrocious ever seen in the city. They pile the body in a red cart pulled by a burro wearing a sailor's hat and pose him beneath an advertisement with the slogan "You die, you got screwed." The mob powders him with flour until he's completely white, a gigantic snowman in the tropical heat. A man dressed as Tarzan paints his nose black with a marker. "You died, Nando!" they shout, and all around the body, vibrant with life, Carnaval goes on.

"When did they tell Bacán?"

On the sidewalk in front of his house, Bacán is sitting in his wicker rocker, playing dominoes with his friends. Behind him on the stone wall, seven bullet marks give silent, anonymous testimony to the seven frustrated attempts that someone made on his life.

The swallows of blindness fly through the cloudy sky of his eyes, while his seeing fingers read the recessed white dots on the black dominoes spread across the table in intricate railway networks. He's focused on the game, quieter than in mass, waiting for the next move. The old man is not bothered by the distant roaring Carnaval festivities, as on other, darker, nights he wasn't bothered by the sounds of machine guns or the squealing of tires.

In the midst of the commotion, confusion, and shouting, a group of black kids approaches Bacán with the news. "They killed Nando Barragán and they're dragging him naked through the streets."

Bacán doesn't say anything. He stands up solemnly, stretching to his full height, puts on an elegant straw hat, and takes his oak walking stick, which he inherited from his father, who also grew blind in his old age. He grabs his wife's arm and feels his way along the street, toward the direction of the sea of emboldened voices. He moves slowly and with dignity toward the fracas. He holds his head tilted slightly back, with his bluish-white eyes clamped on a universe of stars that he can't see.

On the corner of Twenty-sixth Street and Fourth Avenue two groups meet, one small and the other quite sizable. On one side of the street is Bacán, his wife, and his small bunch of friends; on the other side is Nando Barragán surrounded by a hostile crowd armed with sticks and torches. Fifty feet apart, they stop to size each other up. A gentle rain has timidly begun to fall and it stirs up the sweet smell of damp wool and wets the last Carnaval streamers.

Bacán steps forward, alone, refusing the hand his wife holds out to him. Waving his stick, the blind man approaches the crowd and opens a path among the masked revelers, who step aside docilely. Alligators, wild Indians, lion tamers, and devils all take a step back, respectful of the old blind man and frozen under the slow rain extinguishing their torches and pacifying their spirits. A heavy silence falls, during which only Bacán's slow, saintly steps can be heard.

His oak stick strikes a lump and he knows he has found Nando Barragán's body lying on the ground, tattered and naked. All the world's loneliness and fatigue seem to emanate from the corpse. It lies there broken and conquered at his feet, a huge mess of blood and flour. The battered and bruised head seems to beg for a moment of peace to balance its impossible accounts with the world beyond.

Bacán's blind eyes gaze down on the dead man at the same instant that a brilliant flash crosses the night sky, fragmenting the night air with its luminous rays, and hits the ground with a powerful force. As if the bolt of lightning were a faucet being opened, the sky releases a torrent of water on the assembled masses, who stampede in all directions, taking refuge under bridges or in homes or simply disappearing into the darkness.

Two solitary figures remain in the pouring rain, solid and voluminous, one beside the other, stoically enduring the seasonal discharge. One is vertical and black, Bacán; the other is horizontal and white with flour, Nando Barragán.

"How long were they out there in the rain?"

"Bacán waited, with the patience of a blind man, for the water falling from the sky to wash the body, cleansing it of blood and restoring the natural color and composition of Nando's skin. Then he lifted the body on his still powerful shoulders and started walking toward his house, ignoring the gale-force winds, which grew stronger with each step. His only companion, apart from the body itself, was his faithful wife, who splashed through the puddles alongside him. It was a difficult procession, full of obstacles. The rain soaked the body, doubling its weight, which was already substantial, and the gusting wind threatened to topple them. His blindness didn't help much either; neither did the blackness of the night, both of which made them stumble repeatedly. But Bacán persevered, tranquilly proving his vigor, as if nothing were so important as rescuing that body."

"Did he finally arrive at a safe port?"

Just before dawn, while the sky is still dark, he arrives at his modest home, dripping water and soaked to the bone. He lays Nando on the dining table, on the white linen tablecloth, and asks his wife to dry the body and comb Nando's hair. She obeys and even puts a little makeup on his face, to hide the damage caused during the night.

"Now bring clean clothing."

She brings a freshly ironed suit and gives it to her husband. Feeling his way, in a slow, almost ceremonial manner, the blind man dresses the man he never respected or liked. He dresses him in his own clothing, the only man in the barrio whose clothes would fit him, shirt, pants, socks, shoes. A linen handkerchief in the coat pocket.

He moves his hand to close the eyelids and in that instant his intuition allows him to see the last image imprinted on Nando's eyes before he died. A glimpse of a final memory, a yellow desert, spotted with dark shadows from an outcrop of rocks, on which death is lying like a leopard in the sun.

Bacán supposes that tomorrow, which is a holiday, no carpenter will be willing to build an appropriate coffin, so he puts the dead man, faceup with the eyes tightly closed and arms crossed, in the large pine box that had contained the contraband Westinghouse refrigerator he gave his wife for her birthday. He lights a couple of candles, drinks a cup of steaming coffee, aromatic and comforting, while he waits for the family members to come claim the body. He warms his hands on the pewter cup, glancing blindly one last time at his dead enemy, and says, "Every man deserves a dignified death. Even you."